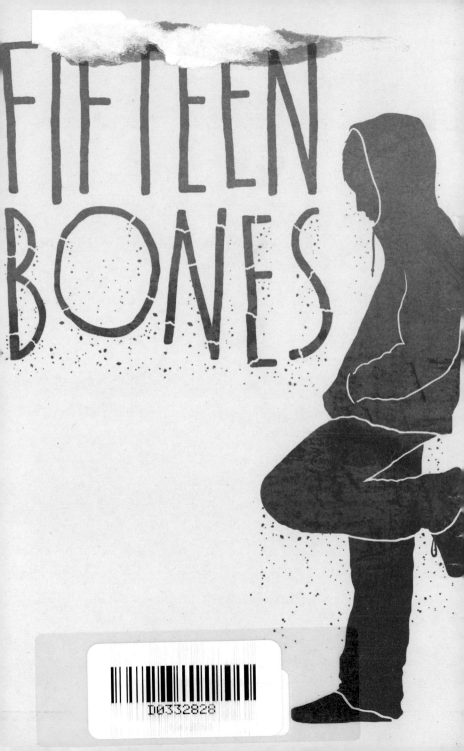

FIFTEEN BONES

R.J. Morgan lives and works in London. FIFTEEN
BONES is her first novel.

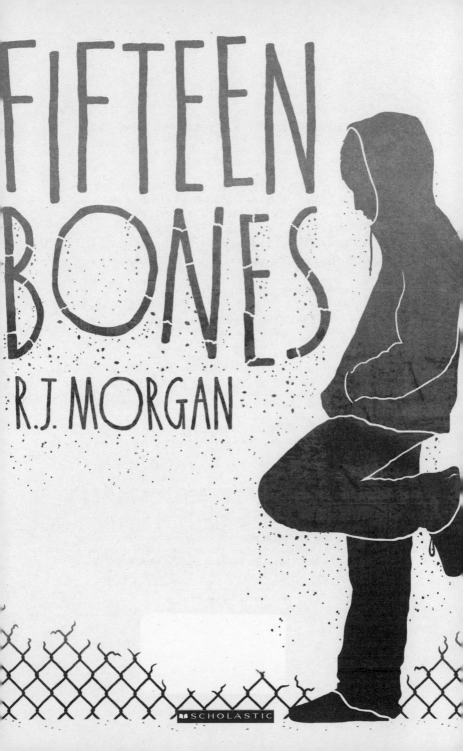

FIFTEEN BONES

R.J. MORGAN

SCHOLASTIC

First published in the UK in 2014 by Scholastic Children's Books
An imprint of Scholastic Ltd
Euston House, 24 Eversholt Street
London, NW1 1DB, UK

Registered office: Westfield Road, Southam, Warwickshire, CV47 0RA
SCHOLASTIC and associated logos are trademarks and/
or registered trademarks of Scholastic Inc.

ISBN 978 1407 13826 8

A CIP catalogue record for this book
is available from the British Library.

Printed and bound by CPI Group (UK) Ltd, Croydon, CR0 4YY
Papers used by Scholastic Children's Books
are made from wood grown in sustainable forests.

1 3 5 7 9 10 8 6 4 2

www.scholastic.co.uk

YA

For Grand

1

When the scouring pad drew blood it became apparent the penis on my forehead was permanent. I plunged my face so deep into the bowl, the water looked black. I tried to hold my breath, but the water threw me out and forced me to look at this creature in the mirror, with blood and graffiti covering its face.

I went to my room and lifted the loose floorboard by the window. I picked up my stash and I would have done it there and then, except I didn't want to be a corpse with a drawing of a penis on its forehead. I replaced the pills and my floorboard and decided to wait for the ink to fade. And that's how I ended up spending that week at home, and that's how I became accustomed to the rants of the hunched man next door, and the skinny girl with long arms, who rattled around like a pinball to avoid him.

I'd watch the man from the edge of my window as he stormed up to his attic. I wondered what he was up to. I wondered what the girl had to do with it, and what it must be like to fight for your life, rather than watch it melt off you piece by piece. And then I'd think it was terrible to be envious of her torment, and I would feel even worse.

The only thing that made me feel better was my stash, and calling Isaac. This wouldn't last. You can only push people so far, and Isaac wasn't speaking to me much any more. With every pill I took he got further from me, and soon I would take a bite of something and he would disappear.

2

We had moved so many times my stuff could fit into three battered cardboard boxes: one for clothes, one for filming and computer equipment, and another for my and Isaac's props.

Mother's business was to buy Death Houses, do them up and flip them. We'd move in, then she'd start scrubbing off the filth and oil, paint the whole place magnolia and it would look like everywhere else. She didn't care who had died and rotted in the sitting room. Your existence would be mopped up and your death would become an Ikea rug or a jaunty throw, erased from living memory.

This Death House was more depressing than usual because the upstairs was empty whilst downstairs was stuffed to the brim with newspapers, Christmas decorations and stacked cereal boxes. Whoever died here never had visitors, and hadn't been able to use the stairs for years.

I spent my time searching through the clutter and getting depressed over a lifetime spent reading the *Daily Express* and obsessing over Jaffa Cake boxes. I was under strict instructions not to touch anything, but I picked up the things I liked and hid them from Mother's magnolia warpath.

I'd cheer myself up by editing the last sketches Isaac and I had made. Isaac played on a loop while I edited the fine detail. Editing is a bit like composing music. You have to time the perfect pause so everyone will laugh. I composed long into the night, poring over every line Isaac said or sang.

"Come back to me," he said whilst dressed as a posh onion. "Come back."

The shouting from next door would occasionally bring me to the window and I'd look across the rows of embattled houses. Foils scraped along the street like leaves, gathering around bins and trees and skipping over endless speed bumps that lay like dead bodies across the tarmac. The shouting seemed to still the air, and I wondered if anyone else was listening, quietly sickened by the ceaseless rant and their inability to stop it.

The house next door sat wet in mud and looked like a giant toad. It was painted dark green and had a broken gutter that streamed rain water over black mould. A red security light blinked angrily above the door. The light from the attic was a bulbous eye, twitching whenever the hunched man paced across the room.

Directly opposite my room was the bedroom of a teenage girl. Her window faced mine like a checkmate. Tree branches ran like veins between our houses, the garage roof a scaly skin that connected us like conjoined twins. Her room was bare except for a bed, a vanity table and a mound of clothes that hid the carpet. Every item of clothing was grey. If you squinted, the room looked like a mud slide. Pyramids of damp ran from the corners of the ceiling. Maybe that was why she didn't have any pictures on the walls. I wondered if they knew that black mould was dangerous, and that circular mould can kill you.

In the beginning, the yelling was more irritating than frightening. The man's voice was a squashed, bellowing growl, raked in cigarettes and beer. He struggled to articulate himself, swearing, his anger racing ahead of his thoughts. When the thoughts caught up, he would hit and stamp on them until they weren't thoughts any more, just more pieces of anger.

On the third or fourth day, as I tried to edit myself out of the Apple Pie scene, the yelling progressed to a high-pitched yowling that poured cold water down my spine.

3

Living in Meadow Gorge had made me immune to other people's screams. I was accustomed to suicidal outbursts and death threats, but this was yelling like I had never heard before.

At first I thought he was screaming at himself, or to whichever demons he could see, but as the week went on and the sky grew darker, the girl's voice became audible.

A scream struck the cold of my bedroom and it hit me all over again. I steadied myself on the wall. I had to call the police, but the scream had arrested my lungs and burned the pulp of my brain. I dialled. The walls became wet and dark, and I slipped further down to the cold ground. The operator asked me which service I wanted. She asked if I was all right. She said to blow into the phone. She said she could hear yelling and I needed to tell her where I was. She said she was tracing the call.

At the bottom of a mossy pit, lights swirling in my eyes, I managed four words: Forty-Four Rancome. Hurry.

I lay flat on the dusty floor and covered my ears with my hands. I heard the call over the scanner:

Domestic dispute at 44 Rancome Road, Oscar Delta one. Over.

Received. 44 Rancome. That's Marcus Brigley's house, control. Over.

Received. Proceed with caution. Requesting back up. ETA, Oscar Delta one. Over.

Received. Three minutes, control. Over.

Received. Ten-four. Over.

Mother had a police scanner to find Death Houses before estate agents could get their mitts on them. She'd know if a funny smell was coming from a dark flat, or if a neighbour had become irritated by an ongoing alarm and an elderly person hadn't been seen in a while. When I have fits or collapse or hallucinate being buried alive, Mother stares at me blankly and can't figure out why.

The police car was three minutes away, but from the gathering pace of the man's outbursts, this was too long. His voice had become looping and breathless. He was losing control of himself. I needed to distract him. I dug around in the cardboard boxes and found Isaac's firecrackers. I bunched them into a ball and tested my throw: weak. Muscle and flesh had gone into repairing my broken bones. The casts had left me shrivelled and uneven, as if my flesh had poured into the cracks of my bones like putty. My lungs burned as I hunted for my steroid pump. I was struggling to breathe. Asthma. I could do without the asthma.

Another yell belted across the cold room. I lit the firecrackers. The flame raced up the string. I panicked and threw them with a mighty yell but they fell directly at my feet. The girl's scream came again. I inhaled, picked up the crackers and threw them out of the window.

They missed the Toad House and hit the mud outside. They lay silent for a while then popped with frenzy. The yelling stopped. The hunched man with shoulders the size of dogs, threw his curtains open and snarled. I ducked as I heard sirens ribbon through the air.

My heart beat like a rabbit's until I heard her voice again. "One day," she said, "I'll burn this place to the ground."

4

Mother's car pulled into the driveway. I didn't know where she'd been all week. I found my school uniform and arranged it on the floor. She yelled my name so loudly I imagined she already knew what I had done. I sat against my door.

She was banging on the front door and rattling the lock. Soon she'd realize it was open and fall inside the house. I heard the stumble and the subsequent cursing. "Jake! Get your arse down here."

My arse didn't go anywhere. I resumed watch of my mirror image as the girl's shadow paced her room.

A police car pulled up outside the Toad House and two officers climbed out. I watched them react to the sudden cold: one pulled at her jacket; the other gave himself a shake. The male officer knocked the Toad House door so loudly my window rattled. My window had glass that could break with one tap, was secured with one of those useless Valli locks they used in the sixties before they realized anybody could open them with a credit card and a magnet, and was so huge a grown man could climb through it. This was what stood between me and some enraged psychopath next door.

The police officers stomped from foot to foot as they waited. When they stepped inside, I could no longer see them. There was a short scuffle and the window opposite mine flew open. The girl jumped out on to the garage roof. She absorbed the shock of the impact and leapt to the ground in one fluid move. "Jesus!" I cried, certain she would snap her legs, but she didn't flounder as she bounded up the garden and leapt over the fence. I blinked, scanning the grass as if my eyes hadn't caught up with her. I looked at the empty ground and unshaken fence, astounded. "Wow," I said.

"Jaaaake!"

I jumped.

"JAKE!"

I stepped out of my room, glancing back at the empty garden.

From the landing I watched Mother move like Pac-Man through the stacks of newspapers. No humans should have stepped foot in that house. There were mice and damp, and damp mice everywhere. The newspapers would make a bonfire of the place. I could name about five hundred things in a fifty yard radius that could kill you.

"Jake! Help me with this paint stripper."

There's another one.

"JAKE, FOR GOD'S SAKE."

I swear she called me Jake because it rhymes with sake. "Stop announcing my name to the whole street." I took another look out of the window at next door. "Put this street in Google and the first fifteen results are about a murder."

"I got a call from your school," Mother said, her neck moving from side to side. She was barely able to speak she was so angry. "They said you haven't been in since you was enrolled at the beginning of *Ock-toooe-buur* and do we still want you on the *roll*. They wanted to know if we had moved. I said *yes* we *have* moved again. *Yes* I've lugged these bloody boxes from Vauxhall to this side of *hell* and *yes* we still want him on roll *thankyouverymuch!*"

Mother wrapped her arm around a stack of newspapers and pushed it to the ground. "You will be going to school like everyone else."

I'm not like everyone else.

"Like a *normal* person."

I'm not a normal person. I walk, talk and look funny. That's why, for me, school is like being in prison for something I didn't do.

"Are you coming downstairs or are you going to stand there like Liza Minnelli?"

Mother's eyes narrowed as she watched me struggle down the stairs. Her look sat so heavily on my chest I had to give up on my epic journey and sit down.

11

"God's sake, Jake." Mother said. It's a good job she didn't call me Bart. "And what the hell have you done to your face?"

"This," I said, "is the fading remnants of a penis."

"The what of a what?"

"I'm a *Daily Mail* scare story."

"What the hell are you talking about?" Mother stomped off.

I looked down into the carrier cot Mum had dumped by the front door. I'd expected Squirm to be asleep, but she was staring with bewilderment at her hands. "Is the baby all right?"

Mother pointed to the French doors that led to the garden. "Make yourself useful and open them doors."

Death Houses never have keys. My role in this morbid game was to pick all the locks and deactivate the alarms, then to change all the locks and reactivate the alarms.

I looked up the stairs and wanted to cry. Stairs mean moving all your bones and a million muscles in a very specific and painful sequence. You have to grind cartilage and skewer bone into the fleshy nerves of your ankles and knees. You have to move about thirty muscles just to flex your leg. Just to *flex* it. Actual propulsion is another world of pain. Don't get me started on the Herculean task of getting back down.

"Now," Mother said.

I dragged my breezeblock feet up the stairs to fetch my tools, moaning and wailing all the way. "I can't. Oh, *God*."

"Walk with your feet not your mouth."

Each step was like giving birth. I concentrated on extending my ankle to move my left leg. This is called "plantarflexion". Moving the ankle is called "dorsiflexion". I know this because I've had to learn to walk twice.

I took my tools all the way downstairs, feeling as though I could fall down and cry at the amount of effort I had to put into everything.

"Well? What are you waiting for?"

"Another part of my soul to die," I said.

"Jesus," Mother said. "The police are next door." She pointed at my tool pouch. "Hide the skeleton keys."

I tried to put the keys back in their little pouches but my huge hands had gone red and wouldn't grip anything. I put them under my armpits to warm them up, but they weren't really cold, they were starved of oxygen. I hung my head at the thought of a creature so pathetic it didn't have the strength to circulate its own blood.

I'm not going to go on about it or anything, but I'll tell you something about the accident I had. Of the many bones I broke, one was my coccyx. My arse, basically. I broke my *arse*. Not only is this so incapacitating you can't even use a wheelchair, it also nicks a nerve in your lumbar so every now and again your own arse electrocutes your leg, just for the hell of it, and you howl like a wolf. There's nothing you can do about it because it's your arse that's out of control and your poor legs are just these useless slabs that have to dangle there and take it.

Anyway, when I broke my arse I had to lie face down in hospital, so I couldn't see what was going on, and people gathered around my bum and spoke over it like it was a campfire. Eventually, they flipped me over and I lay there like an upturned turtle while doctors asked me why I looked so peaky. Worse than that, both my elbows were broken, and they had to put the plaster on at right angles otherwise they wouldn't heal properly. If you have both arms at right angles then they stick out so you look like you're about to row a boat, and you have to have sticks that go from an iron circle around your waist to the encased wrists, and the nurse was like, You won't be able to feed yourself for six months and I said, Never mind that, how am I going to *wipemyarse*? And he was like, Sorry, mate, your mum's going to have to do it. And his eyes widened as they followed the horror drawing through my face, and he said, Or your dad? As if that was some kind of great alternative.

I craned my neck so far back I could see the whole ceiling, and then my mouth stretched wide and I wailed like a baby so loudly that another nurse came in, and my nurse was like, His mum's gunna have to wipe his bum for him, and the other nurse was like, Oh, and then walked out. I wailed still: Woe is me, God strike me dead, and then I said to him to call Dignitas and he laughed because he thought I was joking, and then he wheeled me out like a shop mannequin to our Death House in Vauxhall.

The only good thing about being incapacitated is that no one made me go to school. And then when they finally took the plaster off, they saw I had withered like a prune and that's when they noticed all the cuts and burns and I had to go to the mad house.

The first time I got released Mother picked me up late. She sat in her van, her chin jutting out like a coin slot, and yelled at the nurse for bringing me out without my coat. She couldn't move properly after having the baby. "They done an autopsy on me down there," she said. "It's a wonder I'm still alive."

We took a strange road past Battersea Dogs and away from our house in Putney, and I peeled my spade of a hand away from my face. "Where are we going?"

"We moved," she said.

"You *moved*?"

It was bad enough she would never visit, but the thought of them going through all my stuff and shoving it in boxes, probably inspecting it, opening it, reading it as they went along was too much for my skinny heart. I wanted to go straight back to the hospital, to the girls who looked like baby birds and kind Dr Kahn who always told me I was hiding something.

When we got to that Death House in Vauxhall, where a thirty-year-old student from Guam had died of anaphylactic shock on the kitchen floor and hadn't been found for three months, I used a paring knife to cut my arm nine times from the shoulder to the armpit. All in a row like a crazy person. I bled through the mattress, and I was still bleeding when I woke up, and they sent me back to Meadow Gorge before they had changed my bed.

Anyway, that particular stint lasted five months and now I'm out again and we're up to date.

When the police had gone I used a rake key to temper the lock and the doors flew open. "This house is easier to get into than Clapham Common."

This is an excellent joke because, of all the open grounds parks and commons I could have chosen, Clapham Common is by far the funniest as it's where people get caught having sex or doing drugs or whatnot. And it's alliterative. And it has matching syllables. And it has a fulcrum. And if you want to be a comedian you have to think about these things.

Mother barged past me through the front door, thoroughly unamused, and chucked a stack of newspapers into a skip that was stationed in the driveway.

"It's like Clapham Common," I said.

"You can get your spades around some of these bloody newspapers and help me for once," she said.

I looked at my massive hands and thought about how much I hate my massive hands.

"All right, Lurch," Dad said.

I jumped. He'd been lurking so morbidly behind me I hadn't distinguished him from the stacks of moulding paper.

"Looking forward to. . ."

"No."

"And your room is. . ."

"Horrible. It looks like the Ward."

"Maybe you could do some of your writing . . . you . . . there's good light out. . ."

"Painters, Dad," I said. "Painters need light."

16

Dad picked up a Santa toy from the dusty shelf and turned its stiff key. Santa's wheezing cymbals didn't make a sound as they ground together. Dad returned it to its shelf. He looked at it for a good while before he turned to me and said, "Oh."

"Eat, will you?" Mother said as she came back into the house. "There's pizza."

The dining room was a cocoon of newspapers with a sunken table at the centre. On the dining table were three warm cans of cola and a greasy pizza box. I picked up the lip of a pizza slice and the mozzarella licked the box, leaving a soggy slice of mulch. The cola was full fat so I emptied it on the dry soil of a dead plant. I stuffed two pizza slices into a sheet of newspaper, wrapped the can in another newspaper, went through the kitchen and threw it all in the skip. I clapped the dust from my hands.

"Don't you dare go through that skip," Mother said. "I'm not cleaning up new mess."

"I haven't done anything," I said.

"Exactly," she said. She sighed as if what she was about to say had taken some great effort. "How's your room?"

If her life was a meal, I'd be the side salad.

"Eerie," I said.

"You think your nose is ear-y," she said. She picked up a carriage clock, opened it, checked its bottom, frowned, and hurled it into the skip. "Three points, Kobe Bryan," she said as it sailed in.

"Bryant," I said.

"That's what I said," she said.

Frenzied shouting erupted from the Toad House. An older woman's voice shouted back. Mother froze.

"Should we do something?" I said.

"No," Mother said, "don't want to get mixed up with that." She disappeared into the house and reappeared with a stack of soup bowls. "We're going to have to listen to that day in day out, I'll bet. Everywhere you go, everything you do, there's always some bloody man there ruining it."

"Charming."

"Oh, I didn't mean you," she said. "You're not a man."

"Charmed, I'm sure."

"Get yourself upstairs, ready for that school tomorrow," Mother said.

"I am not going back there."

"You are going back there."

"I am not going back there."

"You are going back there, you mark my words. You didn't even make it to registration!"

"He *tagged* my *face*."

"It's the Detention Centre next, that *bloody* social worker said. I'll be taken to court, she said. And I'll tell you what I told her, sunshine: if you don't go back to that school, I will bloody well give you something to take me to court over. That clear?"

She went back in the house.

"God help me," I said to myself as over the fence, beyond the green wall of the Toad House, I heard sobbing.

18

5

When I got to my room I couldn't breathe properly. I shook my inhaler. I looked in the mirror and winced. I lifted my shirt and breathed in. I moved from side to side, allowing my ribs to taste freedom. I poked at the gaps. It made a *tut tut tut* noise. My hipbones rolled under the skin.

A spider scuttled across my bedroom floor and burrowed beneath a cardboard box. I lifted the box with my foot and the spider ran out and disappeared under my bed.

I pushed the box under my bed and looked at it for a while. I picked up another box and tipped it over the floor. I waited. I put everything back in the box. I opened and closed my door. I turned the light on and off. I shoved everything under my bed. For the first time in five months, I went to the toilet without being watched. I went back to my room and looked at the coat lying on the floor and the stuff under the bed with some satisfaction. I tested the lamp at my bedside. Dust rained from the shade as I switched it on and off. Light beat into the room in pulses. I went faster and faster on–off on–off until I felt more than saw someone looking into my room.

I froze.

I saw her standing, fists to hips, at her window. She scowled and darted away, not in fear, but in haste. She shoved things into a rucksack as if trying to drown them. She was tall and quick; her long black braids swished as she dived for things to thrust into the bag. She looked at me again and I dropped to the floor. When I crept up her curtains were closed.

I sat beneath my window, waiting for her to reappear. I traced the dots up the scar on my leg. The dots are where they screwed the bolts in. I ran my finger around the smooth puddle of skin on my knee and the faint line where they sewed on the skin they'd cut out of my back.

I took my pills. I looked at Isaac's picture on my phone. He's smiling, I'm laughing. I scrolled through to his number. On his number is the same picture I have as my screen saver. I looked at the call button until the screen went black.

6

Reep! Reep!

A mechanical screech woke me the next morning. I pressed my hands to my burning eyes. The noise was tangled up with a disturbing dream I'd been having. I couldn't wrestle them apart.

My bedclothes were rumpled and soaked with an alarming amount of sweat. The sheets were bunched into a corner as if bullied during the night.

Reep! Reep!

Reep! Reep! "This vehicle . . . is . . . reversing!"

I got out of bed and went to my window. A digger bouldered down our long road, its huge metal arse pressing away bins and narrowly skimming the parked cars.

Reep! Reep! Reep!

Bleary neighbours yanked open their curtains and

peered out of their front doors. I prayed the truck wasn't headed for the Death House, but as I looked down, I saw Mother in the epicentre, her dressing gown gaping at the arms, guiding the diggers like a mad wizard.

"Bloody hell."

"God."

"Bloody hell!" said the neighbours.

I went back to bed and pulled the covers over my head. I tested the hollow groove under my collar bone. I wrapped my hand around my bicep, my thumb easily looping over my fingers.

My alarm sounded and I didn't risk having a shower. I'd wait until the Death House funk was gone and there was less chance of inhaling the dead man's grime. I put on my stupid uniform and stood in front of the mirror.

The stiff tie nagged my gag reflex. I drew it over my head like a noose and made a choking sound. My shoulders hung. The bright white shirt was too big. I looked like a cocktail umbrella. A lanky, sick cocktail umbrella. "You," I said to my reflection, "are going . . . to . . . *die*."

I made my way through the circus outside our house. Mother put a grip on my bony shoulder. "Last chance," she said as she spun me around and rammed my tie against my throat.

"It *chokes*—"

"I do not want to see that *bloody* social worker again, you understand? We are not *those* people."

I had apologized a million times. I didn't know what else I could do.

"Says on the Internet a kid was murdered on this street," I said.

"Black, wasn't he?" Mother said, distracted by an orange extension cord.

A weight pulled on my stomach as I watched her untangle the cord. I wanted to make her explain but the chances of a row increases by the syllable so I had to ration my words like war biscuits. She sensed me hesitate. "All you have to do," she said, "is not get involved with anyone."

"Or anything," I said.

"Quite right."

For the second time I set out towards the only school in London that would take me. A school with four towers, police cordons, and a curfew.

7

Our long road led to a handful of besieged shops and offices, many with their shutters down and doors open. Outside the post office, there was a yellow police notice with ARMED ROBBERY in big black letters. A security van had been robbed at gunpoint and if anyone had information they should contact the police, although someone had drawn a line through "Contact the police" and replaced it with "Use money to get high".

At the bus stop, a pack of kids in black hoodies harassed a bus driver whilst another swarm of black uniforms stopped cars and tormented cyclists. I kept walking. Kids clattered out of flats and behind them came the screams of gravel-mouthed mothers.

I walked on. The long road was flanked by grey trees, dirtied by the constant spit of pollution. Their suffocated roots bubbled beneath the pavement. A urinated underpass led to the school gates. On the walls was a tag that looked like this:

$$☠

It had been sprayed with a stencil, which meant someone has staked their territory. No one else had tagged the wall, so $$☠ had some clout.

I emerged from the underpass and there it was: Cattle Rise High School. Four grey towers spiked from the ground. The wet walls surged up like a cantankerous sea monster, so old its eyes had turned to glue.

The sign for Cattle Rise High School had been sprayed to read "BATTLE CRISE" and "I am" was written above the "High".

A line of kids in black uniforms was waiting outside the main gate to go through the knife arch. They lobbed their rucksacks into the plastic trays in competitive carelessness and kissed their teeth at the guards as they walked beneath a metal detector. I looked back down the road. I thought of all the places I could go other than this hormonal cauldron. I thought of the Southbank and London Bridge, and Shoreditch and the comedy clubs you can sneak into in Leicester Square.

It's the Detention Centre next, that bloody *social worker said*.

Once inside the gate, my lungs shrank. I took a puff of my inhaler.

I stepped towards the entrance and the very same penis-graffiti goons barrelled towards me. There were three of them: two were pale minions with bad teeth and filthy hair, and the leader was a boy-mountain, with a beard of acne, who smiled in delight at my reappearance.

"Who said you could come back here?" he said.

I lowered my head and tried to back away. I held the strap of my bag so tightly it was cutting into my hands.

A thin boy peeled out of his shadow and blocked my way. He looked back to the boy-mountain. The boy-mountain lurched and snarled. His groaning body obscured my sight. His neck was spackled red with razor rash and angry ingrown hairs. His face was scabbed with crystallized acne. He wore a bright white hoodie draped across his shoulders in a curve that suggested they were not only massive, but made of muscle.

There was a tap on my shoulder and I turned, as you always do, the wrong way.

The school nurse turned and knocked a jar of cotton tips to the floor. She bent to collect them and her hair spilled from its bun.

The locked medical cabinet contained seven first-aid kits, a shelf of gauze, a bottle of tuberculocidal bleach and a bag of cat litter. They use gauze to cover cuts and burns and stuff like that. Bleach and cat litter is for blood. It's a special kind of school that has plenty of cat litter.

On the ceiling was an industrial fire alarm and if you looked hard enough you could see faint grey swirls in the paint. White paint had smudged over black ash and the paint had dried into this strange pattern. This meant fire damage. Recent fire damage. It happened once when we got a Death House from an old lady who had fallen asleep smoking a cigar.

A short man with torrential acne scars burst in. "What's happened here?" he said. He put his nose so close to mine I could see into his cavernous pores. "Dear me," he said, "you didn't even make it through the door."

He flung a finger at the nurse. "Clean that off his face, will you. *Clearly* it's going to be one of those days."

Clean *what* off my face?

He stormed off and the nurse approached me with a cloth that smelled like bleach.

"What's on my face?"

"You don't want to know," she said.

"*Whatsonmyface?*"

"It'll be all right," she said, wincing.

I took my phone out of my pocket and looked in the black screen. Scrawled across my forehead was the word "GAY".

The nurse straightened up. She twisted her mouth anxiously. "I don't think this is going to come off."

"Great," I said, careful not to swallow any of the acid or whatever it was running down my stupid face. "Don't call my parents. I can get home on my own."

"Your mum has said you have to go in," she said, flicking through a large grey file. "I've already spoken to her."

I sat up. "You *are* joking."

"It's for the best," she smiled. "You can't miss another day in your first month. Your attendance percentage will

27

be so bad you could get excluded."

"She's just worried about Social Services. She doesn't actually mean—"

"If you're absent they automatically send your parents a text. So, no way out of it, I'm afraid."

"You are joking though?"

"Just go to registration. It's only the morning and the afternoon reg that goes into SIMS," she whispered with a little smile, "then try and sneak out."

She said this as if it was some big secret.

She ruffled my sticky-up-y hair and tried to smooth it over the effigy on my forehead, but my hair won't be pulled down, it defies gravity, and that's why I look like an electrocuted scientist. "You can barely notice it," she said. Her fingers felt funny on my hairline.

"Miss, 'gay' is written in black ink on my IMAX forehead. I look like a light bulb. I can't go anywhere like this. I'll get hate-crimed."

She nodded and then shook her head to try to cover up the nodding. "I'll see if there are any hats in lost property."

She hurried out and left her computer open on my photo-less file. I thought about the girl next door. I checked the door and reached over to type her address. I might at least learn her name.

The computer whirred and presented the world's slowest pinwheel. "Come *on*," I said, as it managed one more bar. I heard the nurse padding back to the room. The door rattled and I hit escape just as the computer flashed: NOT FOUND.

The nurse was holding two rancid beanie hats and a white baseball cap.

"Lice or scabies?" she smiled. She placed the black beanie over my head. I liked how freckles were dotted over her cheeks and under her eyes, and how her hair was fine like a baby's. She had white all across her nails and her skin was so fine I could see her capillaries. I wondered if she became a nurse because she spent her childhood staying inside when everyone was allowed to play. I wanted to ask her things like why I sometimes can't take in a full lungful of breath, and why, when I finally do, I feel dizzy. And why is there this ringing in my left ear? And why am I so unsymmetrical? Is it God's way of telling me to get out of the gene pool? And don't get me started on my skin and bones, or the horror show of waking up every day.

I got up and shuffled out of the nurse's room. I turned to smile at her and she looked back at me with concern. The door closed between us and I stood behind it for a good while.

I slid out to the long corridor, and kept my back against the wall.

Last chance, Mother said.

It's the Detention Centre next.

A group of kids headed towards me. The front-runner pointed. "Gay!"

I scratched the back of my head.

"Battyman," a girl screeched and her friends howled

laughing. Slow news day.

The bell rang and the corridor filled with kids. "Gay," people said as they passed me. I hung my head and kept walking.

"Gay, gay, gay."

A swell of people pushed past me and I felt a small object being pressed into my hand. I waited until they had gone before I looked at it. It was a tiny bottle of nail polish remover. That's a new one. I wondered what the insult was. Girl? Emo? Drag queen? I put it in my pocket.

"Gay!"

I binned the scabies hat and went to registration.

I found my form room and lingered outside. The knot of my tie felt like a fist. I looked through the reinforced glass and loosened my tie.

The noise was painful. The kids were gathered in groups, stretching and squawking, swarming about like insects. One girl had dyed her shirt black and wore it over bumblebee leggings. Another girl had bright pink hair, standing on end. The pink had drained into her shirt and the reddening mess swam around her neck like a grim execution.

"Hang on," some hooded genius cried from inside the classroom. "Who the *hell's* that?"

I dug in my bag for my inhaler and took a few burning puffs. I opened the door. There was a pause before the entire class bawled with laughter. The red-faced teacher squinted at my stupid mug and went, "What on *Earth* have you done to your face?"

I pointed to myself.

The class laughed.

"Yes, you," he said. "Well?"

Pause.

I slowly pointed towards my forehead. "You think I did this to my own face?"

The class laughed again, and it wasn't at me, it was with me.

I waited for the pause. "Maybe after school I'll go up Luton and try and get myself killed."

The class laughed again. The teacher's eyes vibrated back and forth as he weighed the cost of battle. "Go and sit down," he said.

I headed towards the back of the class to a table occupied by a skinny white kid in a Yankees cap. For a second I thought I had escaped. The laughter was on my side. I was going to be an eccentric character, with witty jokes and attentive friends, but as I took another step the Yankees-cap boy sprang up. "I am not sitting next to him if he's gay."

He shuffled his chair to another table, but the occupants immediately moved away, and this set off a cascade of pushing and shoving.

"Get off!"

"God, extra."

"Get off me, man."

"Everybody, calm down," the teacher said, but he was drowned by the commotion.

I was far away from the door and I started to panic. A tiny girl with high socks clattered out of the crowd and slapped the dust from her skirt. "*Budget*," she muttered. She pulled her bag over her shoulder. The bag was so big it made her look like she was playing a double bass. Her tiny fingers tapped on the strap and her foot tapped the floor. Her eyes were wide and open. She looked calm. She looked like she knew herself. "Budget, homophobic, frigid tossers."

"Calm down, Clarissa," the teacher said.

A tall, olive-skinned boy with black hair parted the sea of bodies to arrive at my radioactive table. "As if he'd put that on his own head? It was obviously Darscall."

"Ooooh!" the class said.

He pointed at the kid in the Yankees cap. "He done the same thing to you, Sean. I don't know what you're being such a bitch about. What was it he wrote?"

"Yeah, nothing," Sean said.

"Go on, what was it?"

"Nothing."

"Oh, what was it?" The tall boy pressed his hands to his eyes.

"Balls." Sean shrugged and everyone laughed. "Yeah, yeah, all right. *Balls.*"

"Yeah," the tall boy said. "You was Balls O'Brien all of Year 7."

More laughter. Clarissa, the girl with the double-bass bag, smiled sleepily at him.

"So I call amnesty on this one," the boy said.

"All right," came the general murmur.

"Peace in the Middle East."

The tension broke and people laughed. The boy had deep brown eyes, dark hair gelled carefully into an upright mess, big lips, and white teeth like an American. He had a calm superiority. He looked like one of those sardonic cats who live in leafy London, the ones who don't blink at loud noises.

"Kane," he said as he sat next to me. "Welcome to Special Measures."

I opened my mouth but no sound came out.

A sumo-sized boy with an apple-shaped face walked over, pulled out a chair and joined us. The class looked across at him. He gave them a bored smile.

"Thanks," I mumbled as he sat down. "Jake."

"Bash," he replied.

"Is that short for Bashir?"

"Yes, and?"

My fingers curled into the flesh of my palms and my knees pressed together. I was once told with great confidence that I was so pasty that every little thing that came out of my stupid mouth sounded racist. What team do you support? Racist. What page are we on? Racist. You want my pudding? Racist. Is that short for Bashir? Racist. I vowed not to speak again.

Bash opened a textbook, removed a small black notebook from the pocket of his blazer, and resumed his note-making.

Sean shuffled back to our table and a girl with dirt rings

on her neck followed. Then everyone wanted to sit at the table, just to show how charitable they were, and that irritated me more than the initial scramble to get away.

Kane looked at me. "Wasn't you in my primary school?"

I panicked. If anyone found out what had happened, it would eclipse announcing myself to my new school with "gay" written across my forehead.

"I don't think so."

"Yeah. You was. Ellie's in Brixton, isn't it. St Eloïse. Brixton massiv. You hung round with that kid, what was his name?" He clicked his fingers. "Skinny little . . . Isaac. Isaac! That was him. Ise. I liked him. You was some sort of act. Like twins. You used to do them shows, the pair of you singing and cracking jokes. You was jokes."

I fiddled with my phone. "That wasn't me."

"Yeah, it was. You was jokes. You give me laughs, fam. You give me laughs. What was that? What . . . yeah, the Real Fly Rabbi! We used to film it. Who else? Oh, Albert. Albert! And that teacher, Mr Reacher, who was always, like, hungover and like teaching stuff like how to eat cold pizza. It was well funny. You used to do those raps. 'Scrub your woks, Iron your socks. . .' You had that song called 'Punch Me in the Face':

There's a girl who caught my eye
With just one look
And one right hook.

You was jokes."

I couldn't believe he remembered the words. I didn't recognize Kane at all. Maybe I never noticed him before. Maybe he'd gone through such a massive Croydon Makeover that he looked completely different. "That wasn't me."

"It was you." Kane sat closer. "What happened to him and you? You went the good school, eh. *Skeen*."

I prayed the searching look in his eyes would stop. He couldn't know what I did. It was news that would spread like nothing else, even wildfire isn't wireless.

"So?" Kane said. "Where you bin?"

Five schools, four hospitals, a courthouse and a madhouse.

"Nowhere," I said.

"You look like a right gaylord with that on your face," Sean said. He couldn't take his eyes off me.

"What gives it away?" I said.

The others laughed.

"Are you gay then?" Sean said.

"Does it matter?" I said. They laughed again and Sean shifted in his seat.

The bell went and the class crowded out. "Here," Kane said, handing me a shiny LA Lakers cap. "Lend this."

"I can't," I said, terrified to be seen with it. "I'd get rushed."

"Rushed like doughnuts." Kane laughed as he took back the cap and put it in his bag. He looked up and caught me staring at him. I snapped my eyes away.

"Here." He handed me a permanent marker pen. The other kids were closing in on us. I looked at it and wanted him to stay and for him to go away.

"Come out, let's *goooo*," called the mob.

"Use it to—"

"Come *aaaaaaaaaaaht*."

"All right, I gotta go, yeah." He backed away. "Get some emo to borrow you some nail polish remover, you get me? And stay away from the tower four yard, that's where Darscall hangs out with his lap dogs." He was at the door. "And don't go around a—"

He was swept into the human traffic. I looked at the marker pen and felt the nail polish remover in my pocket, and wondered what strange trick he was playing.

The corridors were swarming with taggers. They slung eyes at everyone who walked past. As the bell rang for lunch, the taggers wailed and I retreated to a toilet cubicle. I sat cross-legged on the toilet so no one could see my feet. I wasn't going to walk into any more lessons like that, and there was no way I was going to any canteen, don't even mention canteens to me.

Perhaps Kane thought I should colour in the letters. I could make them spell GAP or OAP. Then I'd be the most popular boy in the world. I thought of how Mother removes the oil from Death Houses by rubbing even more oil into the stain. I looked at my distorted reflection in the bog-roll dispenser and traced the tiny tail of the "Y" with the pen and wiped it with nail polish remover.

The ink came off. I wrote over the word. I shook the nail polish remover on to the toilet paper and wiped it across my forehead. I thought it would burn but it didn't. I looked at my reflection and the ink had vanished. I felt faint with relief.

The rest of the morning was a waiting game. I read old texts on my phone until I had to emerge and go to the first afternoon lesson and make the register.

Near the English corridor was a wall of sporting trophies and medals. I scanned the photographs, looking for the girl next door. The faces were determined and proud, happy to be in their sports gear. I lingered on the face of one girl for longer than the others, a skinny Jamaican girl with green eyes so electric they beamed out from the photograph, shoulders like a jaguar, slender muscled arms, a stomach as flat as a board and a hint of glee teasing the corner of her mouth.

Year 8 athletics squad, I read. They called themselves the "Insain Bolts". They had won "gold, gold, gold and gold".

She seemed so familiar, but it couldn't be her, she looked so bright and excited.

Kane was coming down the corridor towards me. "Where were you all morning?"

"Oh . . . school tour," I said.

"Yeah, right," he said, "touring around a toilet all morning, more like."

I hung my head.

"Got that off then." He pointed at my forehead.

My eyes were all over the place. I hated that he was looking at my face. "Thank you," I managed.

"You had your first day rush?"

"No. Give it time."

Kane laughed and looked like a toothpaste advert.

We turned into the English classroom and I bumped momentarily into his hard body. Because I was disorientated, or because I'd been hiding out for so long – or because I was such an all-round idiot – I started talking.

"Why would someone wear the same bandana every day?"

"Because they're in a gang?" Kane said absently.

"What gang?"

"What colour was it?"

"Grey."

"CRK, from Wimbledon," Kane said, looking around. "Dangerous."

"Wimbledon? Dangerous?" I tried to keep him talking as people shoved past us into the classroom. "What do they do? Threaten people with couscous and Frappuccinos?"

"Maybe the Wimbledon you go to," Kane said. "Why do you even want to know?"

"No reason."

"Yeah, right," Kane laughed. "You couldn't lie in bed."

Before I could laugh he'd gone to the front of the class and left me hovering at the back. I wondered if he was one of those welcome committees like they have in America, and would evaporate the next day.

The English classroom was painted a rose colour. Light streamed in through the windows. Above the interactive whiteboard was an origami crane, and above that some hand-painted calligraphy:

There is another world, but it is in this one.

When everyone had taken their seats I found myself an empty chair and sat down. It was empty because it was not quite at the back, and not quite at the front, but in the precarious middle realm where the back of the head is an easy target for flying Blu-tack.

The teacher was dealing with an argument between a group of girls who had all sculpted their hair to cover their left eyes, so they struggled to stare each other down, and ended up curving towards each other like courting penguins.

I searched the hand-painted quote on my phone. Yeats.

"Wha' your coo?" a voice said.

I ignored it. A foot thumped the back of my chair. "Wha' coo?"

I turned to a boy in a Lakers cap, sitting so low in his chair his arse missed the seat. "What?"

"*What* your *coo*?"

"Coo?"

"Crew." He spat the word.

"I haven't got one," I said.

"You ain't got no coo?"

"No."

"Das gay, man. Das bad, man." He laughed a fake laugh and advised me of the many ways in which my life, virginity and metal health were at peril, speaking in such stilted English it had regressed to German. "Das moist. Das gay."

I thanked him for the advice and he sat back, chuckling to himself. It was a fake chuckle and I think I hate the sound of fake laughter more than I hate the sound of foxes or those heroin foils or pretty much anything else.

I ran my finger over the dollars-and-skull tag engraved into the desk. A slim hand handed me a mark scheme and I woke up to myself.

"You must be Jake. I'm Miss Price." The teacher's singsong voice came to me through the fog. Her nose crinkled. She had perfect skin and short Afro-textured hair that patterned her skull. She was wearing bright green. Her sweater sucked flat against her stomach and her forearms were hardened against the bone. Her shoulders were squared. If you hold your shoulders square it means you've got back muscles. If you've got muscles across your back, it means you're fit. Really fit. "And what's your name?" she smiled.

"Jake." I shrugged.

"Jay?"

"Jake," I said.

"Jason?"

I coughed, "Jake."

"*Jake*. You shouldn't mumble, Jake. You should respect what you have to say."

I shrugged again. "OK."

"You mustn't shrug, Jake. It's a non-committal gesture."

I hung my head.

"And what's the story of your name?" she asked. "*Everyone listening.* Jake? What's the story of your name?"

She remained in front of me, nodding and smiling, and I felt terrible for her because if I kept quiet for much longer she would lose control of the class. "Jake is one of the most common names in the world. So's Jones." I shrugged, avoiding her eye. "Jones means 'son of John', but I'm the son of David so . . . maybe there's something my mother isn't telling me."

Nothing.

"And what about Jake?" she asked. "Paint a picture."

What picture? If you have a Coca-Cola name, it's obvious that there was no real thought behind it, it's just a name.

I couldn't think of any story. My mind used to be so quick I could spar with Isaac and make him laugh. Where could my name have come from? Miss Price looked around and lightly scratched the left side of her long neck. She wasn't going to be able to hold the class's attention for much longer. "I was named after the dog," I said.

"Lovely," Miss Price said.

"Nob!" someone said, and the class bawled with laughter. It took Miss Price a good while to calm everyone down.

Miss Price handed out a copy of the poem "Suicide

in the Trenches" to everyone. She also gave me a new exercise book. "I want you to write me a letter telling me all about yourself."

As she spoke to the class I opened my new book, cracking the spine. I looked at the blank page and smoothed my hand over the paper. I used to love school.

Miss Price was talking about Siegfried Sassoon and how he had been a war hero. "Then," she said, "he took his medal of honour and threw it in the river. So let me ask you this: why do you think he threw his medal away?" No one answered. "Why do you think he threw his. . . *List – en – ing*. Why did he throw his medal away?"

He didn't.

I put my head to the table.

Sassoon didn't throw his Military Cross away. His grandson found it about a year ago in an attic in Mull. I know this because I've already done war poetry in Year 9 in some school or other. I don't know why this lot were even doing war poetry. It's not in the GCSE this year. I wanted to tell her about the medal but she was working so hard to control the class I didn't want to interrupt her.

The whiteboard timed out and Miss Price fussed with the controls. Everyone barked instructions. A girl got up, pressed a few buttons and fixed the board. Miss Price thanked her with enthusiasm. The girl smiled but the boys advised her she had a fat arse three times before she sat down, so she stopped smiling.

"Oh . . . *kay*. . ." Miss Price sighed. The class was irrecoverably distracted, and into the commotion launched the boy-mountain who had tagged my forehead. The air pulled as the class tensed.

Miss Price gave her watch a theatrical glance and the class laughed nervously.

"Miss. Thing's, like, I got speak to you innit," Darscall grunted.

He stood there kicking at the wall and Miss Price motioned him out of the room. "Why did he throw his medal away? Think about it," she repeated as she followed him out.

The class exploded into noise. I put my head down and noticed that the bag of the boy behind me was stuffed with a grey hoodie and bandana.

"What you lookin' at?" he said.

I sat up. "Nothing."

"Sideman. What you lookin' at?"

The class hushed and turned to us.

"Nothing," I repeated.

"You steppin' up to me?"

His eyes were far apart like a hammerhead shark, giving his face a strange lack of focus. You had to choose an eye to look into otherwise your eyes swept across his naked face like a windscreen wiper. He tensed his forehead and this did not move his wrangled eyes. I knew I had seconds to stop him from hitting me. I had one chance to say one thing that would calm him down, to say something funny, but I baulked, and for some unholy reason I said this:

"Don't get emotional."

The great plane of his face evened out. "See you?" he

said quietly. "Oi. Sideman. See you?"

I didn't turn.

"See you?" he said.

The class became a bubble of silence.

He smacked down my face. Not across my face, *down* my face, right on the bridge of my nose, and it hurt. My arms went into a spasm of retaliation, but I kept them pinned to my side. He seemed sated by the slap and sat back down. If it escalated, I'd be helpless. I put my head down and let the pain glug through my stupid face. Drops of blood fell on the page. I pressed them with my fingers. The class howled.

"Woah, woah," Miss Price said as she came back into the room. "Only boring people have to yell to be heard."

She calmed them down in time for the bell to ring. I waited for everyone to leave before I got up.

"Jake?" Miss Price said. "I read your transcript."

Here we go.

Three expulsions *blah blah blah*, madhouse *blah blah*. I don't suffer fools *blah blah blah*. You can't get anything past me *blah blah blah*. Now your other schools may have *blah bl—*

"So you're a poet?" she said.

My eyes darted all around. "*No*."

"You are. You wrote poems published by the . . . what happened to your face?"

"I walked into a door," I said.

"And does this door have a name?" she asked.

"Doreen," I said.

"Very funny," she said, which is what people say when they don't find things funny.

I shrugged. "I wrote *lyrics*. I'm not a poet."

"You are. You won the Silver Pen Award in Year 6. The *National* Silver Pen Award. That's amazing, Jake."

"It's . . . stupid." I looked at the floor. "I never write anything."

"At the end of this term we're having a poetry reading. Some kids will be rapping, some singing. It's called Pip-Pop day. Pip-pop," she beamed, "like hip hop, except with poetry."

"I get it. It's . . . catchy."

"So you'll write something?"

"Uh . . . no, sorry, it sounds really stupid."

"Well, why don't you tell me what you really think?"

I fussed with my bag, hoping she would go away. I thought of writing "Punch Me in the Face All Day" with Isaac at the end of summer. It was quite cold but everyone was still outside. We wrote in a spiral notebook, and we rolled backwards on to the grass because we were laughing so much.

"Miss?" I said.

"Yes, Jake?"

"If you hear a family yelling at each other next door, should you call the police?"

"It depends how you perceive the yelling. If it's threatening and if you think someone's in danger then, yes, you should. If it's persistent you can call the council. Family liaison units are really effective. Well, they were before the cuts. But they're still good."

"So if you really thought someone's life was in danger, then calling . . . is all right?"

"Of course it is. It's your civic duty."

"And can they trace the calls? I mean, the people?"

"The police?"

"The people you called about?"

"No. Why would they?"

"And what if it went to court, would you have to go?"

"If you want to report a crime anonymously you can call Crimestoppers. It's free and they won't ask you who you are or anything like that."

"But if you did call the police you'd have to go to court and everything?"

"Yes, it's your civic. . . Is there something you want to tell me, Jake?"

"No, it's all right." I began to leave the room, unable to walk steadily.

"Has your neighbour threatened you, Jake?"

"Nope, nothing like that. It's . . . anyway. Thanks."

"If you've been threatened you have to tell someone."

"Right-o," I said. I didn't know where I got that from.

"Be careful. Jake."

It was strange that she paused before she said my name. It was as if she understood what was about to happen, and all she could do was offer me some solace before I stepped out into the corridor.

8

They waited like kindling. I stopped, breathless in the vacuum. Hammerhead-shark boy was shuffling and agitated. No doubt he'd told Darscall and his minions about my egregious crime. Darscall waited, leaning into his grin. They wore grey hi-tops, matching but not the same, and had grey snapbacks in their back pockets. Their hi-tops had tongues like desert plants, thick and oily. Their snap-backs were pristine, with tags left on them.

"Gaylord!" Sean said, bumbling through the stand-off. "Where's your billboard gone?" He jabbed his finger to my forehead.

I smacked his hand away.

"Miss, miss!" he said as a teacher approached, oblivious to the unspoken threats all around her. "He's trawling for sausage. He's not denying it."

"That's enough, Sean," she said. "Go to where you're supposed to be."

"Miss, I can't walk around with this cruiser in my yard."

The boys laughed. Sean became louder. "Miss! He's a—"

Sean stopped hollering as a suit with a walkie-talkie came bombing towards us. His eye-roll was so dramatic he had to move his whole body to accommodate it. "Oh, *alloooow* it."

"What's going on here?" the suit said, scowling all over the place.

Sean walked in a little circle, bouncing, fiddling with his cap. "Don't scrape, sir."

The crowd dissipated.

"I've had quite enough of you for one year, Sean O'Brien, and it's only October." The suit shoved his beak in my face. "And you? Who are you?"

"Jake." I leaned back. "Charmed, I'm sure."

"What did you just say? Who do you think you are? What do you find so funny?" The questions came like bullets. "Well?"

"I—"

"What on Earth have you done to your face?"

"What did *God* do to his face?" Sean said.

"Quiet, Sean." He pointed at my forehead. "It's red."

"As if I did this to myself," I said, my voice quavering. "What are you on?"

"What am I *what*?"

48

"What kind of hallucinogenic drugs are you on?"

The suit's eyes widened. "Go to Mrs Anderson right now."

"Who the fuck is Mrs Anderson?" I threw my arms out wide.

He blinked, once, twice. "The *principal*," he seethed as he pointed up a flight of stairs. "Go, now. And don't you dare swear."

"I didn't bloody swear," I said.

Sean laughed.

The suit steamed. "NOW."

I dragged my bones to the principal's office, my moon head rolling all over the place. I pressed the heel of my hand to my chest. The pain in my stomach was acids attacking the lining. The stomach eating itself. I stopped before the last stair and caught my breath. I couldn't make it through the day without being beaten up, sent to the nurse's room and the principal's office, but at least I had learnt that the girl next door was most likely in the CRK, and that the CRK are extremely dangerous, and I wished I had never thrown those firecrackers.

9

The secretary was bone-skinny and had all her pencils arranged in a row on her desk. She had vom dots above her eyes so I liked her immediately. Vom dots are little red dots you get when blood vessels burst from the strain of throwing up.

"You can go in now," she said. I felt like talking to her but I couldn't so I stepped into principal's office instead. My stomach was rattling around a space so cavernous it made a high-pitched *Ahoo* sound.

"Well," the principal said brightly, "who do we have here?"

Ahoo, said my stomach, chewing on itself like a confused vampire. *Ahoooo!* My head swam and smacked me down to the chair. I turned the chair around and put my back to this so-called principal. Schools like to rename things, like we're in Beverly Hills or whatever. Because their school is a nightmare, they think that changing it from "head teacher" to "principal" will make some sort of difference. I have no time for people who call themselves principals. None whatsoever.

I folded my arms.

"Turn around," she said.

The wall opposite the desk was dominated by an aquarium. I followed the endeavours of a lone clown fish that burrowed furiously against the glass. I could have cried for that stupid fish. I wondered who looked after them over the holidays.

"Turn around."

The fish struggled against the glass and I leaned towards him.

"Turn *around*."

"Bright eyes," I sang.

"I *begyourpardon*?"

I turned around.

"You were supposed to start last week," she said as she flicked through the stupid file, "but you started *today*."

"All right, Sherlock," I said under my breath.

She shifted towards me and I told myself to shut up. *It's the Detention Centre next, that* bloody *social worker said.* No way was I going to a Detention Centre. The boys would take one look at my skinny arse, recognize me from whatever school I'd been kicked out of and go for me.

I hung my head.

"You ended Year 6 with across-the-board 7s," the principal said in a faraway voice, reading the file, "and in *Brixton*."

I shrugged even though I wanted to tell her where to shove it.

"How did you go from that, to this?"

I shrugged again.

"You were expelled from your last school?"

I shrugged.

"And the one before that?"

I shrugged again.

"You've been in a Mental Health Referral Unit."

"I prefer the term 'madhouse'," I said.

"Why were you there?"

"In the madhouse?"

"In the Mental Health Referral Unit."

"On account of my being mental."

"How long were you there?"

"Elephant days. Wobble months. Jam," I said.

"*Pardon?*"

"That was a joke."

"I said, how long was your . . . referral . . . at the mad . . . the mental house . . . I mean, Mental Health Referral Unit?"

It was none of her business, but it wouldn't matter if I protested. Everything was there in my file and there was nothing I could do about it. This made me need my inhaler. The whale sounds from my stomach started to go up at the end, like questions: *Ahooo? Ahoooo? Ahoooooooo?*

The principal raised an eyebrow and looked down at my stomach.

"We do apologize," I said, knuckling my guts.

In a flurry of disgust, she snapped the file shut and glared at me. "How are you finding mainstream education?"

"Fantastic. Maybe later someone will punch me so hard I'll shit myself."

Her eyes levelled with mine. Her sleepy eyelids made her eyes look like reading lamps. I shrugged again and let her glare. My mugged moon face and bony arse answered any questions she might have. I put my reddened twig fingers to the table and let her look at them in all their battered, skeletal glory.

"I see," she said eventually. "Mr McMurray says there was an incident in the halls. That you lost your temper."

"I didn't lose my temper."

"You didn't lose your temper what?"

"I didn't lose my temper, miss." I rolled my eyes. "I was threatened by—"

"Do not roll your eyes at me."

"*Godsake*," I grumbled. "I was threatened."

"What did you just say?"

"I said I was threatened."

"Before that."

"I was threat—"

"No. Before that."

"I said I was—"

"Before that."

"God's sake. I said God's sake, all right?" I looked

down at my knees.

"Finished?" she said.

I scrunched up my fairy-tale fingers and put my fists to the sides of the chair.

"Have you got anything to say for yourself?"

Ahooooooo!

The principal looked at my warbling stomach. "When's the last time you ate?"

". . .*pardon?*"

"*When* was the last time you *ate*?"

I sprang to my feet and kicked the chair. It flew across the small room and hit the stupid fish tank. Who knew chairs bounced?

I woke up to myself. The principal's face was drawn with horror. I turned to see what she was looking at. The fish tank. And a chink. A chink in the glass. It grew before my eyes. A cobweb blistered across the glass. The principal rose in horror. There was a second of nothing, then *crash*! Water flooded the office and helpless fish flapped over the needle-sharp carpet.

"OLIVIA!" the principal screeched.

The vom-dot secretary burst into the room. They danced around finding Nemo and I retreated to the corner and rubbed the scars on my arm.

Congratulations, Jake Jones, you're about to be expelled from the Worst School in the World. Where will they send me next? Baghdad in my underpants? The dark side of the moon? Croydon on a Saturday?

It's the Detention Centre next, that bloody *social worker said.*

"Get out," the principal said.

Ahoo, said my stomach as I bent to help them pick up the floundering fish.

"Get out!"

I went out into the corridor and smacked a display off the wall. I looked back to the office and realized the vom-dot secretary had left her computer open. I clicked on my file and changed my mother's mobile number to my mobile number and our address to my old house in Brixton. Then I headed out into the swarm.

"Gay," said one kid as he shoulder-checked me. "Gay," said another who I'd never seen before. "Die," someone else said so I went home, but not before I got another glimpse of the Insain Bolts, and the green-eyed girl with long arms and a lopsided smile.

10

When I arrived home, Squirm was crying. I picked her up and she stopped crying. She grabbed my shirt collar and shoved it in her gummy mouth, then she took it out and laughed, put it back again and was repulsed to find it was wet. "Ug!" she said and I laughed.

Mum was ripping up the carpet in the gutted front room. She didn't lift her head when I walked in.

I put Squirm back in her cot and helped Mother roll the carpet.

"Mum?" I chanced, starting a conversation. "Why am I called Jake?"

Mother's face brimmed with laughter. I'd forgotten how her eyes creased at the sides when she laughed. The laughter shocked her lungs and she coughed.

"Why do you want to know?"

I shrugged.

"When I was pregnant with you," she said as she ripped a sheet of dust, "I was in agony and I was craving cheese. One night your dad came home and he'd bought me a packet of Jacob's crackers and some cheese and he cut it up for me and. . ." She looked to the ceiling and a smile warmed her face. "It was the nicest thing anyone had ever done for me, and I thought, if I have a boy I'll call him Jacob." A tear shone in her eye.

I looked at her for a second. "That's the nicest thing anyone's ever done for you?"

She didn't reply. I held the dusty old roll as she swept the floorboards. The funk of the ancient rug made my nose itch and the murky underlay lit alive with panicking spiders. I dropped it, and sent plumes of dust across the room.

"Bloody *hell*, Lurch, what did you do that for?!"

"I didn't do it on purpose, did I."

"Christ! Go on, get out. I'll do it all myself, as per bloody usual."

I sloped off, hitting my trousers against my ankles, certain the spiders had climbed up my stick legs. I needed to get to my room before I started to cry or something.

The Toad House was asleep. I thought of the girl over there in the trenches. I thought that if the police had been concerned, they would have taken her out of the house.

I reached for my phone to see the photograph of Isaac. He's smiling, I'm laughing. My head is craned right back, so you can see my neck and my wide-open mouth. Isaac is looking directly into the camera, his eyes lit up, his hand on my shoulder.

"Get down here and eat your tea before I blender it!" Mother yelled.

She always got the word wrong. It was to remind me of being force-fed at the hospital. I went downstairs.

"Eat," she said, pointing to the cola and more of the awful pizza. It was full-fat Coke again. I hate fat Coke. I always have. I hate full-fat Coke almost as much as I hate watery pizza. "You got fat Coke," I said.

"Gratitude!" she said to an imaginary audience. She picked up a Santa, checked his base, then chucked him to the corner of the room, where he hit a pile of his broken friends.

I picked up a pizza slice. Pink water ran from the cheese. "This is the worst pizza in the history of ever," I said, but she had disappeared into the kitchen.

I put two slices into a piece of old newspaper, walked out to the garden and tucked them beneath the smashed dinner plates in the skip.

"DUCK!" Mother yelled. I ducked, and Rudolf sailed over my head and into the skip. "Three points!" she hollered before she bombed back into the house.

As the plates crumbled beneath Rudolf, the light from the kitchen window hit something shiny within the rubble. I tried to reach it, but I couldn't lift my weight over the side of the skip. I stretched my pumpkin fingers and got a small touch on the shiny object, enough to pull it a fraction closer. It was a photograph frame. I picked it up and blew off the dust.

The photograph was curled at the edges. It had been mounted on black card and placed in an ornate silver frame. It showed a mum and a dad standing outside the Death House, smiling and holding a toddler. The dad wore flared corduroy trousers, a pale shirt and a large tie with blue flowers trailed across it; the mum wore a bright purple mini-dress with a matching hair band. I stared at the man, his wiry frame, his shock of blond hair, and felt for a second that I was looking at myself. I looked at his hand wrapped around the toddler's back, reaching the bend of her ribs. I looked at the chubby-cheeked little girl with pudgy little hands gripped to her father.

I found Mother on the stairs. "Is this you?"

She grabbed the picture and hesitated before stomping off to the skip.

"Mum? Mum, you're the kid in the picture. Mum!" I followed her through the house.

She threw the picture in the skip from enough distance for a three-pointer, but she didn't score herself this time. I ran to retrieve it but my Kit-Kat arms couldn't lift my idiotic body over the skip. "Mum!" I called as she barrelled back towards the house.

"I told you not to look through that skip!"

"Mum." I followed her into the kitchen. "*Mum.*"

"I am not cleaning new mess."

"But. . ."

"Every time I try to do something there are messing it up."

She stopped. She knew she had gone too far. I could

make her stew for being so mean but I decided to cash it in straight away. "Is that you in the picture?"

"Yes." She shrugged.

"But the picture was taken in front of this house."

"Well," she folded her arms, "this was my parents' house."

"The man who died here was your dad?"

"Yes."

"And you didn't help him?"

"Oh, *thankyouverymuch*," she said as she stomped off up the stairs.

I followed her. "How did he die?"

We reached the landing and I followed her into her room.

"*When* did he die?"

"I don't know, Jake."

"But he was a hoarder, Mum. Mum! He couldn't climb the stairs, Mum. Why did I never see him? Why did we never visit, Mum? Why didn't we *help* him?"

She spun on her heel. "Because he was in *prison*! And if you don't clean your act up and stop being such a royal bloody pain in the arse, you'll be next!" She pushed me out of the room and slammed the door.

"Prison? For what?"

No reply.

I looked around the house, packed with newspapers and old Santa figurines, cereal boxes and the world's biggest collection of lime green plates. Why would he make a prison of his own house? What was he hiding?

And what she was looking for? This would take some investigating.

That night the moon filled my bedroom with light. I tried to fashion curtains out of my sheets and clothes, but my clothes were all so worn down by my bones the moon streamed through anyway. I looked across into the girl's bedroom. Nothing had moved and she was nowhere to be seen.

I snuck out of my room and stood by my parents' door, listening to the fretful pattern of their breathing. They hated each other even in sleep. I went outside and used the light of my phone to find the small chair and climb into the skip. I put my phone in my mouth as I searched through the poor man's belongings, taking care not to cut myself on the broken plates. I found the photograph, slid it out from behind the broken glass and put it in my pocket.

I switched my phone on again and I heard a small buzzing. I looked around before I realized I had called someone. Isaac. He's smiling, I'm laughing.

I let it ring. I liked the way it buzzed in my hands. Since it was a mistake, maybe this time he would answer.

This is the O2 messaging service. . .

I switched the phone off and felt the weight at the top of my head.

A van pulled up outside the Toad House and I pressed myself against the wall to see what was going on. Two men, one black and one white, struggled out of the vehicle and lumbered to the door. The girl appeared on the scrap of grass outside the house. The men were laughing about something. The white man pushed her. She stumbled but didn't fall. The white man held out a fist for her to bump and she refused. The black man did the same and she grudgingly accepted. The men squeezed back into the van, did a scrappy U-turn, and drove off. The girl hung her head as they disappeared down the joyride road, then she hesitated. She seemed to force herself to go back inside the Toad House.

I ran into my house, checked all the doors were locked and went to my bedroom.

In the Toad House, yelling erupted and the girl launched into her room and slammed the door. I ran my finger over the ridges of my arm. She lifted the vanity desk above her head and hurled it at the door. She paced like a cat from window to door. Her braids swished when she turned. She walked with a straight back and square shoulders.

She took one of the legs of the vanity desk and held it like a bat. The hunched man flung open the door. She swung for him and his paw flew to his face. He stormed into the attic and started hitting the desk in such fury I could feel the blows in my room.

The girl pressed her back against the door. She looked sadly at the space where her vanity desk had been. She grabbed her rucksack, slid open her window and dangled from the ledge. She swung her long legs backwards and jumped, landing like a cat on the garage roof. From here she leapt to the ground and ran along the muddy path through their garden. She scaled the fence without pause and began to walk down the long road with her head back and arms flying. I recognized the hesitant way her hips were tilting. She was barefoot.

I went to run after her but found myself fixed to the ground. Very faintly Isaac sang, "*There was a girl who caught my eye. . .*"

11

The next day, on the way to school, I started to cry for no reason. I don't even know what I was thinking about. Once I'd started crying, every miserable thing from my memory clamoured its way to my face and poured out of it, and then I started shaking, so I had to lean against a wall like a drunk. I looked back down the joyless road to see what had triggered it, but there was nothing.

I thought of Isaac. I thought of the girls at the hospital, the fragile baby birds. I thought of all the promises I had made and broken to doctors and counsellors.

I dragged myself to Cattle Rise and barely made registration before the bell went for period one. My tutor gave me a small smile and marked me in. "Arsenal supporter?" he said.

I recoiled. Arsenal? Something about arses? Something

about guns? What was it? Could he tell I'd broken my arse or what?

"It was a joke," he said. "I was just asking why you looked so miserable."

"Oh," I said as the bell went, "that's funny."

He asked me if I was all right and I nodded and hurried off. I followed the herd to English and sat at my desk. Behind me I felt hammerhead-shark boy's eyes boring into the back of my head.

On each of our desks was an envelope with our name printed on it. The whiteboard read DO NOT OPEN. Miss Price stood tall and square in an orange jumper and a chunky silver necklace. Her shoulders were perfectly straight and you could see her toned muscles beneath her jumper. She didn't have the sloping shoulders of someone who spent their teens hunched over a book and their twenties hunched over a computer. "What are you looking at?" she said.

"Triceps," I blurted, worried she would think I was looking at something else.

"Triceps?" she said, glancing at her arm.

"Triceps are hard to get," I said. Triceps are the Holy Grail. You need to do specific exercises for them. You can't just go out running or whatever; you have to find this tiny muscle and spend hour upon hour working it out.

"Yep." She flexed her muscles and laughed. "You 'ave to be well 'ard."

I smiled. "What sport are you into?"

"I do fencing," she said.

This was a lie. The muscles of her arms and hands were even. No bat or weapon sports there. You get triceps from weights, climbing, dips or mad rowing. From *training* for something.

She asked one of the girls to hand out the worksheets. No one ever asks me to get up and do anything. Maybe it's because my eyes are wonky and I look like I can't put one foot in front of the other. Or maybe it's because I look like I'd drop dead if I lost any more calories.

"How's your neighbour doing?"

"She's in some trouble, I think."

"What kind of trouble?"

"I don't know. She leaves her house in the night, goes off on her own."

"Have you tried to talk to her?"

"Yeah, right. Why would she talk to me?"

"You're a personable kind of fellow." Miss Price smiled.

"I get punched a lot."

Miss Price smiled, but now the rest of the class were clambering into their seats and hollering for attention. I checked my phone. He's smiling; I'm laughing.

"Whas eez?" they yelled as they plonked down on the plastic seats.

"You'll see," Miss Price said.

"Whassis?" a girl shrieked as she went to rip her envelope open.

"Don't open it," Miss Price warned gently.

"Why?" she said. "It's got my name on it."

"Well done, genius," I said.

"Shut your *marf*, queer!"

I did shut my mouth. I couldn't bear to be in a classroom. I just wanted to register and get out of there.

Another kid crashed in. "Why's my name on it?"

"You'll see, Blessing," Miss Price smiled.

"Why's my name on it?" she yelled.

"It's just . . . it's just a bit of fun. Jesus," Miss Price snapped and the commotion stopped. She laughed. "Wow, you actually made me lose my world-famous temper."

The class laughed with her.

"Right," she said, "today we—"

Darscall lolloped in. My stomach twisted. He lobbed his suitcase-sized bag across to his chair before thumping into place and kicking his trunk-like legs under the table. The class had to reshuffle to accommodate him.

"You're late, Richard," Miss Price said.

"Whassis?" he grunted, ripping at his envelope. The class groaned and he invited everyone to shut up or die.

"Now," Miss Price said, clapping her hands. "Today we're going to—"

"Why's it got my name on it?" Darscall interrupted.

"It's *magic*," Miss Price said, rolling her eyes.

"I don't like fings with my name on it. What's in it?"

"Now today we're—"

"WHY'S MY NAME ON IT?" he bellowed.

"Richard, it's just—"

He ripped the envelope open.

"Ritchie, wait! You'll ruin the—"

He read the piece of paper and slapped it down on his desk. "S'only crap from Macbeff."

"Shut up, Rich," Bash said.

"Shut up, shoe bomber. Don't tell me to shut up. Shut up."

"Current racial slur," Bash said.

"Back where you come from innit!"

"Where, Tooting?"

The class laughed.

"I'll see you," Darscall said and Bash backed down. My heart seized. At this point Isaac would make a joke and everyone would laugh, and it would break the tension. But everyone had their heads bowed.

"Don't open the—" Miss Price said as Darscall's minions ripped open their envelopes.

"Mine's from Arse . . . total," one minion grunted.

"Aris*totle*," Miss Price said in despair.

"'A friend is a second self'," the minion scoffed. "What? Friends is ghosts?"

"'Tomorrow and tomorrow and tomorrow'?" Darscall bellowed, disgusted. He curled his lip, kicked at the table and yelled, "Tomorrow and tomorrow notes with my name on?" Miss Price put her hand to her head. "I don't want fings with my name on it, got it?"

"I . . ." Miss Price spoke quietly, her lips flattening.

"Yeah. Got it, bitch?" he said.

The class was silent.

Miss Price's lips thinned as she fought tears. I felt terrible for her, plus I really, really wanted her to register me so I could get out.

"You," Darscall yelled, ready for another onslaught. "You go—"

"Gnurrrr," I grunted.

Silence.

My tongue hung in my mouth. "Guuuur, I don't want fings wiv my name on it! I only want ovva fings." In the silence, Darscall turned, dumbstruck. The class looked on in delighted horror. "Unnnuh! Wassis?" I picked up a pen. "Wassis fing? I doan like dis fing! Whas it do?" I opened the pen and mimed trying to figure out what it was, then jabbing my eye out with it. "Owwwww! The jabby blue fing bit me. Bloo stick bit me! Mummy! Bloo stick bit me."

The class laughed. Darscall was hang-mouthed.

I stood up, hooked my thumb into my trousers, and looked down at my pants. "Wassis fing? Was it do? Was eez?" I pulled up my pants. "Why's it got my name on it? Mummy! Why's my name on it? Mummy? Why's my name wrote on it? I don't like fings wiv my name on it. It's my name. Arrrrr!" I mimed ripping up my underpants. The class covered their mouths and howled with laughter.

I heard Miss Price yell as Darscall knocked me to the floor.

"Rape! Rape!" I yelled and got a few laughs before the weight of Darscall drowned my senses.

Darscall's hand stopped mid-punch as Miss Price

hauled him from me. He was loudly removed and when that palaver was over there were only ten minutes of the lesson left and Miss Price was too shaken to take us through what she'd prepared. We kept quiet as she put her head in her hands and bit her lips.

"Are you all right, miss?" Clarissa asked as the bell went. No one moved.

Miss Price nodded. "I didn't think it would be like this," she said.

There was a long silence. We all felt sorry for ourselves.

"I like my envelope," Poppy said.

"Yeah, I like mine," Bash said. "I like English."

"Yeah, thanks," I said. I made sure she saw me put my envelope in my pocket. "I'll finish it at home."

"Be careful – Jake," Miss Price said, pausing before my name again. I nodded as I walked out. Isaac would have made everyone laugh. I made everyone other than Darscall laugh. There was a big difference.

The gate was open, but I couldn't risk walking across the open space. I'd have to hide until long after the bell had gone. I went to visit the Insain Bolts, and then I hid in an empty classroom and edited the Apple Pie sketch until I heard the school keepers kicking everyone out.

12

I bit the zip of my coat and walked home. The odd black-and-orange decoration was a timid recognition of Halloween. Skeletons clacked in the wind and reminded me of Meadow Gorge. "Hello," I said as I walked past.

Buses bombed past but I didn't get on one. I never would. I was too scared of being cornered, or being felt up by some pervert, or stuck beside some racist rant. No, thank you.

Kids hung around the bus stops, harassing each driver and never successfully getting on the bus for free. They screeched, threw things and would love to take their frustration out on someone like me. I kept my head down and kept walking.

With no lighting and no exits, my *Crimewatch* road looked like it was built by murderers. The breeze pushed foils across the pavement. It was deathly quiet.

I stopped.

My eye caught the tail end of a pack of kids lingering near my house. Two of them were on bikes. One pedalled towards me. The others followed like a swarm. It was so typical of a nightmare, of the thing I'm afraid of every time I step outside, that it didn't seem real. It was as if I had willed them into life.

The pack moved towards me, blocking the path to my house.

The blackness shifted. The bikes pedalled behind me and blocked me in. Their clothes were so dark they melted to the road. One had a sunken face with a compacted jaw and skin as pale as cheese. One was much smaller, a child.

The child spoke. "That him?"

The alpha's skull swam in the canopy of a hood. I was trapped. I couldn't run, I would get jumped. I couldn't get to my house. I couldn't turn back.

The only way out was the Toad House. I would have to walk up that dark path, beneath that blinking red light, and pray that someone would let me in before they got to me.

The gang jerked towards me. A warning punch. I turned and ran the muddy path of the Toad House. The house seemed to lean towards me as I neared it, swelling with the screaming and misery that filled its wet walls. The gang hustled around the weak fence and strained with laughter. I shoved my clammy hands in my pockets and pretended to look for my key. The red security light blinked in my eyes.

"That your house or what, little boy?" one kid said.

The way they kept saying "house" sounded like how Americans say "arse".

"That ain't 'is ass."

"Look at this gaylord. Ain't 'is ass."

"Who's this queer gone the wrong ass."

"Oi, Mul, get 'im. That ain't is ass!"

"Get yer own ass!"

I knocked at the door and prayed.

Nothing.

"Please," I whispered. I was kiss-close to the fish-eye on the front door. "*Please.*"

Lowering my head, I glanced at the gang. They waited, salivating. I looked at their sunken chests, their hungry mouths. I couldn't feel the backs of my knees. I thought of my weak bones, and my bloodied kidneys, and of the fad for stabbing people in the armpit. Their fingers twitched in their pockets.

"Mug," one of them said.

"Oh, GET 'IM, MONK. He's mugging you off."

"'E's mugging you off!"

"MUG."

The leader surged forward. I braced and a prayer flew out my mouth. *Please, please let me in.*

The wind whipped my back, a hand gripped my shoulder and I flew into the house.

Slam.

The hallway was dark and reeked of damp. Machines

revved somewhere. I bolted away from the door towards the back of the house.

A force hooked my shins and slammed me to the floor. My face hit the muddy tiles with a thud. I was spun over and my hands pinned behind my head. To my horror it was a *girl*. No, wait, it was *the* girl. And, what's more, under her grip, I couldn't move.

"Who the hell are you?" she said.

"God, you're strong," I blurted.

"Yes, I am, and if you don't tell me what you were doing in *my* yard, I'm going to slap the white off your cheeks."

There was a full-armed bang on the door.

She stormed towards it and flung it open.

"No!" I cried.

"What?" she yelled in the leader's face. The gang bolted. The skeleton stood petrified in the doorway. "You selling pegs or what?" With her long fingers she flicked him *splat* in the centre of his eye. He clutched his eye, inhaled mightily, and wailed. He gritted his teeth to stop himself crying. "Go on," she said, "fuck off."

Slam.

She turned back to me. I sat on the bottom stair with my hands between my knees. She folded her arms and squashed her chin to her neck in disgust. "You tastin' your tongue?"

I fidgeted with my shirt.

"You can't speak?"

"Look what you did." I held up my wrists to show the

red imprint of her hands.

"My hands ain't red." She held up her white palms.

She crossed her legs and sank to the floor without using her hands. She wiped the dust on the brown tiles back and forth until it collected into a ball beneath her fingers.

"Thanks," I said.

"For what?"

The hallway was empty except for a few dark coats thrown on the bottom stair. A dying refrigerator revved angrily in the kitchen. "I haven't seen you in school."

"I don't go school."

"You're lucky."

She shrugged. "Where do you go?"

"Cattle Rise."

"Cattle Rise?" she squinted. "Where's that? Texas?"

"It's on the long road down that massive hill, past the park, past the shops."

She slapped her hands to her thin knees and laughed. I hadn't heard someone laugh properly for a long time. "How long you bin there?"

"Three days. Why?"

"Three days? Three whole days?"

"Well . . . not *whole* days."

She put her hand to her tiny belly and waited for the laughter to fade. "That's *Castle* Rise," she said finally, "not Cattle Rise. It's on Castle Rise Road? The logo's a castle. The place looks like a castle? Why would they call somewhere Cattle Rise?"

I dug through my bag for my planner. I could not

believe it. A drawing of those four ugly towers: Castle Rise.

"Who are you anyway, walking round these ends? You look like a *ghost*."

"I live next door," I said.

"Well, you're better than that weird old git who used to sit there all day grizzlin' like he'd just been kicked in the tits."

"That was my grandfather."

"Oh, shame."

"He died."

"Oh, shame," she said, smiling. It almost made me laugh, and this felt strange. I realized I hadn't laughed for a long time. Years, perhaps. "Now there's some doughy geezer who mopes down the garden like a mad gnome."

"That's my dad."

"Oh, shame." She twisted her face. "So you're the kid always looking in the mirror over there?"

I looked at the floor.

"Sexy," she said with a grimace. "You wanna get down a chicken shop, bruv. Bony as a morgue."

I smiled faintly.

"Thin as wages."

I smiled.

"You look like that muppet, uh. . ." She clicked her fingers.

"Beaker," I said. I knew him well.

"Yeah, Beaker on hunger strike. Guantanamo Beaker."

She laughed and I joined her. She waited for me to

have my turn. "Look at you," I stammered, pointing vaguely, "with your . . . nice . . . face."

She laughed so much she had to put her hand to her stomach. She glanced back at the door. "What are you waiting for? Pumpkins?"

"Pumpkins?"

"Yeah, the fuckin' pumpkins! You want to piss off or what?"

I got to my feet. My hands were shaking so much I couldn't open the door. She yanked it open. The street was clear. The epic journey to my house had shrunk to a few simple steps.

"Oh." I took a breath. "From Cinderella," I said.

"Are you on tranquillizers?"

"I—"

"Can you pick locks or what?"

"Can I—?"

"I saw you picking that door. I thought you was some jabbering crackhead at first, but then it took you so long I thought you must be related — or desperate — so I left you to it."

"I—"

"Why's it take you so long? In films it's like *clickedy-click*."

"It takes a long time in real life."

She kissed her teeth with a low, slow, sucking sound. "Oi, can you see my attic from your attic?"

"I don't know. I haven't—"

"There's two windows facing each other, like yours

and mine, up in both attics."

"I—"

"Have you ever been up there? In the attic? Spyin'?"

"No. I can barely get up stairs."

"It don't matter," she said, her face busy with something.

"Did you want to take a look?" I asked.

"Might," she shrugged.

"What's your name?" I asked.

"FIX UP YA SELF!" she said as she pushed me on to the doorstep. "That's my name."

Slam.

"Funny old name," I said to the door as the red security light flickered above my head.

That night, I lay awake as the light from the Toad House blared through my window. How could a teenage girl scare off a gang with one look? How could someone so quick, so vital not even go to school? With my quilt pulled over my head, I stationed myself by the windowsill. Hours later, I saw her push open her window, climb on to the garage and jump to the ground. Off she walked into the darkness, carrying her rucksack, her head flung back, compensating for the fear of it all.

"Where are you going?" I said as she disappeared into the night.

13

The next day at school I was told by everyone I came into contact with that Darscall was after me.

"What particular psychotropic drugs were you on yesterday?" Bash said as I sat down in biology.

"You stood up to him too," I said.

"I'm massive," Bash said, "and I know when to back off."

Kane joined us. "That was well funny in English," he said. "Suicide, but funny."

"Bash," Sean said, waving his finger between the two of us, "when did you get a boyfriend?"

"When your dad stopped treating me right," Bash said.

Laughter.

"Where've you been hiding?" Sean said to me. "Stepping up to Darscall, you must've gone full-Britney."

"He's not that scary," I said.

"Are you dumb?" Sean said.

"Are you mad?" Bash said. "He's the worst person here. He's a Boss. He was arrested last week, gun-related charges, but they couldn't hold him. What were you thinking?"

Clarissa came to our table. "Wa'gwan, Papa John?"

"Peachy keen, Krispy Kreme," Kane said.

"Pimpin hos, Dominos," Sean said.

They looked at me.

"I feel honoured like Mc . . . Donald. Like McDonalds." I coughed. There was an awful pause.

"Nice one, Kanye," Clarissa said, and they laughed. She had good timing. "You'll need them wits when Darscall's about to kick your teeth in." They laughed again.

"Come on, Jake, what happened?" Kane said.

"What's your story?" Bash said. "What's with you? Where are you from anyway?"

"Tell us the story of Jake," Sean said, smoothing an imaginary beard.

While that was a terrifying prospect, I looked at their faces, their expectant brown eyes and bitten lips, and felt a small wave of warmth. I wasn't going to tell them about my ridiculous life, but I did have *her*.

"There's a girl who lives next door," I said. "There's, like, a garage between our two houses and I can see right into her bedroom."

"Jackpot," Sean said.

"Shut up, Sean," Bash said. "Go on, Jake."

I took a deep breath and told them about the Toad House. I told them I had heard a scream and seen a young girl fight off a big white man. I told them she had run away when the police came, holding a duffel bag. I told them about the two men in a van, who seemed to intimidate and upset her.

"What *exactly* were they wearing?" Bash asked, and I described their grey trackies and the white guy's beanie cap in some detail. Bash raised an eyebrow.

"Fist bump?" Kane said, drumming his fingers.

"Yeah," Bash said, leaning forward, "did she bump the white guy?"

"No," I said, dragging my hair down over my forehead, only for it to pop back into its maddening upright shock.

"Act it out," Sean said.

I bumped my fists together.

"That's you with your boyfriend!" Sean grabbed himself and looked desperately for others to laugh with him.

Bash stroked his chin. "Traffickers?"

"Traffickers? With a black girl from London?" Kane said. "Unlikely."

"I never said she was black," I said.

Kane shifted uncomfortably. "What?" he said. "Some white girl gan jump off a roof and not die?"

The table laughed politely.

"Oi," Sean said, tapping his pen. "What accent she got?"

"Sarf London," I said.

"Ain't traffickers then," Clarissa said.

"Yeah," Bash said, "that's what we're saying."

"Must be debt collectors," Kane said.

"Yeah, that's what I think," Bash said.

"But he was attacking *her*," I said.

"Not those kind of debt collectors," Kane said. "He owes them. They've seen he's got a teenage daughter and, well, there you go."

"You're saying she has something to do with the repayment?"

"I'm saying she *is* the repayment, son," Kane said.

We all looked at each other.

"You've got to get in that yard, blud," Sean said, "see wa'gwan."

Clarissa kissed her teeth and the others laughed. "Sean, you ruin bein' Jamaican for me, man. Shut up, man."

"Clarissa," the teacher said, "sit down, please."

"Sorry, sir," she said. Her voice was soft and raspy. She turned back to us. "So what are we going to do about this girl?"

"Clarrisa, didn't I tell you to sit down?"

"I believe you did, sir," Clarissa said as she turned back to us. "We have to find out who she is and help her out of whatever hell her old man has—"

"Clarissa."

"We know her address so we can find out who she—"

"Clarissa!"

"'*Sake,* sir, I'm not the only one talking!" She turned to me. "What's her address?"

"I tried the address, it doesn't work."

"Clarissa, I've called SLT."

"Am I the only one talking? Am I? Or am I the only *girl* talking?"

The class whooped.

"Clarissa, calm down," the teacher said.

"That'll work," Clarissa said as she took the address.

A black suit appeared at the door. "Clarissa Neale?" he said. Clarissa folded the address into her notebook and snapped it shut. "Now," the suit said, wielding his walkie-talkie.

"I need my mice," Clarissa said.

"Now, Clarissa."

"Sir! I need my mice! He's only sending me out 'cos I'm a girl."

"Now, Miss Neale."

"Sending bitches home like Venus and Serena."

Laughter.

"Sir," Clarissa said, digging through her tiny bag and retrieving two tampons, "I need my mice."

She clattered out of the classroom and I knew she wouldn't care about having to go, because nothing is better than making your whole class laugh.

I looked uneasily at the door. Clarissa had the Toad House address in my handwriting, which anyone could use to find my address, which could link me to calling the police, and still what I was most upset about was not being able to think of a good rhyme earlier when that was what I basically spent my whole childhood doing. My mouth ran ahead of my brain.

"I could have thought of a hundred of those food rhymes," I said to Kane.

"You're all right, love," Kane said, with a little pat on my back. He and Bash creased with laughter. "You're all right, pet."

14

Schools like this are undersubscribed so it isn't hard to find abandoned classrooms, and their empty storage cupboards. These cupboards will be filled with past papers, photocopied in preparation for kids who never came, stacked and moulding, half chewed by mice, and, if you like, you can sit there until school has finished.

I opened both doors with a rake key and a biro. They might as well not bother locking them.

Isaac was playing on loop while I continued editing myself out of the Apple Pie scene. We play these gangsters who are playing Russian roulette with a McDonald's Apple Pie. Isaac, in his genius, approaches the pie teeth-first, but the moment he bites into the pastry, I look at the camera and laugh. For months I'd been trying to edit out my awful corpsing. I couldn't use any of the later takes because once he'd seen me laughing, he couldn't help laughing too. He would buckle over, his legs twisted, his hands furrowing into his crotch, worried he would wet himself.

He did, once. He wet himself when we were performing in the school playground. "Oh, my dignity, my dignity!" he cried, convulsing on the ground. I had knelt beside him, trying to shield him from everyone else's view, but I was useless with laughter. I felt I might die laughing.

I clicked off the videos and called him.

This is the O2 messaging. . .

The bell went for afternoon registration. I checked my path was clear and made my way to my locker.

A low voice.

"All right, Jake."

That graveyard voice. My bag came off my shoulder. I turned around without thinking.

His shoulders were relaxed and his lips wet. I felt a spasm of electricity in my legs, as if a very ancient part of my psyche was telling me to run for my life. On the wall was that awful tag:

$$☠

Riches, skull.

My eyes widened.

Rich . . . skull.

Ritchie Darscall.

Jesus.

Without a word, he lifted my jumper, revealing my thin trousers. He ran his hand along my belt, gently, almost lovingly. He put his paw down into one pocket, then the other, and fished out my phone.

"No!" I cried.

He grinned.

"I need that." I grabbed for it and he shoved me so hard against the lockers it knocked the air from my lungs.

"Twenty quid," he said, then spat in my face. "Queer."

I thought of the videos of me and Isaac as he pocketed my phone. I didn't dare move, not even to reach up and wipe the phlegm from my face.

"Open your locker," he said.

I did it.

"Don't wipe your face. Keep that on your face."

He took a package the size of a cereal box out of his bag and put it in my locker. "Anything happens to that, you are dead. You got it?"

It wasn't the first time someone had spat in my face. It wasn't the first time some gangster had forced me to hold drugs for them. And it wasn't the first time that some massive white kid had stolen something from me and ransomed it.

"BOO!" He feinted a punch to my guts. I flinched and he laughed. I looked at the floor, at Darscall's gaudy trainers.

Clean-haired kids floated by in their logo-less shoes.

15

That evening I watched our sketches on my computer. Over and over, all evening, just to block out the day.

In one scene the Real Fly Rabbi is rapping and you can hear me laughing in the background. The camera shakes and often swoops to the floor because I couldn't control myself.

"Yes I've got loafers,
but I need a new pair.
Tesco ones are comfortable and practical
and they do discounts there."

People at school used to crowd around our computers to watch our sketches and the Real Fly Rabbi was a popular character.

My fingers twitched for my phone. I thought of the sketches I had on there and nowhere else. I thought of the pictures on my phone, and, I thought as I started to cry, of his number. I didn't have it written down anywhere.

A rustling came from the garden of the Toad House. A glob of darkness moved about. I blinked and the glob became a figure. The figure scaled the guttering and reached the bedroom window. The pocket of light from the streetlamp briefly brushed the fine face of the girl. I stretched to call out to her, but instead watched her pick at the moss on the garage roof. When I blinked it seemed she wasn't there, but just a shape in the gap between our houses.

16

When I woke the next morning I was bundled on the floor in the corner of my room, holding a cricket bat. My night terrors were back. Mother was in the middle of one of her rants. Dad was walking in circles round the garden, teetering on the verge of a permanent dream world. Plus, I had the shakes.

No school today.

I looked up at the hatch in my ceiling and wondered why the girl next door wanted to look up there. I fetched a chair and used the cricket bat to push the trap door open. Dust plumed down to my face. The attic was pitch black and reeked of rotten vegetables. I tried to see inside but couldn't lift myself up. I squinted at something I thought was moving in the breeze. I pushed the trap door shut, and went downstairs.

"What the hell have you been doing?" Mother yelled. She stared at the dust as if it was the blood of newborn infants. "You are not to touch anything in this house, do you understand me? Do you?"

I dragged my feet across the excavated sitting-room floor, up the epic stairs and back to my room. Mother yelled on and on like artillery fire, until her words became meaningless. After a while I ripped the door off my cupboard and held a tight grip on the exposed hinge until it cut through my skin.

Mother flew up the stairs and rammed on my door. I screamed at her to go away. She screamed back, then stormed away. I heard something smash downstairs. She flung open the front door, causing my door to fly open then slam shut again.

Mother's car did its familiar screech out of the drive. I watched from the window as it stalled and revved and screamed into the traffic. Something about this particular tantrum gave me a sickly feeling. My nails dug into the pulse of my wrist, and then I heard the baby crying.

"Mum?" I said.

In Squirm's room, two little feet kicked from the carry cot on the floor, trying to escape the soiled nappy that was stinging her. The noise of her screams spiked down my ears to the base of my brain. I tried to pick her up and she jammed her arms to her sides. "Don't you want me to change you?" I said, but she carried on screaming. "Well? Don't you?" I yelled. She screamed and screamed. "Shut up, you tiny idiot." I jabbed her blanket. "Shut *up*!"

Squirm covered her eyes with her podgy hands. I picked her up, but she cried as if terrified. "I'm sorry," I told her. I managed to change her and put cream on her nappy rash. I patted her back and cuddled her, rocking her back and forth. She began to hiccup with the exhaustion of crying so much. Finally I held her away from me, let her dangle her podgy legs, and she stopped crying. I was sweating and shaking from holding her. I wiped my face and I realized I'd been crying with her.

Squirm looked happy now, waving her hands excitedly, searching for something to hold. I offered my finger and she grabbed it, then shoved it into her little mouth.

"Orrr," she said

It would be hours before Dad came home, *if* he came home. I carried Squirm to my room and tried to find her some toys to play with.

"What's that smell, Squirm?" I said.

"Orr."

"Has one pooed one's pants?" I said. "Again?"

"Orr," she said.

"Very lady-like. Charmed, I'm sure."

I carried her to the bathroom and took off her nappy. It was filled with poo and the poo was green. I heaved her into the sink and ran her bottom under the tap. The sink soon filled with green poo so I put her in the bath, poo spreading all over my hands.

I ran the bath. The smell was getting worse. I looked back to the sink and realized I had left the tap on. The pool of green poo was edging closer to the rim. I couldn't unhand the baby for the seconds it would take to reach over and switch off the tap. "Shit!" I said as the sink overflowed and spilled on to the floor, flooding the tiles with the putrid liquid. I relinquished my shirt and plucked the gunk-covered baby from the bath and waded over to turn the tap off. I felt sick in my mouth as I plunged my hand into the sink to drain the green water with . . . bits . . . floating in it. Gripping the swaddled baby, I was sick into the toilet, my stomach heaving painfully.

"Uuuf," Squirm giggled.

I covered the floor with toilet paper. The bath was filthy and I couldn't wash her in it, so I held her with one arm while I used the other one to scrub it out. I rinsed it a million times before I put her back in it. I couldn't find any soap except a florescent green hand wash that that said it was zero per cent everything. I tested some on Squirm's cheek before risking her whole body. I made my fingers into a fin. "Look, Squirm, a shark! Oooooooooooo! Say 'Ooooooooooo!' What do sharks say? What do sharks say? Actually, what *do* sharks say? E-ooooooooo!"

She giggled and splashed when I plunged my shark-hand into the water and brought it out again. "Eeeeek-ooooooooo!"

It was scary taking her out of the bath. Every edge is hard and murderous. I put one towel over myself, another towel around her, lifted her out and held her to my chest. I stepped over the grim mess on the floor and carried her back to her room. I dried, powdered and dressed her. It took for ever because she wriggled about, and by the time I'd done it she had pooed herself again so I had to change that nappy as well.

As I looked at her trembling mouth and heaving stomach, I realized with panic that I hadn't fed her. I hadn't even thought about feeding her. I took her downstairs and found a box of rusks. Squirm went for it, mouth-first.

"Were you hungry, Squirm? I'm so sorry."

"Orr!" the baby said and she slapped my cheek, giggling. I smiled at her. Poo-floor aside, I'd done all right. I took a bite of the rusk. "Oooh!" she said.

One pot of applesauce later, the doorbell rang. I looked at the shadow behind the glass, hoping it would go away. It didn't. The bell rang again. I picked up Squirm, crept to the door and checked through the eye hole.

"I can see you," Miss Price said.

I opened the door.

Miss Price looked inside. "Left alone?"

"No, Mum and Dad just went to the shops."

"Both of them?"

"Yeah, Mum doesn't drive so Dad had to drive her. . ."

"And is this why you weren't in school today?"

"No. Not at all. I'm . . . ill."

"Ill. Right. With what?"

"What?"

"What's wrong? What are you ill with? What are the symptoms?"

"It's—"

"It's what?"

"It's, uh. . ."

"You're ill and you don't know what it is?"

"It's—"

"It's *what,* Jake?"

She was such a force of energy, I couldn't think of any disease except peritonitis, which I have to take medication for, but I tripped over the word and said it too quickly. "I've got penis," I said.

"*Pardon?*"

"Peniton . . . peni. . ." I panicked. "Penis." I shook my head. "I've got problems."

Miss Price frowned. "Well, I collected your homework," she said, and handed me a wad of worksheets.

"Thanks."

"Funny – Mr Caffrey and Mr Halls had never heard of you."

"Oh? They probably just haven't learnt my name."

"Hum," Miss Price said.

"Weird." I nodded.

"Yes, it *is* weird. Especially as you don't have Mr Halls and there is no Mr Caffrey."

Sneaky. I couldn't think of a reply.

"You're not actually going to your lessons, are you, Jake."

For once I was thankful to feel the timid but determined tremble of Squirm having a poo in my arms. "The baby needs her nappy changed, miss, so unless you want to stay and—"

"No," Miss Price said abruptly, "no, not at all. But I have my eye on you, all right?"

"All right." I shut the door and gave the baby a kiss on her forehead. "Well played, Squirm."

17

It was dark when Dad arrived home. I flew at him the moment he opened the door. "Mum drove off and left me with Squirm all day."

"What are you talking about?"

"She left me with the baby *all day*!"

"Yes, all ri—"

"What if I'd put my music on and not heard her? What if I'd gone out? What if she had rolled over or choked or—"

"What are you *talking* about, Jake?"

"I didn't know when her last feed was. What if she'd starved—"

"Her last feed?" he said. "I hear you have been of no. . ." He shook his head.

"What?"

"We got a call from your head teacher."

"They're called *principals* in the shit schools you send me to."

"She said you broke thi . . . I said it couldn't have been you. You . . . you wouldn't have. . ." He read my face. "Oh, Jake! Why do you have to make everything so bloody. . ."

"So *what?*" I asked.

"So. . ." He rolled his hand, his face strained.

"So what?"

"Difficult," he exhaled. "So bloody *difficult*."

"I'm the one being shunted about by you pair of berks."

"We don't move to spite you, Jake. We move because of you. Everywhere you go, you get in trouble. You make everything worse."

I turned, opened the front door and slammed it so hard the window box fell and smashed. I raged to the end of the street where my sphere of anger hit another, and we collided like bumper cars.

"What you lookin' at?" she yelled.

"Nothing."

"You dancing?" She shoved me backwards, then stopped as if shocked by how far she had pushed me simply by touching my chest. "Sorry," she said.

I reached for my phone; then I remembered I no longer had it. I put my face to the sky and seethed.

"What's wrong with you?"

"What do you care?"

"I asked, didn't I?"

She pronounced it "arkst".

She stepped forward. "You having a heart attack or sammink?"

"As if you care."

"I arkst, didn't I?" she repeated.

"You shouldn't be able to . . . feel your heart." I pulled at my shirt.

"You having a heart attack? Eh? Dot Cotton? What's wrong with you?" She put her hand to my forehead. Her fingertips were cold. She wiped her hand on her grey joggers. "Sweating like a pregnant nun."

I meant to laugh, but no sound came out, just a hollow jolt to my chest. I stretched my back and tried to push my shoulder blades together in the panic of short breath. "What's your name?" I asked.

"Lean forward, curve your spine," she said, "all you're doing there is flattening your lungs."

I put my elbows to my knees and took a lungful of air. My spine made thankful crackling noises.

"Better?"

"Yeah. How did you know that?"

She shrugged.

"I need my phone," I said.

"Stolen?"

"Ransomed."

"That's worse. Don't ever pay a ransom."

"I need that phone. It's got stuff on it."

"They'll only ask for more money, fam."

I pulled at the weeds that had pushed through a crack

in the kerb. Across the street a lumbering figure was silhouetted briefly against the glow of a streetlamp.

"Robin." She shrugged.

"What about them?"

"That's my name. Robin."

"Oh." I stopped. "Why . . . why are . . . are you . . . are you then . . . why are . . . called Robin?"

She twisted her face.

"What's the story of that name?"

"You really want to know?" She picked at the cuff of her hoodie. "When my mum was pregnant with me she used to walk through the park to go to work. She *hated* going work. Anyway, one day I kicked her so hard, she had to sit down in the snow and she started to cry, but then a little robin bopped up to her and it cheered her up. Then she decided to call me Robin."

"Lucky it wasn't a pigeon."

"Or a blue tit," she said. "Blue Tit Carter. Imagine what the kids at school would call me."

"Bluey?"

"Yeah, that's what I was thinking. *Bluey.*" She laughed. "What's your name then?"

"Jake."

"Jade? That's a girls' name."

"Jake," I said.

"Jason?"

"*Jake*," I said.

"Oh, *Jake*," she said as if to memorize it. "So what's the . . . *story* there?"

"Uh, my mum was pregnant with me, and miserable and that, and then my dad got her some Jacob's crackers and it cheered her up, so she decided to call me Jacob." I got up and slapped the dirt from the back of my trousers. "Like the actual crackers."

Robin laughed. "Lucky it weren't HobNobs."

"Yeah, I wonder what the kids at school would call me."

"Hobby?"

"Yeah, *Hobby*, that's what I was thinking." I laughed and it felt weird in my mouth.

"You look like you need to be in bed, no 'fence. You look a bit wavy, mate."

"I'm all right," I said. I didn't worry about her saying I looked ill. I was just pleased she'd called me mate.

I kicked at the tiny stones on the pavement. Robin got up and walked down the street in the direction of the park. Her walk was quicker than my run. I called, "Surely you can't be—"

She turned. "What?"

"You can't be going down the park? A kid was—"

"What?"

"Killed. On this street. He wasn't just stabbed, you know. He was beaten up."

"You think I don't know?" Robin said, her face pinched. "Get back to your knitting or whatever you people do."

"What do you mean 'you people'?" I called after her.

I could only see her when she was beneath the weak

light of the lampposts. "I'm not white!" I said. "I'm from London!"

I walked to my door and kicked away the smashed window box. Something silver turned within the soil. I pulled it out. It was a key. I tested it in the front door and it worked. "Idiot," I said to my dead grandfather. I stepped inside and my footsteps echoed across the cold room. Dad and Squirm were gone. The key was cold from the soil. I stepped back out of the front door and ran.

18

Darkness felt smaller as I broke into a run. I waited for my ankles or knees to buckle in pain, but they didn't. My lungs sucked the cold air and didn't arrest; my heart pumped blood around my body. My thigh bone absorbed the reverberations from the pavement and held together, grateful to feel the strike of the pavement once again. At Meadow Gorge there were athleticas who would run up and down the stairs like mad Slinkys. They would challenge you to marathons or squat championships or to three thousand sit-ups. If you want to know what doing three thousand sit-ups feels like, I couldn't tell you, because after a few hundred you can't feel anything and the next morning you feel like someone has carved a canoe out of your stomach. Once, this girl Hannah, a baby bird on the loose, was sprinting back and forth between two lampposts in her bare feet, her dressing gown flying behind her like a cape. I ran back and forth with her. I thought it would calm her down, but it only spurred her on. She looked like a child in her mother's clothes. After a while I stood there like a plum as she thundered back and forth, swimming through the air.

I kept to the long road. When I got to the park, I stopped. I went back a few paces. A strange mound was pressed against the fence. I approached, squinting. The mound had two skinny little legs poking out of it.

"Robin?" I said.

The mound shook itself to life. "Get lost, will you."

I crouched beside her. "Why are you dressed like a cartoon spy?"

"Get lost before you get us both killed."

"I saw those two blokes and that one of them pushed you. I'm sorry. I'm so sorry I didn't call the police or anything."

"What are you on about?"

I lay flat on my ribs next to Robin. Wimbledon Park has tennis courts, a running track and a lake filled with swans and ducks. Beyond the lake is a luscious golf course, which is private and you get shot or something if you go on it. Beyond the park you can see the silhouettes of mansions that line Wimbledon Hill and eclipse the estates of Southfields. The park is where you camp to get tickets for the tennis. I went there once with Isaac and his dad. We got so scared when the sun set that my dad had to come and get us. But by then I had got caught up in

Isaac's stories and I was disappointed when I saw my dad.

"For ever," I whispered. I turned to Robin. "Me and my best friend Isaac went on this treasure hunt all through Brixton, looking for these red rubber bands that were left all over the street. We were sure they marked out places and there was some kind of pattern. We went everywhere collecting them and marking them off on a map. This other time—" I started to laugh and she raised her razor-flat hand.

"Shh."

In the distance a fox barked and made me jump.

"I hate that sound," I said.

"Innit," Robin said. "Sounds like a woman screaming."

I felt happy that she agreed with me. "My mum says they should shoot them all," I said. I don't know why I said that.

Robin shook her head. "They're only doing what they do. Not their fault."

Movement within the fence near the running track looked faintly animal. "Are there people there?" I whispered.

Robin nodded.

"What are they doing?"

"What do you *think?*"

The fox cried again. I jumped. Robin didn't.

She opened her duffel bag. Inside were night-vision goggles and a camera. She handed me the goggles.

I put the goggles to my eyes. I saw the slouched outline of a pack of kids huddled in the far corner of the park. A hulking, faintly beast-like figure lumbered towards them and disappeared behind an oak tree. The stick figures approached the tree one by one, squat-walking to keep their jeans on, dragging their feet like they'd stepped in dog poo. From where we were they looked like question marks. They fiddled in pockets so low that they had to crane their backs to reach within them. They looked terrified.

"It's money." She took the goggles from me. "Pay-off."

The big man clipped one of the kids across the head and he scurried back to the pack.

"They're paying him," Robin said. "Giving him his cut."

The man lumbered on, up the hill and out of the park. The boys remained in a huddle.

"Go and see what they're selling," Robin whispered. She put a ball of notes into my hand.

"*Me?*"

"I can't, can I? They know my arse."

The sulking stick figures retreated back to their corner, doing their dog-turd walk. My eyes swam across the darkness. "But, what if I get . . . killed?"

"No one's gunna bother killing you."

That was a new one. No one was going to bother hiring me or marrying me, but now no one would even bother to murder me.

I looked at Robin, her soft face visible now my eyes had adjusted to the darkness. "What do I ask for?"

"Drugs, obviously."

"Just, 'Can I have some drugs, please?'"

"No, you virgin." Her eyes lit up. "Ask for a *piece*."

"A piece of what?"

"Of Chocolate Orange." She kissed her teeth. "You're from Other London. Your clean hair bullshit. You got buttons in your eyes, blud. A piece is a gun. *God*."

"It's a bad world where people have buttons in their eyes, so if—"

"Just move your arse, muggle, go on."

"So if I was a muggle I'd also have no butt—"

"Lost."

"What am I doing?" I said out loud. My face had taken on a strange numb sensation, as if this was happening to someone else.

"I need to see if they're selling guns," she said.

We watched the distant movement in the park and I waited for her to speak again.

"This lot are small fry. Trust."

"Oh, my life."

I skulked towards the imps, holding my breath, clutching the crumpled tenners. Every step plunged me into quicksand, my stomach lurching, my lungs on fire. I approached the animalistic gathering. I realized they were all wearing grey hoodies. "Good evening," I said to the nearest boy. "I'd like some, I mean . . . got . . . any . . . uh. . ."

"The hell are you?" he barked. "Go and talk to Stee. 'Ere, *Stee,* you useless tart, talk to this skinny little slag."

105

A weasel-shaped boy scurried over from the pack. "Skunk? E? H?"

I envisioned him with a screeching, scratching skunk, squirting stink all over my face before it scratched my eyes out. "Nah," I laughed. "I need a . . . some *pieces*."

"Some *what*?"

"Some pieces for this thing I've got to. . ."

"Pieces of what?"

"I. . ." I was careful not to look in Robin's direction, but it was taking all of my tiny concentration. "I want your special . . . *thing*."

"What are you, some sort of queer?"

"I want a thing that you point and it goes off. . ."

"Talk. Fast."

"A piece!" I said triumphantly. "A piece. That's what I want."

"Piece? Of what?"

"Eight," I blurted. "Pieces of eight! Arrr! I'm a pirate." I clicked my tongue.

"Who the hell are you?"

"Me? No one."

"Tell you what, No One. How about you ask for a piece one more time, and I get all these boys here to come over and kick you until you are dead. How about that?"

The other kids were looking our way and I could feel, in the darkness, that they were moving towards us.

"No, you're all right," I said. "I don't fancy that." The pack were close enough now for me to see their faces. I did a double take.

Darscall and his minions.

I tried to turn before they saw me, but I couldn't take my terrified eyes off them.

"You what?"

"No, thanks. Thanks a lot." I shuffled backwards. "Thanks a lot, have a nice. . ." I exhaled.

The boy watched me back away.

The rest of the pack inched forward, ready for a signal from the leader. I turned and walked as slowly as my poor bones would let me. I heard him pad after me, and then the soft padding rumbled into a wave of hi-tops slapping the pavement. I ran the winding road, momentarily surprised at how fast I could go. I had forgotten how it felt to fly through the air, those first moments when you're running so fast but your heart doesn't put on the brakes and burn your muscles to tell you to stop. I took a short cut through a gap between two houses that no human should be able to fit into, and slipped inside. Trapped in the shadows, I panicked with claustrophobia, but the gang ran past. I waited until I saw them amble, confused and breathless, back to the park.

I slid from the gap. For a short second I was stuck and panicked so much I felt my heart expand, but then I was free and I ran the long road that circled the park until I was sure I hadn't been followed.

"Well?" Robin said when I returned.

"I'm no expert," I whispered, "but I think I failed that one."

"Nob," Robin said, her eyes on the pack of question-mark kids.

"I recognized some of them from school."

"Who?"

"Ritchie Darscall. He's the one who took my phone."

"*He* took your phone? Shit, Jake. Watch your arse. Dizzy Darscall's a nasty piece of work."

"Dizzy Darscall?" I almost laughed. "He's just a Darscall, he's Dizzy Darscall."

"I wake up every day is a nightmare, in the mirror my face is a big scare," Robin sang.

"I gel my hair to make it look like an afro, but it's weak and it's blond and it won't go."

Robin laughed. "Some people think I'm Darscall, but I just think I'm . . ."

She stopped. A few of the kids had sloped off to a grey house perched on the end of the quiet road next to the park. The cold set in my bones.

"Where are they going?"

"The Trap House, where they cut drugs and keep those poor girls."

"Keep" was a sinister word. "Will you tell me why you have a camera with you?" I asked.

"I wanted out, so they're jumping me out. And I'll show them being jumped out."

"What's jumped out?"

"Oh, Christ. Too late."

Robin ducked her head and took the camera out of her bag.

In the distance a boy walked into the park holding

another boy by the elbow. The question-mark kids packed around him. Robin shot me a look that said "keep your mouth shut". The question-mark kids closed in, cooking him, ready for something to explode. There was only one way this would go. They needed energy from their victim: he would run or fight, and either way they would devour him.

"Have you got a burner?" Robin whispered.

"Sorry, I don't smoke."

"A burner's a *phone,* you monk." She took out her own phone and dialled 999. "Police, please," she whispered in a Liverpool accent. "Hello, I'm just walking me dog past Wimbledon Park and it looks like a gang has this lad and they're going to attack him. He—" She hung up. The boy had been consumed by shadows. I could just about make out his shoulders moving up and down in panic. I prayed he wouldn't run. Animals need the chase. If he ran they would pounce on him.

He ran.

He made it a few steps before he was thrown to the ground. They set on him, their legs flying as they kicked and jumped him. I thought of getting beaten up on Bertie Bridge down Battersea. There had been three of them and I couldn't walk properly for a week after it. This kid had seven or eight. I put my hands to my head. Robin's hand gripped the dirt. The gang stopped, exhausted. They whooped, howled. The boy was a rag doll on the ground. "God forgive me," Robin whispered as she pressed the button on her camera. It took rapid photos but also made a whirring noise. The pack lagged off. I could barely see them, but I felt someone watching us. I grappled for the night-vision goggles. "Cover your face," I whispered. Robin drew her scarf beneath her eyes.

The boy broke into a fast walk. The others followed like a swarm. "Robin," I whispered, shoving the goggles into her rucksack. "Run."

"*What?*"

They sped up and headed towards us.

"RUN!"

I leapt up. I turned to help her but she hared off ahead of me. I brought my speed up until I couldn't feel my legs. I heard them stampeding behind us, grunting and baying.

"What colour are they?" Robin yelled as she belted up the hill.

"What?" I was sick with exhaustion.

"*Colour.* What colour are they?" she yelled.

I glanced at the grimacing hoodies gaining on us. "Grey," I panted.

"Not their clothes! Their *skin!*"

"White," I managed.

"Good," Robin said. "Split. I'll take the long way."

"*Why?*" I called. My heart lurched as she sped away. I thought of her getting caught, mauled and destroyed by a rabid gang. My mind took over my useless legs and propelled them forward. You can't see darkness when you're racing through it.

When I reached our house I saw a jagged figure sitting in the apple tree. My fingers absently folded into prayer.

"Robin?" I called to her.

"Jake?" She jumped from the branches.

"Robin," I said, "are you all right?"

She shrugged and walked towards me, as if the jump hadn't affected her knees at all. Her camera was in her hand.

I swallowed my heavy breath only for it to burn my lungs and explode back out of my mouth as a wet cough.

Sirens circled the air.

"Why were you glad they were white? Are white guys not as dangerous?"

"Yeah, they are," Robin said. "They just can't run."

"Oh," I said.

We both laughed. The wind whipped up the foils from the grass and pushed them across the long road.

"Don't ever join a gang," Robin said. "Not ever."

"No one's asking me."

"No, they wouldn't." Robin gave a sly smile, which she quickly dropped. We both knew that was the problem. "They flatter you and in, like, weeks you're just a prisoner."

I scratched the back of my neck. "What's happened?"

"I told them I wanted out and they said I ain't getting out. And that was it. Just like that. The next day these sidemen, who I didn't even know, got arrested, and they all think it was because of me. Like, this one shit-stirring monk puts it on Facebook and suddenly every BBM, Snapchat, post, everything is saying I snaked to the police and I'm *ghosting*. Do you know what I'm saying?"

I didn't.

"They think I'm a snitch and that is a serious threat. So they've said I've got to show up on Friday and tell them who it is."

"How could they make you go?"

"They have ways."

"How do they know where you are?"

Robin laughed.

"Who is it? The snake, I mean."

"I don't know. That's the point." She looked through the photographs. "It must be one of these," she said. "Without names it's useless."

I looked at the pictures on her camera. The boys who hung around Darscall were peering beneath their grey hoods.

"Can't you just lie low? Run away?"

"Run away? Are you five? Run away? No one can run away. He'd find me."

"Who?"

"The Beast. The boss man."

"The Beast?"

"Subtle, innit?" Robin shook her head. "When he was a Young he was called Dub List and it, like, changed over the years to the Beast."

"How would he know how to find you?"

"Find me?" She pointed a thumb towards the glaring eye of the Toad House and the hunched man shifting angrily within. "He's watching me right now."

I looked at the photograph of Dizzy Darscall and his minions, then to her worried eyes, then to the glare of the Toad House. "I could find out who they are," I said.

19

I was late to Cattle Rise but the teacher marked me in without making me sign the late register. It was a small gesture that made me feel a tiny bit better about being there. Some teachers can just look at you and know it's a miracle you're in school at all.

After registration I didn't go home or to my cupboard, I followed Darscall until I spotted the minions from the photograph. They walked slowly down the corridor and had something to bark at almost everyone who passed them.

They entered a classroom at the instruction of a bearded teacher whose ID card read "Mr A. Millar". All I needed was an unlocked computer and I could look at his class lists and find the names and addresses of the boys, but for that, I'd have to actually go to lessons.

I arrived at history and found an empty desk. Everyone was looking at pictures of gulags and writing questions they wanted to ask. "Anything you don't know, anything you don't understand, anything you might want me to explain," the teacher said as he paced the class.

The class was industrious. Mr Gilbert dragged us through the work. I felt exhausted as I watched everyone crowd out at the end. I followed them to the front of the class and when no one was looking I crouched beneath the desk. The system unit whirred next to my ear.

I waited until I heard Mr Gilbert lock the door. I had minutes before the next class came in. I clicked off his register and went into the teacher profiles. I typed "Millar" into the surnames. His class list appeared and I clicked on Period One. His register loaded. I filtered the boys and clicked through each one, their mug shots loading with infuriating delay. The light in the room changed strangely. I looked up and saw everything I was doing was being projected on to the massive whiteboard. I searched around for the control for the projector. I couldn't find it. I was running out of time, so I'd have to risk it. I checked the porthole window and persevered until one of their lanky faces crept onto the screen. I clicked on "student profile" then "print". My heartbeat became warm until finally I heard the printer whirr into life. I took a paper clip out of the desk tidy, bent it, twisted it in half, put one half in my back pocket, and the other half in my mouth. I kept clicking until I found the last boy. "Derrick?" I said to his face. "Who's called *Derrick*?" I printed his profile, grabbed the pages, picked the lock in two clicks, went out into the empty corridor, and slammed straight into Kane.

"Oh," I said.

"Oh," he said. He snatched the pages out of my hand. I fought him but he put his hand flat to my chest and easily held me off as he read the profiles.

"What have you got these for?" He shoved me back into the empty classroom and closed the door behind us. "Who *are* you?" he said.

"Who I am?" I said. "Who am I? You know who I am."

"Did someone ask you to get this? Because if someone's forcing you I can help you. But you have to tell me."

"What?"

Kane folded his arms. "Who are you?"

I couldn't speak. I could only look at him. I quite liked being alone with him, but I was also aware I was in quite a lot of trouble. And I hadn't spoken for a long time now, so I just needed to say something. Anything. Any little thing! Who was I? I didn't know. But I did know that I really, really, really needed to speak. . .

"No one," I said.

"Nah, nah, nah, there's arrests happening around here and people are ghosting."

"I don't know what that means."

"Running. Scared. Someone knows too much. There's a snake. Somewhere. So I'll ask you again, for your own sake, who are you?"

It was a strange question to be asked, and I had no idea

how to answer it, but then I thought of my other life and I found a way out. "I was at St. Eloïse's in Brixton. Like you said. I'm sorry I don't remember you."

Kane nodded slowly. "You Brixton then?"

I nodded and Kane relaxed. The *air* relaxed.

"So where you bin? Why act so suspect?"

"I've been in hospital," I said.

"What happened?"

I closed my eyes and saw blood with pieces in it.

"Cancer or something?" Kane guessed. That's what everyone guesses. Kane looked again at the profiles in his hand. "What you gunna do with those?"

"Do I look like I could do anything about anything?"

"You just happen to be holding profiles of two people in the CRK? Who are both simple? Who both work for Darscall? That a coincidence, is it?" Kane tore the pages up and put them in the bin. "There are people who make shit happen, and people who have shit happen to them. Do you know what I'm saying?"

Darscall's in the CRK too?

Before I could open my mouth to ask, the deputy principal burst into the room. "What on earth is going on in here?"

"We're having an orgy," I said.

"I *begyourpardon*?"

"Yeah, do you mind?" Kane said. "We're busy."

"Get your bags and your blazers and step outside, please." The deputy principal had been stressed for so long, his skin was starting to die and peel off his face.

Kane laughed and dodged past him, out of the room. He was so good-looking he could do stuff like that.

The deputy principal turned to me. "Now, please, there's a good lad."

"Oh, fuck off, will you?" I said.

I stormed past him and into the corridor.

"Jones," he called, thundering after me.

"Hang on." I turned and pointed at him calmly. "I thought I told you to fuck off?"

"Get up those stairs right now."

"You'd have to buy me dinner first."

"Jones!" he screamed, his veins swollen to maximum capacity. "You will go and see Mrs Anderson right now!"

I went up the stairs, fuming, I threw myself on the chair and the half paperclip stuck right in my arse cheek. "SWEET JESUS!" I cried. I jumped up and grabbed my bony arse.

"What on Earth are you doing?" the principal yelled.

"My bloody life!" I cried. "My poor arse!"

"Are you on drugs?"

"No, have you got any?"

"Go and stand outside my office."

I paced outside the office. The vom-dot secretary shifted to tell me she was uncomfortable with me walking about. As she typed I looked at her poor red hands. They were tiny and ravaged, but not with bad circulation like mine, with anti-bacterial wash.

"Miss," I said softly, holding my stomach and staggering. She pushed backwards in her chair as I came towards her.

"I feel really sick."

"Well, you're going to have to go outside."

"Miss. . ." I staggered and she instinctively put out her hand to catch my fall. I caught it and my massive hand wrapped hers like chip paper. She leapt from her chair and I fell into it and made sure my head touched the fabric. "I'll be all right," I wailed. "I just need to sit down for a bit. God. I'm *sweating*." I sniffed and dragged my hand beneath my nose.

"You – you – you need to go *outside*."

"Just give me five minutes, miss, I'll be all right."

She hovered, her little red fingers twisting.

"Could I have some water . . . please? Some . . . *water*. . ."

She hurried off to the bathroom and I went on her computer, found the minions' profiles again and hit print. Nothing happened. "Come on." I checked the wires were connected to the printer and that the printer was on. I opened the tray: no paper. I looked about. The office was immaculate and there was no paper to be seen. I opened the top drawer and there was just a purse, a packet of Dettol wipes and a bottle of anti-bac gel. I tested the bottom drawer. Locked. I reached under the drawer, lifted the base with my left hand and hit the lock with the side of my right hand. The drawer dropped open. I took out the paper and fed it into the machine.

"Stupid drawer," I said to the drawer.

The printer munched the paper. I snatched the printouts just as the secretary arrived back. As she walked towards me I put my hand to my head. "Can you wet the tissue?" I said, putting my paddle-sized hand flat on her desk while the other held my head. She turned and hurried off. I felt bad about contaminating her imaginarily clean keyboard, so I took one of her Dettol wipes and cleaned everything I had touched.

The principal came out. "All right, you can come in now," she said.

"I'm sorry, you're going to have to wait."

She stopped in shock. "I *beg* your pardon?"

"Just wait," I said, scrubbing the desk. "I'll be with you in a second."

"*Ibegyourpardon.*"

They do a lot of begging here.

"You are on a very slippery slope, young man, a very slippery slope. If I put you on report, I will have to tell your social worker, did you know that?"

I wiped the pack of Dettol wipes with a Dettol wipe, then I put it in the bin and stormed off down the corridor. I heard the principal follow me so I started to run. Stairs jumbled beneath my feet.

"Jake!" she called. "Come back!"

Darscall walked past and gave me the slightest raise of his chin.

I kicked the door. The crack made a spider's web across the glass. A scrawny Year 7 stopped in her tracks and gawked at the smashed glass. "Wasn't me." I said, and she laughed guiltily. I walked away, happy that I'd made her laugh.

20

I waited for Robin all afternoon and evening. I fell into a fitful sleep and in the dead of night I woke from a dream where a woodpecker was tapping through my skull and picking out strings from my brain to feed to its young. When I opened my eyes I was still in bed but my head was where my feet had been and I had managed to tie my sheet into a nappy. I looked like a baby, or a sumo wrestler. Let's go with sumo wrestler. The world's worst sumo wrestler. The woodpecker tapping from my dream persisted through the sumo nappy drama until, to my horror, I saw Robin rapping at the window with a full view of my horrific body.

"Open up, you monk."

I grabbed the sheet in mortal panic and tried to cover myself with it. I was one breeze away from being naked and fulfilling my actual worst nightmare. I angled myself so she couldn't see my scars. "I have night terrors," I said. "I did this in my sleep."

"Sexy," Robin said as she climbed in. "You look like a week-old balloon." She was holding an expensive camera and a black rag. She stood with her back to the wall, out of view of the window.

I struggled with the sheet and prayed she would turn around or go away, but then I worried that if I sent her away she wouldn't come back.

"Love what you've done with the place." She looked around the bare walls. "You know not having photos up is a sign of a psychopath? The police look for that when they search people's houses."

"Are you giving home improvement advice? Because your room looks like the one they shot Bin Laden in."

Robin laughed. She snatched the profiles from my desk. "Good lad," she said. I liked that she said that. Robin had an athlete's energy. It filled the room.

She folded the profiles and put them in her pocket. "Next thing," she began.

"Why are you whispering?"

"So I don't wake your parents."

"They're not here."

"They ain't here?"

"No. You're still whispering."

Robin swept out of the room and came back so quickly the door slammed without being touched. "They just left you 'ere on your jack?"

"Yeah. What do you need?"

"Just a favour. But you have to keep your hands clean with this one."

"OK?"

"And you have to keep your mouth shut about it."

"You've got funny way of asking for favours."

Robin looked up at the hatch in my ceiling. "I need to get up in your attic."

"All right."

"And I need to plant this." She handed me her camera.

"OK." I looked at it. "Why don't you use a camcorder with a motion sensor?" I said. "You could keep it running for days."

"You've got one of them lying around?"

"I do. Me and Isaac used to use it to film our sketches."

"All right," Robin said. "And I need to find whatever the Beast has stashed up there."

"Stashed?"

"Yeah, hide your stash in a neighbour's house. Some older person you can intimidate."

"Charming."

"Isn't it charming. *Charming*. Where are you even from?"

I shuffled, struggling with my sheet. "I grew up in B. . ." The word made me sick. "Brixton."

She looked me up and down. "What are you so panicky about? Am I frightening you or something?"

"No." My mouth had turned to cotton. "I just want to get dressed."

"Ah. *Rest, mon*," Robin said as she went to the door.

Then her eyes widened as she caught sight of my leg.

"Oh . . . my . . . *days,* bruv. Look at the size of that scar!"

I panicked and tried to cover it up with the sheet.

"It's two feet long! Let me look at it." She came closer and I flinched.

"It's nothing," I said.

"Nothing? What happened?" There was delight in her voice.

"Nothing, it was an accident." I sank to the floor, trying to put my scarred arms and toast-rack chest and the rest of the horror show out of view. "I don't like *talking* about it."

"How do you get a cut that big? Weren't no operation, it's all jaggedy. God, what *happened*?"

"I broke my leg."

"With what? A chainsaw?"

"It's nothing."

"What happened?"

"I don't like *talkingaboutit.*"

"Why are you sweating?"

"It's very *stressfulforme.*"

"All right, Black Swan, I'll leave you to it." Robin laughed at her own joke. When she was out of my door I realized she was right. I was folded on the floor like a ballet dancer.

I picked up her camera to look at her photographs. But I couldn't invade her privacy like that. Besides, I heard clattering coming from the kitchen and I had more pressing concerns than expensive cameras: she was hunting for food.

"You want a sandwich or what?" she yelled.

I wiped the sweat from under my arms with my nappy sheet. "No, thanks, I've eaten."

"When?" she called. "I'll make you a sandwich anyway."

Sandwiches are one of my all-time most hated things in the world. I can't even look at sandwiches. It's cake, basically. Two bits of cake with hormonal meat stuffed into it. I tried to console myself: *she cannot make me eat it.* I repeated this over and over until she bounded up to the room.

I had been so distracted I had only pulled my jeans halfway up my legs. "Jesus, Robin!" I grabbed myself.

"Who were you talking to?"

"No one."

"I talk to myself, no shame in it." She shrugged, shoving half a cheese sandwich into her mouth. "Only way to get a decent conversation." She picked up the hair gel on my desk and replaced it, then she picked up my pen and replaced it, then she picked up my notebook and put that down. Her eyes fell on my unopened C box. "What's that?"

"Nothing."

"Why's it got tape on it?"

"I haven't opened it yet."

"That tape's old."

Smart.

"What's 'C' stand for?"

"Crap," I said.

"Charming."

She opened and closed the empty drawers in my desk, then ran her hand along the base of it, as if looking for hidden keys or trap doors. She kicked the skirting boards and stamped on each floorboard.

"What are you doing?"

"Nothing," she said. She picked up her camera and her eyes settled on the faint line of the hatch in the ceiling. She seemed to be taking measurements. Then she dragged my chair beneath the hatch and balanced on it as she pushed the door open. Dust fell on us. She gripped my arm and it burned right down to the bone. With one foot on my headboard and one teetering on the back of the chair, she pulled herself up into the icy darkness.

"Woah!" I said involuntarily.

"Come on," she said, as she lowered her hand out of the hatch.

"You won't be able to lift me."

"Wanna bet?"

I looked at her outstretched hand. Be lifted and prove you're weak; fall and break your ankles. Lose, lose.

I dragged the chair on my bed and balanced on it as I hooked my hands into the hatch. I couldn't lift myself up. I stretched again and the chair teetered and fell to the floor. I scraped the floorboards.

"Come on, Spider-Man," Robin laughed. She wrapped her hands around my arms and pulled me into the darkness. She dragged me on top of her and for a moment

I felt her soft body against my bones.

We felt our way along the floorboards. Robin flicked on the light, giving a burst of orange. We held our breath, blinking as our eyes adjusted to the spectacle. It was a cove of dresses and framed photographs, with shelves of high-heeled shoes and delicate hats. The young face of my grandfather beamed from all the pictures, his arm proudly around a beautiful woman with bright orange hair and a look of mischief about her.

We opened box upon box of photographs. In each one he looked more and more like me. His dipped cheekbones, his big eyes, his apologetic crop of blond hair, his miserable mouth, his sparkling eyes.

"I feel like I've been here before," I said.

"Of course – you would have."

"No, my mum said I never visited them."

"Maybe it was a past life," Robin said. "Maybe you killed yourself. They say you have to repeat your life."

"Who says that?" I demanded, horrified.

"Buddha."

"God," I rubbed my arm, "I hope that's not true."

"It's a shrine." Robin ran her hand through the bejewelled coats and capes. Robin ran her finger along the floorboards and inspected its tip. "The dust is blackening," she said. "It's old and undisturbed. I saw it on CSI." She brushed off the dust then reached out to touch an ivory silk dress that hung on a hand-crafted rack. "No one's been up here for years. We might get rich."

"Or asbestos poisoning."

Robin went over to the corner where there were wavering stacks of paper. "More newspapers?"

"Yeah." I lifted one to the light. "Some of these are from the Sixties."

"He's like a mad hamster."

Robin pulled an orange micro-dress over her head. "Oh, beee-have," she said. "Grooooovy, BABY!"

I held up one of my grandfather's old tweed jackets and thought of putting it on. I could pucker my face and wag my finger and say, "Youth of today don't know they're born," or something like that, and Robin would laugh.

But then she might not laugh and I'd have to make an excuse about why I did it. I worried she was getting bored. Maybe I would forever be a boring character, someone who can't make a joke in a room full of costumes. I hadn't worried about being boring before. I mostly worried about being lonely, but maybe lonely was the best thing for me.

Robin smiled. "I like this dress." She swished it around.

"Have it. It looks good on you."

She pulled the dress back over her head. "I could never wear it," she said, the smallest rush of pain on her face. "God, this is Chanel." She ran her thumb over the label. "All this stuff is designer."

I checked the labels: Dior, Chanel, Biba. Robin giggled with delight, but I noticed the stitching. "They're fake," I said.

"What?"

"You can tell because the top layer is stitched but the

lining isn't."

"How do you know that?"

"I know a lot about costumes."

"Why?"

"Costumes get the first laugh." I looked away from her so she wouldn't see how miserable I was getting. I could feel the heaviness of it in my mouth, and I knew I wouldn't be able to shake the melting feeling for days.

We had forgotten about the window. The sun began to rise and we looked up, surprised to see streaks of light. Robin's face fell.

"Are you sure he isn't there?"

"Very sure," she said, checking her phone. I detached the flash and LED from Isaac's camera and placed them under a few newspapers, then I patched dust around the lens.

"You look like you've done this before."

"I have, actually," I said, smiling. "This one time, my friend Isaac was convinced he had a poltergeist because his stuff kept moving around, and we set up the camera to try and catch it in action, and—"

"Got a sister, has he?" Robin deadpanned, killing the story. I thought of Isaac and me watching the tape and when we saw the door moving we howled with terror. After we'd had a Twix and a Red Bull we built up enough courage to play the rest of the tape and saw his sister and her friend, dressed up in Isaac's clothes, almost incontinent with laughter as they imitated the way boys walk. When they were changing clothes you could momentarily see them in their underwear, and Isaac feigned being violently sick. Between that and the two girls playing I laughed so hard I fell backwards on to the floor.

"Do you want to see him?" I asked.

Robin nodded reluctantly.

I used the camcorder to show her a sketch we made about a teacher who throws hissy fits and behaves like a stroppy teenager. She didn't laugh but she was smiling. "You two look really close."

"We lived together once."

"Really?"

"When my dad got really bad and Mum went to her Travelodge, I lived with them. It was the best time ever." I clicked the camera into place in front of the window.

"Have you got enough memory?"

"Yeah," I said, "I've got tonnes of blank discs."

Robin looked around the room. "Well, I don't think we'll find any treasure?"

"Treasure?"

"I mean, stuff they stashed here."

"Doesn't look like it."

"Where are your mum and dad anyway?" she said, her pink tongue working its way around her tiny teeth. "I wish mine would leave me to it."

"Who knows?" I said.

And then I saw it. "What the hell's that?"

Robin came over without making a sound, easily negotiating the beams. "What?"

"Can't you see?"

She went to the hatch and dangled down, lifting herself

in and out of the hatch, looking at my ceiling, then at the wall of the attic.

"That," I said, tracing the brick as its colour faded from dirty grey to a lighter grey, "is a fake wall."

Robin climbed out of the attic to find tools. "You coming or what?" she said.

I looked at the distance to my floor. I shook my head. I thought of scaling a fence with Isaac. After I jacked him up, he scrambled to the top, looked down, screamed and clung to the ridge like a koala bear. "I can't! I can't!" he yelled as I fell to my knees with laughter.

Isaac couldn't run, climb, punch, swim, throw. He couldn't pass, catch, score. Every time the cricket ball or the baseball went to him, the team would groan. He'd miss, then dramatically leap around, following the ball as it trundled along the grass, his bony bum bopping in the air. He'd finally pick it up and throw it back with a massive grunt, only for it to sail high into the air above his head.

Once, with Isaac's oldest brother, we filled water bombs with red-liquid jelly to hurl at a store in Wimbledon that he said used sweat shops in Bangladesh. Isaac raised a jelly bomb triumphantly, gave a warrior yell, and the liquid exploded over his head. He stood covered in jelly, with a half grin, while I became useless with laughter.

Robin reappeared beneath me, holding a mallet. "Your dad's got every tool in the world down there. Your living room's like Homebase," she said. "I got this chipper thing, an actual *pickaxe,* and a drill too."

I pulled the pickaxe into the attic. "They're my mum's."

"Your mum's?" Robin sounded impressed. "Mum the Builder," she sang, "can she fix it? Mum the Builder. . . Yes, she *can*!" She did her enviable jump into the trap door.

I looked at the pickaxe and felt bad for how I always argued with Mother. It was impressive that she'd flipped so many houses, despite their grisly past, and she had done this with a hospitalized son, a mentally ill husband and a baby. Not bad. I patted the pickaxe on its head.

Robin smiled and nodded towards the wall. "Ready?"

"Now, look. . ." My voice quavered. "There's things in houses called support walls. . ."

"Like support bras?"

"Yeah, if you smash one of them then. . ."

"The world ends." Robin rolled her eyes. "Are you going to hit that wall or am I?"

"All I'm saying is that with one false move we might just blast our way to our bloody deaths."

"You need a support bra, fam."

I tapped my bony nipples. "No, they're like fried eggs."

Robin smiled. "Get on with it."

"All right. On three. . ." I braced myself, raised the mallet and closed one eye. "One . . . now, remember, if the roof caves in then we will have to—"

"Get on with it!"

"All right. Don't rush me. All right. Here we go. One. . ." I repositioned myself. "One. . ."

Robin snatched the mallet and swung it into the wall. "Yaaaaar!" she yelled.

"Oh, God!" I threw my arms over my head and waited for the avalanche of brick and mortar. None came. When I looked up, Robin was covered in grey dust. We burst into laughter. She took a few more healthy swings at the wall until there was a gap big enough to crawl through.

"Oh . . . my . . . *days*," Robin said as she peered into the gap.

"Is it bodies? Is it bodies?!" My eyes jammed shut.

"Calm down before you break," Robin laughed, but then she stopped laughing.

"What?" I said.

She pointed to a solid brown chest with a heavy lock, nestled in the middle of the darkened space. "What do you reckon's in *there?*" she said.

We climbed inside the tiny hidden room. My heart raced as she yanked the lock. It wouldn't give. She tried to lift the box but it was too large. She paced the beams of the roof, looking for something to hit it with. She found an old saucepan in one corner and used it to smack the heel of the lock.

"Damn," she said, "this won't budge."

"Careful! What if it's rigged?"

"Rigged with what?"

"Explosives."

She raised the saucepan over her head and swung it like an axe.

BOOM!

"MERCY!" I screamed and Robin killed herself laughing. My hands flew to my heart and after a while we both laughed. She dipped momentarily to one knee she was laughing so hard, but joke was on her because you can't go around shocking someone with my skinny old heart, it might snuff out any minute.

"Wait! I'll try to pick it."

"Yeah, but we wannit before Christmas."

"I can pick Chubb locks."

"Chubb off," Robin said, giving the lock another smack. "I've seen you picking locks, bruv, we'd have to get camping gear."

Isaac would love this drama. He wouldn't be jumping around taking charge. He'd let me do it. Then again, him and me, we would be up here for months trying to chip a brick out of that wall. Then we would spend hours fretting about ghosts and curses and support beams and everything. The two-stone twins, as Rabbi Kaufman would say, weak as seven days.

Robin opened the chest and I didn't have to look at what was in there for more than a second to know what it was. Stacks and stacks of medical records, lawsuits and finally, discharge papers. "He wasn't in prison," I said. "He was in a madhouse." I would have cried if I wasn't so exhausted. "Poor, poor man."

"And that's when his missus left him," Robin said, sifting through the papers.

"Worst. Treasure haul. Ever."

We piled the papers back into the chest. As I bent over towards it, I noticed a name. I blinked. I licked my thumb and rubbed away the dust.

JAKE.

"Why does it say my name? Why would he leave this for me?"

"Jake." Robin rubbed dust out of the crevices that formed the letters. "Look at it, it's old. Older than you."

I hung my head. No one gets named after a packet of crackers.

"Don't let me end up like this," I said.

"Like what?" Robin said gently.

"Like this," I said. "Scared."

"All right," Robin said, as if she had seen this all before.

"Oh my God," I said. I dragged out a copy of the English textbook that had some of my poems printed in it. "He had this."

"Look, it's you." Robin handed me a newspaper clipping of my Silver Pen Award win. "And, look." She held up a spider broach, with boggly eyes and long, gangly legs. "He made you this."

I sighed and recognized the jittery line of a hot glue gun. "They make you do crafts in hospital to stave off the suicide." I couldn't bear to look at it.

"Don't you love it though?" Robin said. "It's like he's a funny spider."

"He looks mental."

"He looks cheeky. I love it. Don't you love it?"

"No." I gave it a closer look. It was plastic and stick-on crystals. "You can have it."

"No. You should have it. He left it for you."

"Robin, have it."

She looked at it admiringly and pinned it on her collar.

A light came on in the glaring eye of the Toad. Robin cowered. We shouldn't have made so much noise. She pointed to the hidden light on the camera. It had turned green.

Robin slapped the dust from her legs and climbed into my bed. She held up the quilt for me to get in next to her. "Come on, go sleep," she said.

I lay down and liked how warm it felt. I knew I wouldn't fall asleep all night for fear of one of my mad night terrors. I worried about how I should feel all emotional about having a girl in my bed, and how it was supposed to send you insane or something, but I didn't feel anything. I just felt sorry for her.

"Where would you go?" Robin asked, her voice slow and sleepy. "If you could go anywhere in the world?"

"Edinburgh," I said.

"No, I mean, anywhere."

I turned to face her. "Edinburgh."

"No." Robin propped herself up on her elbow and looked down at me. "Like anywhere in the world."

". . . Edinburgh."

"No, like, *in the world* . . . if you had all the money *in the world*."

I looked at her. "Edinburgh."

Robin laughed and flopped back on to the pillow. "What kind of bullshit answer is that? You could go there now."

"No." I laughed with her. "I'd like to live there and prepare this, like, amazing show for the Fringe Festival."

"That's *dead*."

"Nah," I said, copying her accent, "that's *calm*."

She laughed despite herself.

"We're going to go there, get five-star reviews and then get our own TV show down here."

"What would it be called?"

"The Isaac and Jacob Collection."

"That's not just the worst name I've ever heard, that's the worst thing I've ever heard. That's worse than someone's dream being going to Edinburgh, which is just up the road."

"No, it's clever. It's like a fashion collection. Our book would be called *The Book of Isaac and The Book of Jacob*."

"All right, Posh Spice, you should hire me along so you don't disgrace yourselves with dumb names like that."

"What would you call it?"

"That ain't my job," Robin said so indignantly that we both started giggling. "I'll just tell you what ideas are an embarrassment."

"What about you?" I said. "Where would you go in the world?"

"Paris." Robin leaned forward, her eyes bright. "I'd go to see the *Mona Lisa* and I'd go see a ballet. I'd love to see a proper ballet. The Royal Ballet."

"You can see them in London."

"*You* can see them in London."

"Paris is closer to here than Edinburgh."

"Is it balls."

"It is!"

"Balls."

"You could go to Paris any time."

136

"Maybe I will."

"Maybe you should."

"Fine," she said. "And you'll come with me. But you can't ruin it by being a maudlin monosyllabic nob."

"Fine, we'll go," I said.

"Fine."

"Fine." I fidgeted. "I didn't know you liked ballet."

"I used to eat, sleep and breathe ballet."

"That's why you're so. . ."

"What?"

"Grace— Beau— That's . . . you know." I shook my head. "You should do it. You should do whatever you want. You live in the capital of the world. After New York and several other places. The Capital of the World! They have that ballet company in Croydon now. You could just go to that."

"They have Fringe Comedy in Camden now. You could just go to that."

"Yeah," I said.

"Yeah," she said. She fiddled with her plastic broach with the long-legged spider that glittered in the moonlight.

"Put that away."

"No, I love it."

"I hate it, it's embarrassing."

"I love it," Robin said. "It's all right to be out of it every now and again." She looked at me. "And he done this 'cos he wanted to get better." She smiled. "God," she said, "he really loved you."

21

The next morning Robin wasn't in bed with me. I felt like I hadn't slept, but I didn't remember seeing her leave.

The pavements were sponge today and I stretched into every step without a jolt of pain through my bolts and hinges. I felt like a proper person. A real boy. I thought of having our photograph taken by the Eiffel Tower. I could put that photograph on Facebook, or on a collage that I would stick on my mirror. Those photographs people have always upset me, but now I would have one of my own and it made me weak with happiness. A girl had asked me to go to Paris. A girl. And not just any girl: a cool girl. A cool girl who doesn't go to my school. It was a trifecta.

At Cattle Rise the teacher-less classroom was a wall of noise. I spotted Sean decked in his Yankees cap, and despite my need to be alone and my general dislike of him, I took the empty seat on his table.

"How do you like Rodriguez this season?" I said.

"Eh?"

"Alex Rodriguez? A-Rod? How do you like him this season?"

"Who?" Sean adjusted his cap.

The teacher waded into the noise holding a silver flask, the redness of his face seeping into his neck. He sighed with exhaustion as he looked at the class. "What am I about to say to you, Sean?"

"You love gay guys?"

The class laughed.

"*Sean?*" he said calmly. Sean took off his cap and the teacher relaxed. "Right, nobody move. I've forgotten my memory stick."

"Tell 'im you love 'im!" Sean called and everyone laughed. I scratched my neck.

Clarissa rushed to our table. "Jake! You are never going to guess who that girl is." She produced a photograph of the Insain Bolts. "This her?"

"Yes," I said, picking up the picture.

"You don't know who that is?" Clarissa beamed.

"That's Robin," I said.

"Yeah, but do you know *who* she is?"

"No."

"Robin Carter." She waited for a reaction but I remained blank. "Robin Carter. Jake, she's criminally insane! Those blokes weren't threatening her, they were answering to her."

"No way."

"Jake. She's a boss. She burned down the whole bloody school!"

My mouth hung. I wanted to defend her but I found myself unable to speak.

"Shit, Jake," Sean laughed. "You're gonna get clapped."

"Don't believe anything she tells you." Clarissa said. "She's a boss in the CRK."

"Yeah, what is the CRK?"

"The Castle Rise Kingz."

I rolled my eyes at the name. "She left them."

"Bollocks," Sean said. "No such thing as leaving them." He laughed. "First person you annoyed inside was Darscall. First person you meet outside is Carter. You must have the luck of fuckin' Adam. You're gunna get shot in the. . ." He couldn't speak for laughing. "*Face.*"

Kane folded his hands and said calmly, "What aren't you telling us?"

They sat in a tiny congress around me, real humans with real ears and eyes and everything. They had straight backs and even shoulders and clean hair. These were people whose parents bothered raising them, and they were listening to me.

Kind Dr Kahn always said that if you can't tell someone what you're doing, then you shouldn't do it.

"Well, we had to look up in my attic for stuff the . . . *CRK* had stashed up there. But we didn't find anything."

They paused for just long enough for me to admire how pretty they all were, how animated their expressions were. Even Sean had his wiry appeal.

And then they stretched into ghoul faces and bawled with laughter.

"Green!"

"Wet!"

"Sideman. Side . . . *man!*"

They all said this for quite a while.

"You are going to get murdered," Sean said.

"You're getting Kansas-Citied, son," Kane said.

"What's that?" I asked and they all laughed again.

"Kansas City Shuffle," Kane said.

"Is that rhyming slang?"

"Rhyming slang!" Sean laughed louder than war. "Look at this Doris Day, it ain't the Fifties."

"What's a Kansas City Shuffle?" I said. My need to help Robin drove me past their contorted faces, their laughter, the pain in my sorry excuse for an arse and the alarming shakes racking up my legs.

"It's like when. . ." Clarissa began. She stopped and put her hands to her slim hips.

"It's when you're, like. . ." Sean rolled his hand. "It's like when someone is, like. . ."

Kane scratched his baby stubble and looked at Bash. Bash took a breath. "Say you wanna do someone over, yeah? And you tell them you're doing someone other than them over, so then they go along with it."

"She told you you have to look for this stuff, so you let her, get it?" Clarissa said, her arms flying. "If she hadn't told you, you wouldn't be letting her do you over . . . you know?"

"No," I said.

"It's like when you. . ." They all spoke at once, the words crunching in their mouths, their eyes to the ceiling, trying desperately to find an explanation. A small smile grew on my face. I liked the way their voices crackled, so fast and alive. Clarissa's voice moved her whole body.

"It's like. . ."

"It's like you're. . ."

"It's like you're a mug," Sean said finally, slamming his hand to the table. They all laughed.

Another table was following our conversation. I watched Bash take his pen and notebook from his pocket and pull Kane's textbook in front of him. Once the noise level rose again the group turned back to me.

"Jake, you can't leave the ends with her. It's really, really dangerous," Clarissa said.

"You can't trust people, Jake," Kane said. "Don't be a mug."

"She's probably setting you up for something," Sean said.

"Are you all right, Jake?" Bash said.

I blinked. Thinking of Paris and thinking I might throw up. "Yeah?"

"Have you . . . eaten?"

I got up from the table. The pain in my joints had lifted. I saw flashing lights.

The lights are a warning.

Fading brake lights. Blood with pieces in it. Isaac's face. Black smoke swam the edges of my vision. I was out in the corridor. I pressed my hand to Miss Price's door, and I remember falling.

"Jake?" Miss Price said as I woke. I checked my crotch to make sure I hadn't done anything horrifying. I saw it all over again. The flashing lights. Blood with pieces in it. My shin bone spiking from the flesh. Skin, clothing. "You're awake," she smiled.

I baulked at the paramedic. "No," I said.

"You're all right, petal," he said with a smile. "You've had a bit of a spill."

"I'm all right," I said.

"When was the last time you ate, petal?"

It was weird to be called petal by a huge West Indian man with a Croydon accent. I tried to get away, but he held me down as easily as you would a tablecloth flapping in the wind.

"Yesterday? Today?"

I relented. I had to appear sane so I could get the hell out of there and back to Robin. "Food's overrated. Over . . . ated. Ha ha."

"You need food to survive. Your heart needs it. Your brain needs it. If you don't eat you can get very confused and depressed."

Well, that would explain a lot. My eyes followed a pinprick swirl that patterned the ceiling and I remembered how to get out of this particular jam. "I'm in treatment," I said.

"Very glad to hear it, petal." The paramedic smiled.

"It's hard to say to someone that we need help, isn't it? But you're doing it and I think that's very brave." He gave me a bottle of putrid yoghurt drink. "You have to make sure you drink this, all right?" He turned to Miss Price. "Make sure he drinks this. Don't let him go to the toilet on his own."

Miss Price nodded without flinching.

He turned back to me, "All done," he said. "You must tell your nurse and case worker about this, all right?"

"OK," I said.

He and Miss Price smiled warmly at each other and he left the room, humming. I sat there like a plum.

"Jake," Miss Price said, "what happened? You scared me."

"Sorry," I said. "I didn't know where else to go."

"It's all right," she said. She put an arm around me. I tensed against her hard body and soft breasts. I didn't really know what was going on. "You know you can talk to me about anything." I liked how her voice made her body vibrate. It made me feel quite calm and I could suddenly take a lungful of breath.

"I'm all right," I said.

"How's the girl next door?"

"She's in trouble. I think people are after her."

Miss Price let me go. "What kind of people?"

"Gangs, I think."

"The Met has an intervention team that deals solely with gangs. They can help vulnerable gang members, Jake."

"She's all right," I said, "she just needs to get out of it."

I turned to see Dad hovering by the classroom door like a murderer. When Miss Price smiled her hello, Dad looked at the floor.

"All right, son?" he said. His voice was small. He wore a huge black cardigan and the bags beneath his eyes were so big his face looked like it was melting.

"Yes, fine."

Miss Price handed Dad my coat and the yoghurt drink. "You have to make sure he drinks this and not let him go to the bathroom on his own," she said. She waited for Dad to answer her but he just fussed with my coat. She turned back to me. "Jake? If there's anything you want to tell us, anything at all, we're always here."

"Thanks," I said.

Dad hung his head. He was too shy to speak to her, and I was so embarrassed I could have hit him. "Thanks, miss," I said again.

"Chen," Dad mumbled. It's what "cheers then" sounds like when it comes out of his mouth.

"Dad," I said as we walked out, "why do you have to wear that massive cloak? You look like a Sith Lord. You look *mental*."

He looked with some concern around the corridors with their warning notices and torn displays. "What happened?" he said.

"Where's Mum?" I said, ignoring him, my mouth as dry as crackers.

"Did you black . . ." he asked, " . . . like when. . ."

"Yeah," I said. "Yeah, I did."

145

"That Miss Price is. . ."

"Yes, she is nice," I said.

I went to the bathroom and Dad waited outside. On the drive home I started to feel sick.

"Home, home," Dad said as he pulled the car into the driveway. I got the hell out and ran inside. I went straight to my window. Dad stayed in the car for a long time. When he finally shuffled into the house, he switched on the TV and slumped on the sofa. He would stay like that until he fell asleep.

I waited for so long for Robin to tap at my window that my legs started seizing up and I had to do these mortifying exercises to keep them awake. I stretched and curled and went into a downward-facing dog, and this was the moment Robin appeared in front of my window.

"All right, Tiny Dancer," she laughed, "don't mind me."

We sat beneath my window with a map of London, drinking coffee, mine black and Robin's milky. Robin produced a packet of Oreos. I ate two; the first by biting off the top layer and chewing it seventeen times before throwing away the rest; the other using the same trick but dissolving the top layer of biscuit in my mouth before eating the rest. Robin ate six Oreos, all in the same way: first the top layer, eaten in two bites, then the filling, which she scraped out with her teeth, then the bottom biscuit, which she licked clean and ate in three bites, one large and two small.

"Mission Two," Robin said, brushing crumbs from the map. "Bettina's Pizza in Wimbledon."

"My mum buys pizza from there. It's disgusting."

"It's a front."

"I knew it! I knew there must be something dodgy about that place. The pizza is so watery, why would anyone buy it? And how difficult is it to make pizza? It's bread and cheese."

"I know, it's obvious," Robin said, scanning the map.

"Just use the map on your phone," I said.

She shook her head, half an Oreo sticking out of her mouth. "Traceable," she mumbled.

"What do they do?"

"Fence and launder." She shook her head. "Do you realize, if we shut it down and got everyone there in jail or deported, we'd seize more than half of the gang money in this borough?"

"Shut it down?"

"Yeah, if I get jumped out, I'm taking everyone down with me."

I looked her and imagined this was a sketch. *I'm taking everyone down with me* is exactly what a crazed gangster would say.

Robin pulled a small black box of her duffel bag. It had a sucker attached to it, like one of those things they stick to your chest to monitor your heart.

"What's that?" I said.

"It's a transmitter," she said. "We can record everything

147

they say. We need to plant it at Bettina's. In the back room."

"How are you getting in?"

"You can only get in through the restaurant." She showed me a picture of the restaurant, painted in watery green, on her phone. "The slaves they have working for them are no problem, but anyone skulking around the back is dangerous. Breaking in is a big risk."

"Breaking in?" I rubbed my arm. "But this thing is tiny, why don't you just walk in there?"

"That's your big plan, is it, Danny Ocean? Just walk in there?"

"There must be a way. What if we got invited in there? Say if we became ill or lost, or if we nicked something?"

"Way too risky."

"We could deliver something, say we lost something."

"Are you living in this dimension?"

"What if I fainted?"

"You can faint on command?"

"It isn't hard," I said.

Without thinking, I opened my C box. Our stuff was still there after all these years: costumes, scripts, fake blood, fake spiders, wigs, make-up. I dug around and found our blood capsules. "It could be something more dramatic, something that will stir them up, make them panic. Something that will get one of us stationed in their back office. We could start up an argument. You attack me. Then they have to look after me and try to persuade me not to call the police. When I'm alone I'll plant it somewhere."

I took out Isaac's battered old sketchbook from my box and found the notes we'd made about stage-fighting. "Here," I said, "we can practise. All you have to do to make it look real is let the victim control everything."

We spent the rest of the evening practising fake punches and falls. Robin learnt to hold my clothes with open hands to make it look like she was grabbing my body. She held my wrists and I yanked her, making it look like she was attacking me. Finally, she practised throwing me against the desk to make it look like she had broken my nose. On the final practice, Robin pretended to throw me, and I hit the desk with my hands. I staggered backwards and cried as I broke a blood capsule over my face.

"Oh, my life!" she cried as I straightened up. Finally she laughed with relief. "That looked properly real."

"Yeah," I said, wiping away the blood, "I used to be quite good at this."

"You should be on TV or sammink. I mean, not prime time or any of the good channels or anything, but you know, TV."

Once again, she climbed into my bed without taking her clothes off. She patted the mattress and I sat beside her.

"Tomorrow," she said, "is going to be fun."

22

I woke to the sound of rummaging. A half-naked Robin was delving into my C box. She wore a purple bra and a pair of my boxers. If that wasn't horrifying enough, she had my old notebook open on her bare legs.

My voice disappeared into the stretch of my mouth. "What are you doing?"

"This is really good, you know."

"It's *private!*"

I grabbed my jeans and tried to pull them on from under the sheet, but it was impossible. I was desperate to grab the notebook from her, but it would mean getting out of bed in my flimsy pyjamas and her seeing my abnormal nipples, my razor-sharp shoulder blades, my twisted collarbone, my endless list of horrors. I broke into a fresh sweat. "Put it back!"

"C. . ." She smiled with her tiny teeth. "'C' stands for 'comedy', doesn't it?"

"Get off it!"

"Why don't you do this any more?"

"Robin!"

"You and Isaac. You could be sitting on a fortune here. Real Fly Rabbi, this is well funny. I like your Croydon rude boy characters too. Well funny."

"Get off it!" I croaked. I could barely speak.

She flicked through the pages. "Look, this Mr Reacher sketch is really funny."

"Put . . . it . . . back."

"You never said you wrote the stuff yourself."

"It's none of your business."

"Jesus, all right." She picked up her clothes from the floor and shook them. Out fell one of those stomach wraps weightlifters use to protect their backs, and she strapped it brutally around her chest, flattening her breasts. I didn't know where to look.

She tore a strip off the lid of my C box and scribbled down her mobile number. She flung it in my direction. I stopped being so angry with her. She wrote her sevens funny, with a line through the tail.

Then she flattened out her map and started studying it again.

"We'll have to walk there," she said, pulling at the logo on her grey hoodie.

"To Wimbledon Village? From *here*?" I scratched the back of my neck. "What about the District line?"

"No," she said. "We can't take the tube."

"Or a taxi?"

"No. Taxis is suspect. They know everyone." Robin clicked off her phone.

"It'll take all day!" I thought about my poor knees.

"It ain't far. And we can't go through the park."

Before I had time to think, she was climbing out through the bloody window. "Robin! Go out the door. It's dangerous!"

"What's dangerous?"

"The glass? The drop? The roof?"

"What you on about?" she said, her bum dangling over the ledge.

"Someone might see you," I said.

This worked and she climbed down.

She went downstairs and I heard the front door open. My door opened at the same time and closed itself as the front door slammed shut. The ghost at the door. I shut my window, got dressed, and caught myself smiling in the mirror. I looked out at the gate and felt pleased that she would meet me in full view of everyone in the street.

She had changed into silver leggings, a tight grey tank top, Chuck Taylors and a grey hoodie. I smiled when I saw the spider broach pinned to her tank top. Her hoodie was so big, and her legs so long and thin, she looked like the Tin Man. She saw me approach and hared off down the road, her braids jumping from shoulder to shoulder. I had to run to keep up with her.

We walked to Wimbledon through a maze of back streets that led eventually to the main road. A group of kids was milling outside the shopping centre. They looked at us and hung their heads. "You're sort of big news then?" I said.

"Wait till I get jumped out," she said, "then you'll see big news."

"What *is* 'jumped out'?" I said, but she was too far ahead of me to hear.

We walked up the steep hill to Wimbledon Village and I had to remind my calf muscles to keep up with my knees. Robin looked in every direction, like a soldier out on reconnaissance. It seemed weird to be nervous in a place where three different shops sell organic honey.

Bettina's was hidden on a road that led to Wimbledon Common. Its green lettering had faded into the white paint and the two plastic tables outside were empty, as was the counter inside. There was a single menu on the wall, next to a food hygiene certificate that looked like it had been created in Microsoft Paint.

I had decided my character would be a timid, privately educated loner, who had been sent on a make-or-break errand by his mother, who was testing whether he could be trusted with money. Robin's character would be a Southside chatterbox, one of those girls who could talk for ever on a vocabulary of about three hundred words.

A man appeared from the back. He gave Robin a look of suspicion as she leaned over the counter.

"Can I have, like, a pizza, but not the one I had last

Friday. I want the one with, like, the stuff on it that I had when I was round Shannon's house that one time for her birthday?"

"Sorry?" the man said, struggling to keep up.

"No," Robin said, "can I have . . . one of those ones with the chicken but it tastes like that sauce you get in Tescos from that Jamaican guy who was on *Dragons' Den*?"

"*Dragon Den*?" the man said. "What is '*Dragon Den*'?"

"Boss, you don't know *Dragons' Den*? *Dragons' Den*? Are you mad? *Dragons' Den!* You go on with, like, ideas and that, and get bare money for it. But, like, sometimes you, like, don't get money for it, you get . . . cussed . . . *out* by millionaires who are, like, '*This is not a business, this is a cloud cuckoo land!*'"

I put my rucksack on both shoulders and shuffled closer to the counter. "Excuse me, could I make my order if you're still deciding?"

Robin turned to me and looked at me so sternly I didn't have to act. I was scared.

"Are you dumb?"

"Sorry . . . I just need to order. My – my – my mum is ill and needs a pizza otherwise her blood sugar level will—"

"Are you *dumb*?" Robin shoved me. "Interrupting me while I'm talking about *Dragons' Den*?"

"Everyone, calm!" The man disappeared and reappeared with a podgy clone. "Calm down."

"You better apologize, son!" She shoved me again, and

I had to concentrate not to lose my footing.

"But you hadn't decided," I said.

"I'll decide what to do with your *face*."

"It's polite to let people who *have* decided—"

"Are you still talking?" Robin grabbed me and I forgot to match her footing. I stumbled, and she dashed my head against the counter so hard it nearly broke my goddamn face.

I caught hot blood in my hands and howled. After some delay, the capsule cracked over my jeans.

"No, no, no! You – *out*!" one of the men shouted.

Robin flung open the door. "Watch *Dragons' Den*!" she yelled. "It's sick!"

To my shame, that's all I remember. When I woke up, I was in a windowless office with a packet of frozen chips on my face.

Whether he was Italian or Kenyan or Eritrean I didn't know. He was one of those shaven-headed men who are so tall and beautiful and tall you can't concentrate on what you're thinking.

"How are we feeling?"

"Where . . . am I?" I said, taking care to look around, all wide-eyed and terrified.

"What's brought you here?"

"I'm supposed to get a pizza for my mum from Papa John's."

"Ah." He relaxed as he fell for my excellent ruse. "You came to the wrong place." He smiled and sat beside me.

"Now, *mate*, what happened outside was unfortunate. What's your name again?"

"Hugh."

"Hugh?"

"Hugo."

"Hugh or Hugo?"

"Hugo," I decided. I was out of practice.

"Now, *Hugo*, we could call the police. We could definitely call the police for you, that's no problem, but what the police will be askin' is stuff like, did you threaten her? And, what did you do to her? And how did you end up being beaten up by a *girl*? I mean, girls don't attack people for no reason, do they? Especially blokes. Big strong blokes like you!" He nudged my shoulder and I almost fell off the chair. "And then you're in trouble and we don't want that, do we?"

I nodded.

"So, I think, for your sake, we'll leave them out of this and let you get off home with a nice free pizza, whichever one you want. On the house."

"Thanks." I put my head to my hands. "I do feel awfully queer," I said, "like I'm going to throw up – I mean, like I'm going to vomit or something."

"I'll give you a minute, all right, son?" He ducked under the door and out of the room.

I checked every corner. There was a laptop open on the desk, but it didn't seem to be on. I put my coat over it. I took the small bin from under the desk and threw up into it. I held the edge of the desk to steady myself, and placed the funny heart monitor box in the gap between the desk and the drawers.

Robin was leaning on the low wall at the bottom of the hill, lightly kicking a bedding plant with the top of her shoes. When she saw me, her face brightened. "Jake, that was so *realistic*!"

"That's . . . because . . . you dashed my head on the counter and nearly broke my *face*."

"Oh, my bad."

"My cheekbone feels like it's broken."

"I said I was sorry."

"I don't need to look any more weird."

"I said I was sorry. *God!*"

I sat on the wall and she stood over me.

"Did you do it or what?" she said.

"Yes, I did it."

"Good lad!"

I liked it when she said that. I handed her the pizza. "I got it free," I said. "It's chicken."

"It's pigeon," she said. "Bin it."

We walked towards Wimbledon High Street. Robin fixed her eyes on a gang wearing black hoods. "We're losing it," she said, watching them like a bloodhound. "They've taken Southfields. Now they're taking Wimbledon, Collier's Wood. . ."

"Like Tescos," I said.

"Yeah," Robin said, "except the hours are even worse,

there's no pay and a massively increased chance of getting your head kicked in."

"Raw deal," I said.

"Stop talking."

"All right."

Her face became lost in her hood. I noticed two boys with black hoods were watching her. One pointed. I touched her elbow. "Let's go," I said, "get your Oyster card out."

Robin turned to look. The hoods broke into a run. Robin ran. I chased after her.

We hurtled down the street, past buskers and chuggers and sleepwalking shoppers who woke when we ran past them. The hoods hoofed after us. We darted across the road just as a bus was going to make its break from the traffic.

I grabbed Robin's collar and heaved her on to the bus just before the doors closed.

"NO!" she screamed. "Stop! Stop this bus! I can't . . . I can't just be on any bus!"

"Robin." I put my hands on her shoulders. "Robin, calm down."

"Let me go!"

I watched as the chase turned into a stampede. The hoods were punching their arms in the air. I put my hand flat to my chest and scanned the terrified eyes on the bus.

"It doesn't matter where the bus goes," I said, "I can always find my way home. I've lived all over. I'm like a homing pigeon. You're Robin and I'm a pigeon. I'll stay with you, I promise."

"It's not that, you monk."

"What?" My voice was high. "I'll be here is all I—"

"I can't just get on any old bus and go anywhere I like. What are you going to do if we get attacked?"

"Attacked?"

"Yes, attacked."

"Human shield?" I forced a smile. She sank to her seat and kept her head down as the bus trundled down Kingston Road towards the world's capital of homesickness, Tooting.

"We should change buses," I said.

"Why?"

"That's what Jason Bourne does."

"The only thing you've got in common with Jason Bourne is that you're both retarded."

We changed buses. Robin looked all around. She pulled her hoodie over her eyes. All I could concentrate on were her kiss-shaped lips. I tried to keep looking away from her.

We drove past Tooting Bec and Robin jumped up. "Come on, get out."

She swooped into the street and cars braked to avoid crashing into her. She dashed into the station and I nearly fainted trying to keep up with her. "Where are we going?"

"Paris, you idiot!"

23

"We can't use our Oyster cards," Robin said, feeding money into the ticket machine. "They'll track us."

"Who?"

"*Them.*"

"Who?"

"Who? You an owl?" She slapped a paper ticket into my hand. "Come."

We ran down the immense escalator to the platform and I got to the bottom before I realized I didn't have to think about which muscle to move in which sequence.

As we waited for the train, I shielded Robin from view of the platform camera, and in that moment, I felt quite human, not just some bag of bones sitting on the wrong side of a clipboard. But when the train rolled to a halt and the doors slid open, Robin climbed on and spread out on a double seat, indicating that I was not to sit next to her, and I went back to feeling how I always did: left out, miserable, and wheezy.

It was a long way to St Pancras, with many stops and an endless carousel of commuters. Robin checked every face that entered the train. I tried to lighten her mood. "Robin hoodie," I said, pointing at her. "Geddit? *Robin hoodie?*"

"Rubbish joke," she said. But I could see she wanted to smile.

"I'm just going to the station with you, right?" I said. "I haven't got my passport."

Robin dug in her pocket and took out two British passports. Both pristine. I took them from her and checked they were ours. "How did you get my passport?"

"I found it in your mum's drawer," Robin said. "Took ages."

"We don't have tickets."

Robin produced two tickets, and two consent forms.

My eyes widened. "We haven't got any money."

Robin kissed her teeth. "I got bare money."

"I can't spend your money."

"I'd spend yours," she said. "Don't be sexist."

We got off the train at St Pancras and I was horrified to see Robin disappear into the human traffic on the left-hand side of the escalator. The left-hand side means you have to walk. Who walks up an escalator? There are so many things to consider. First, the cardio; you have to have the lungs and stamina to be able to walk up a million stairs. Second, balance; you have to hit every stair and not get dizzy on the way. This means keeping your eyes on the back, or the backpack, in front of you and hoping they don't stall or turn around. And last, the social pressure: you can't stop otherwise the person behind will bump into you, and in London this would mean getting yelled at.

My pumpkin hand gripped the roller and I was dragged into the fast lane. I paced myself, concentrating on Robin's grey back, keeping time with my feet. A few times, I closed my eyes, my balance adjusting in the darkness. I forced myself to breathe in shallow and deliberate breaths. I remembered the baby bird who would chant "I must not stop till I get to the top", which kind Dr Kahn said was an example of negative language, but I chanted it anyway. With a dull ache in my matchstick legs I finally reached the top. Without the time to celebrate my small miracle, I followed Robin through the maze of tunnels and into the station, and there we got our reward.

The station soared to the sky. A dome of beautiful light that made you feel like you were sky-walking.

"I never been here before," Robin said.

"Never?"

"I've never been further than Southfields."

I turned. "*What?*" I reeled. "You've never been to the Southbank?"

She didn't reply.

"You've never been to The National? Hyde Park? To Trafalgar Square? To . . . to . . . Hampstead Heath? Never?"

Robin shrugged again.

"You've never been out of London? You've never seen mountains? You've never seen the sea?"

"Never, all right?"

She walked away, her head down and her hood up. I thought of Isaac's mum and dad taking us to the museums of Kensington and Holborn, to Wimbledon Championships, to see Arsenal play, and to an NFL game at Wembley. I thought of them taking us to sketching classes in the National Gallery and to workshops at the National Theatre, to readings at King's Place and films at the Ritzy. London was bigger then, and more colourful; it had tin men and dinosaurs and letters the size of elephants. London was Wonderland and Brixton was the rabbit hole, the very heart of it, and the best place in the world.

In the Departures lounge, I fiddled with my headphones whilst Robin paced a small patch of tiles by the toilets. I looked at the ceiling and wondered if this was a blind spot where the security cameras couldn't see her. As she paced she was probably debating whether to let me go through with whatever it was she was setting me up for. Were we running away? Forever? Or was it something more sinister? Maybe she did have a plan to escape from the Beast. Or maybe she was smuggling something? Maybe I was her mule.

Either way, I knew I would walk straight up to that passport desk and get on that train.

A loudspeaker announced our train. We waited until the queue built up. The man at the desk barely looked at me as I handed him my passport.

The metal detector beeped and I had a pleasant conversation with the guard about the pins in my leg and hips. He seemed impressed by how much hardware I had on me and let me through, telling me not to stand out in the rain too long, and I laughed even though I hate that joke.

I waited at the corner of the large white wall and watched Robin's bag get pulled apart. I watched as she had to sidestep the machine and get an electronic wand wafted over her body. I watched as a woman with plastic gloves searched her up and down.

I walked ahead so she wouldn't think I had seen her being humiliated like that, and when she caught up with me I thought she would be angry, but it was worse, she was calm, as if everything that had just happened was completely normal.

We had a table to ourselves on the train. I opened my rucksack and pulled out my grandmother's orange dress.

"You hemmed it," Robin said.

I nodded.

"How do you know how to do that?"

"I used to be in charge of costumes when we did our sketches. Costume, hair and make-up authenticate the sketch."

She was silent for a moment. "Did you and Isaac fall out or what?"

I didn't answer.

"Agony, isn't it?"

I nodded.

"All right," she said, taking the dress out of my hand.

"Watch my bag, innit. Cash money."

She came back looking like a different person. The colour of the dress brightened her face. Even the spider broach looked trendy on her Peter Pan collar.

She shrugged. "It looks dumb with my Converse."

"No, I like it. It contrasts. It's interesting. Like you don't have to try so hard."

Robin thought about this for a while and then nodded. She sat down and scooped up her braids, twisting them into a bun on the top of her head. Her neck was long and graceful, like a swan's. "Why aren't you allowed to wear whatever you want in London?" I asked.

"Don't ask me that," she said.

I was distracted by the loud patter of French from the seat next to us. A man in a black suit, massive and tanned like a wrestler, was talking into a mobile phone.

"You're French?" I said to him when he'd finished on his phone.

He raised one eyebrow. "Yes?"

"But you're reading the *Times* in English."

"Of course."

"That's clever."

"To the English people, perhaps this is clever."

"Can you speak English as well as French?"

"But of course."

"How do you say 'I'd like to exchange this money'?"

"*Je voudrais changer des livres sterling, s'il vous plaît,*" the man said.

"*Je vou-day en. . .*"

165

"*Je vou-drais changer des livres sterling, s'il vous plaît.*"

"*Je vou-day en change de leaves un vous-ay.*"

The man scrunched his newspaper. "*Je . . . vou . . . drais . . . changer des livres sterling . . . s'il vous plaît.*"

"*Je voudrais en pa pap de dap dap civils play.*"

"That is enough!" He sprang to his feet and stomped off down the aisle.

I laughed. "I think I'm going to like France," I said to Robin.

Then the thought hit me. "Oh my life! We're going to France!"

Robin relaxed as London rushed away. When she smiled, her cheeks dimpled, and when she really smiled, her left cheek dimpled again.

I felt like an intrepid explorer, carefully navigating the space between us, feeling out the questions I was allowed to ask.

I bit on my thumbnail. One of the very few advantages of having been shunted out of every institution I'd ever been enrolled in is that I was qualified to ask other people about it. "Why don't you go to school?"

"NFI."

Not Formally Invited.

"What happened?"

She looked out of the window and watched the steady progress of a cloud. "I got in with this . . . crowd," she said finally. "Just . . . people I thought was friends. There was so much drama. So much stuff going on, violence, death threats, real-world stuff like that. . . And I'm supposed to concentrate on sedimentary rocks or ignorant rocks or some bollocks? When there's death threats?"

I nodded. "Don't you love it when they talk about bullying? I'm, like, no, I don't want to fill in a form. I don't want to discuss this in a meeting with him. I don't want restorative justice, which is basically someone having a nice chat with him. I want the police because he has threatened to rape me and burn my house down."

"Innit," Robin said. "I was held down and stabbed with a fishtail comb once. That fucking hurt. And then when the group got at it again the police were like. . . Look!" Robin craned towards the window. "Look at the tunnel! We're going under the water! Ahh!" She laughed and her teeth glistened beneath the lights. "Hold your breath."

We held our breath as we travelled beneath the water. I closed my eyes and warned myself to not freak out, but I hated the idea of an entire body of water being above our heads, and I couldn't shake the image of water crashing in over us. Long after I had breathed again, Robin exhaled.

"You can hold your breath for ages."

Robin exhaled, laughing. "I hold my breath in the bath," she said. "I hold my head under and don't come up."

She watched the travelling darkness.

"Why?"

"I don't know. I like it."

My thoughts turned back to school. "Then what happened?" I asked. "How come you don't go to school at all?"

"I clocked a teacher. Got two days. Two days, that's all. Then when I destroyed the science block by making a flame-thrower out of the gas taps, I got peed."

Permanently Excluded.

I tried to look surprised. "That was you?"

Robin shrugged.

"Did anyone get hurt?"

"No, I made this one tiny flame and set fire to this piece of paper. That was it."

"And then what happened?"

She sat up straighter. With every word, her expression and accent changed. Her hands moved to animate her story.

"This bloody Shanice sprayed her cheap-arse hairspray everywhere and the flame went right across the table and set fire to everything. Shanice's chemistry book goes up in flames and Shanice goes mental, screaming, and throws the book. So there's this burning book flying through the air, the table's on fire and everyone's, like, 'Fuckin 'ell, Shanice!' And then the book lands on the windowsill and sets fire to the wood and the glass is poppin' and then the flame goes right up the blinds and I was, like, 'Fuck'. The supply teacher's there trying to get his specs on to read the fire extinguisher and everyone's screaming at him to put the fire out. 'Put the fuckin' fire out!' And he's going, 'Be quiet! Hang on!' and we're trying to wrestle the extinguisher off him, slapping him away, and he's proper fighting us for it, trying to put his fucking specs on, and before you know it, the fire's gone up this display about Einstein, so now it looks like a hate crime. Then it goes, *whooosh!* up the next set of blinds and finds some yellow stuff which goes, *Fsssh . . . BANG!* Then everyone shits themselves and is, like, trying to trample over each other, screaming in their phones and whatever, but, anyway, everyone got out. Then it spread across the room and stuff was popping and exploding out the windows and then the floor collapsed." She stopped. "Nightmare."

I laughed and covered my mouth with both hands. Robin smiled but it quickly faded. It always does.

"Anyway, at the unit, this one scrape calls me a ticker and backhand smacks my face. I lose it. Break her socket. I had to go DC for that one."

"God . . . the Detention Centre."

"Nuthouse, more like. Shed full of raped drug addicts, that place."

I nodded.

She sniffed. "And you?"

"If I told you, you'd go off me."

"I ain't on you." Her expression was stone cold. But then she broke into a little smile. "Go on. Can't be that bad. You ain't institutionalized."

"I was."

"Really?"

I shrugged.

"Where?"

"Meadow Gorge."

"Shit. How did you wind up there?"

"I went to school one day, and then it turns out I got on the roof and it was this big thing."

"What did they say was wrong with you?"

"Nothing. I was just sad."

Robin's face hardly moved. I couldn't tell what she was thinking. "What were you sad about?"

"I don't know. I just am sad all the time."

"Yeah," Robin said, "you look it. They don't ship you off to the Meadows for being sad though, Jake."

I shifted in my seat. "What's going to happen to you?"

"I'm fine." She looked out of the window. "I can look after myself."

For a brief second her real expression travelled across her face. She was terrified, but not of the journey, of something deep and immovable. I'd seen so much despair in the hospital, I could tell what had happened to people just by looking at them, but I couldn't read her. We were miles away from home. What if something happened? What if we were robbed, or threatened, or lost our passports? What if we were caught and thrown in a jail where no one would explain what was happening?

I dragged at the air between us. I wanted her in my hands, my arms, and straight back to St Pancras and straight back to Waterloo and straight back to Wimbledon. Eurostar, Northern line, Overland, home. Two hours tops.

"Robin, let's get back on the train to London. Before anything happens."

She looked at me. "Balls," she said. "This is it, Toto. We're in Paris!"

*

We approached the border patrol, looking behind us as if to check our parents were still there. I sailed up to a window manned by a fat guard with a bushy moustache and a forehead as smooth as milk. He flicked through my passport then snapped the passport closed and waved me through. "Can I have a stamp, please? *S'il vous plaît?*" I said in a high voice, giving another glance behind me as if I was waiting for my mother. The man smiled and stamped my passport. Some people still like you even though you're a skinny teenager.

In the Gare du Nord, globes on beautiful golden stems glide over your head as you walk. "Look at those beautiful lamps!" I said, staring upwards.

"Allow it," Robin said, kissing her teeth.

I ignored her. "They look like. . ."

"Faith," she said.

I had to run every few steps just to keep up with her as she propelled us through the station and out on to the street. Here she stopped and looked athe map, tilting it away from the winter sun. "We need Rue Auguste . . . er. . . by the Colonne . . . do . . . July something? They like their months, innit."

I laughed.

"What's funny?"

"You," I said, "you're funny."

She looked comfortable now, amid the chaos of rushing pedestrians and five-lane traffic. She seemed fine with being shoved, having to alter her path, her senses drowned by the city. Her face was fast. Her thoughts seemed to move every muscle within it. Her eyes shifted as if reading something only she could see; as if chasing thoughts, unable to catch them. She walked at an exhausting pace. I trailed her like a spaniel, and knew that in another life, with a different set of information, she would be someone great, a genius.

She hailed a taxi that sped up as it approached her. "Bloody taxis," she said.

I held out my pumpkin hand. A second taxi stopped and we climbed in.

Beautiful, pale buildings towered stacked on one another like wedding cakes. I put my thumbnail to my teeth. The size of the place was overwhelming. What we were doing was idiotic. We were like those berks on the news, who wander abroad without knowing any of the local laws or customs, and the embassy has to go and save them. They end up on the front page of the *Sun* with a headline like "Young Dumbs" or "Teen Idle". Or worse, we'd be robbed and stranded here, and I've have to stow away to England and live off rain water, and my mother would have to come and collect me from some refugee camp and she'd finally have that brain haemorrhage.

24

As the taxi stopped in traffic, we watched people walking past. The best were the ones in business suits. The women had artistry about them. "The women here walk so well in their heels," I said.

"Walk well in 'eels, is it, Meryl?" Robin laughed.

The neurons in my stomach got there before my brain did: *Walk well in eels, is it, Meryl?* I concentrated on my bloodless fingernails to push away thoughts of Isaac.

"And what's with the scarves?"

Scarves. Good. Concentrate on the scarves.

She was right. Almost every woman without a map was wearing a silk scarf. "They must have a system," I said. "Something tribal."

We got out of the taxi near the Louvre. On a panel outside there was an exhibition poster featuring a painting of a bare-breasted woman absently tweaking the nipple of another bare-breasted woman.

"Oop," Robin said, "tits."

Inside the courtyard, she stared curl-lipped at the glass pyramid sitting next to the palatial gallery. "What's that supposed to be?"

"Who knows," I said.

"Tacky as Christmas," Robin said.

"I like it. It's galactic. It contrasts."

"Yeah, it contrasts with the palace because it's shit."

I laughed as we climbed the stairs to the entrance.

The security guards were spot-checking bags. "*Bonjour*," I said as I handed mine over. "*Je suis u—*"

"Do you have your passport with you?"

"*Je voudrais un—*"

"You would like a walking guide?"

"*Non, merci, je suis—*"

"You would like to be directed to the *Mona Lisa*?"

"No, we're Egyptologists here to see the . . . artefacts . . . from the . . . pyramids for our doctorates about . . . pharaohs." I paused for breath. "Yeah, we just want to see the *Mona Lisa*."

The guard scrunched his face with disgust and Robin and I laughed. We couldn't stop laughing. We were bent double with giggles.

"What is the matter?" the guard said.

"*Ce n'est-ce rien, merci*," Robin said, and then she spoke in a patter of fluent French that wiped the smug look off his face.

"You speak French?"

"And?"

We walked up the stairs and into the grand foyer. Robin crossed the sea of clicking marble towards a headless winged statue. We looked up at her in silence, then we wandered over to the *Venus de Milo* with her missing arms and confident lean. Robin shook her head. "They wanna finish these." I laughed.

She stopped in front of a statue of a woman plunging a knife into her naked chest. Despite being solid stone, the women looked soft and vulnerable. Robin looked at her for a long time. She finally woke up to herself when I touched her elbow. "I feel sorry for them," she said, "stuck here with their tits out."

"Yeah," I said, suddenly uncomfortable. I couldn't offer anything to the conversation the statues were trying to have with us. The man next to us was talking to his wife in rapid Russian. What did he have to say? What were you supposed to think? As we bumbled through the gallery, watching people talking quietly to each other, I felt smaller and more stupid than I had ever felt in my life.

Robin busied herself with the map. "This way," she said. She led us out of the gallery and past the Renaissance without a second glance. "Here it is."

I was shocked. Usually when you follow someone with a map you have to back up, wander in circles and have at least three arguments, until finally you ask someone else to direct you. Robin had taken us straight there. The *Mona Lisa* was perched in the middle of a white wall in front of us.

She was so small. I thought she'd be like the Raphael paintings they have at the National that are so awesome and domineering you cower in front of them. But the *Mona Lisa* was like a little postage stamp, all on her own on a wash of white.

"Is that it?" Robin said.

I shrugged.

"I don't get it."

"Neither do I."

"Does that mean we're thick?"

"Who knows," I said. "A painting made me cry once, so I must know something."

"Self-portrait, was it?"

"Ha ha," I said. Great comeback.

"So why is it so famous then?" Robin said. "Why are we looking at it?"

"Who knows?"

"Who's in charge of stuff like this? Like, what's good or what?"

"I don't know."

"She's laughing at us." Robin pointed to the painting.

"Why does she have to be in that box? It looks like she's suffocating."

"Someone must have tried to nick her," Robin sighed. "At least she hasn't got her tits out."

Tourists jostled behind us. Everyone wanted their moment with *Mona*. I walked away, thinking of visiting galleries with Isaac's mum and dad. Rabbi Kaufman would point out interesting things for us to look at and we'd comment earnestly. He would beam at how fascinating and intelligent we were and assure us that we would do and discover great things in our lives, and Isaac and I would hop off to talk about stink bombs and farting, certain we were geniuses.

There's a Mr Reacher sketch we filmed at the National Gallery. Mr Reacher is dragging a pupil past all the paintings, wagging his finger at each one until he gets to Van Gogh's *Sunflowers*, and he goes: "Crap, crap, crap, crap, crap . . . sunflowers. Write that down." If you keep watching you see a guard storming towards us going, "Oi!" and Isaac screaming as he does his lock-kneed sprint towards the door. I'm holding the camera and you can hear that I am laughing so much I can't run.

"What are you thinking about?" Robin asked softly as we walked out of the *Mona Lisa*'s room and into the corridor. "Isaac?"

I nodded. I didn't tell her that it was all I ever think about. It's the only thing worth thinking about. There was being friends with him, then there was being friends with no one, then there was nothing.

In the taxi I worried about how faint I felt and that Robin might try to make me eat something. What if she wanted to go to a café? In France they put butter on their butter. A bony fingertip scraped along the wall of my stomach.

Robin was looking out of the window at the parping progress of a man on a scooter, unable to negotiate the stuttering traffic because of the enormous box balanced on his lap. The box was wrapped in red paper and sported a badly tied bow. He looked miserable and resigned to the traffic, as if he had expected it to turn against him.

"They're post bands," Robin said.

I turned.

"The red rubber bands you and Isaac saw all over London. They're post bands. They use them at the sorting office. Postmen just chuck them on the pavement, all day every day. They're normal rubber bands."

I thought of Isaac diving to the pavement and springing up with sudden excitement, another rubber band between his fingers. "Ah ha!" he would declare. "Our next clue!"

"Oh," I said.

We climbed out of the taxi and straight into the path of a tramp. Robin slapped her hands to her pockets. The tramp began mumbling wildly, his face a jumble of billowing grey hair and creeping skin, his nose engorged with red wine. He threw up his arms, his sleeves filthy with caked-on dirt. In a split second, Robin became a terrifying gangster. I had scarcely seen anyone so angry. She screamed at him in French and jabbed him so hard in the chest with her gunned fingers, he buckled over and heaved as if to vomit. His hands fell open and out dropped Robin's wallet. She picked it up. "Do one or I'll break your face," she said.

The tramp hurried off, holding his chest where she had hit him. "Minging bastard," she said, wiping her fingers on the wall. "Pickpocketing a kid. Tosser. He'd get shanked for that." She crouched to the ground to calm herself down, her legs perfectly bent. She kept muttering about what would happen to him if she saw him again.

"Bloody foreigners," I said, and Robin laughed.

My chest was tight. It wasn't the tramp, it was the severe crease between Robin's eyes. I put my pumpkin hand flat over my chest and realized, with a panic that aggravated my lungs, that I hadn't brought my inhaler.

"Posh 'ere, ain't it? White muggers." Robin delved into her bag to check everything was still there. "We'll get murdered by a count in a minute."

She walked ahead as the world swung downwards. I saw her feet hurry back. "Shit," I heard through water, "what's wrong with you?"

"As . . . asthma," I said.

My ribs pressed against my chest. My face became hard, baulking against suffocation, trying to suck air into my lungs. A pain spiked up my legs and I realized I was on my knees.

"You are the opposite of Jamaica," I heard Robin yell as her feet flew away.

The sky rushed towards me. My ears became my heartbeat. My face was a slab of pain. I thought of Mum and Dad laughing in the kitchen. I'm so small I'm looking up at them. I thought of Isaac in the playground, his skinny frame and funny walk, stepping between me and a boy whose pudgy hands are pushing me. I thought of us watching Dave Chappelle together, taking turns to recite the bus joke. I thought of us chasing after Gordon Ramsay on Shaftesbury Avenue, begging him for a picture, handing him a camera, and him laughing and calling us cheeky little buggers. I thought of falling to the floor laughing after we had been sent out of class. I thought of Dad buying me a toy I didn't want. I didn't want the tank; I wanted the buggy. I saw a man in a white coat yelling at me. I saw something the colour of water, my old face reaching down to pick me up, my hand reaching out to grab my nose, and laughing, laughing until something small and plastic was shoved into my mouth, and acrid air snaked down my throat.

"You have to run after, innit, 'cos I nicked this."

Robin's voice. I looked up. She blocked the sun. Her skin looked like the inside of a petal. She was shaking the vile inhaler. She pulled my eyelid open. She didn't shake or falter as she bent to one knee and put a hand flat to my back. The crease had left her forehead. She took the grey vial of steroids out of the inhaler and put the empty plastic tube in my mouth. She covered the air hole with the palm of her hand. "Breathe," she said, and I breathed into her palm, taking in the small pocket of air the case allowed. Every time I took a breath she moved her hand to refill the tube. She kept her hand to my back and we started breathing in time with each other, her hand moving with the deflation of my lungs.

"You haven't got asthma," Robin said quietly. "If you did, you'd be out of it. Even I can't run that fast."

"What is it then?"

"Panic attacks. First-world problems. . . Come on, let's

get you . . . a sherry, is it? Some Valium or what? You're like a housewife from the Fifties." She draped me over her shoulder and walking felt like flying. "God, you are light as sin, bruv. Swear down, you need some chicken nuggets. Like Gollum on Atkins. Christ. You're just *bones*."

We walked the wide streets and my head cleared. Women in colourful scarves tumbled past us. It was nice to be walking, but I grew worried about getting lost and I bundled us into another taxi.

"Can you afford this?" Robin said.

I nodded. I thought of those nights spent starving and freezing, determined not to spend the money my mother left me each time she was away working. I wondered why I wasn't bothered to see the money tot up on the meter. I put my head between my legs, testing my newfound ability to breathe.

"You all right?"

"Yeah," I said, rubbing the top of my arm. "Sorry."

"Ain't your fault you're some sort of tart, is it?"

I laughed at the casual way she said this, and after a while she started giggling too. In London I had used my inhaler all the time, but I realized that I hadn't needed it since I met Robin.

"There it is!" Robin said with delight.

I looked up and the iconic tower peeked through the rooftops in the distance. Robin clutched my arm, beaming. In the mirror, the taxi driver was smiling. *"Bienvenus à la tour Eiffel!"* He gave a benevolent chuckle.

We got out of the taxi and raced to the tower and

stood underneath it. With the spire above us, we were suddenly dizzy on the ground. We waited in line to climb to the top. On the first level we paid for two junior tickets. I wondered if I would be able to get to the top. I get jittery standing on a chair, and climbing the stairs in my house makes me want to cry.

As we climbed, the air became sharp and harder to breathe. The higher we climbed, the more often Robin turned to check I was still there. "Don't faint off here now," she said, pointing to the ground. "You'd be absolutely peaches."

We reached the viewing platform and looked over the edge at the delicate whiteness of Paris. Buildings like stickle bricks and trees the size of peas were arranged into triangles, laid out around the palace on the other side of the river like the triangles in a packet of Dairylea. The neatness of it was strangely comforting. The wedding-cake buildings and wide, blustering roads made perfect sense now. It reminded me of being young and reaching the top of the London Eye and Rabbi Kaufman saying, "Well, it looks like London." Mrs Kaufman laughed, and Isaac and I laughed at her laughter. I smiled, realizing he must have expected a view such as this, of a city transformed into an idea, and it made me homesick, though not for where I lived now, but for how much I used to love London.

"Are you crying?"

"No," I said. I wiped my face to make sure.

We drew our hoods up against the cold. "What's the palace called?" Robin asked, pointing towards the river to the Trocadéro, which from this height looked like a giant corkscrew.

"That's *le grand bakery*, where they make all the baguettes."

Robin smiled. "And in the small bit?"

"That's where they make the buns."

She laughed.

"Doesn't it look like a giant box of Dairylea?" I said.

"Yeah!" Robin said delightedly. "I like the triangles."

"Yeah, I do too."

"I don't know why."

"I don't either. Maybe it's because it looks like the buildings are protecting the palace."

"Yeah, like they're all in this together."

Robin picked at the railing. I looked down and wondered how many people had thrown themselves off this ledge. I wondered if any of them had miscalculated the taper and sliced through the base like French fries. I wondered if anyone had thrown themselves off and killed someone on the ground.

Robin's face became strained as she looked out at Paris.

"Have you had a terrible time?" I asked, the rattle in my throat coming back.

She looked into the mist spilling on to the city. "This was probably the best day of my life."

I looked at the triangles.

"I've had a shit life though," she said, "so don't get excited."

As I leaned over the ledge, my eyes followed the path

of vein-like roads leading to the thousands of houses and apartments and little garden flats and mansions and hotels, and I thought the cars looked like bugs eating away the city. I thought about how someone can die and hundreds of people will come to his funeral, and how someone else can die and rot away in a house without anyone noticing. Fifteen times I've moved into houses stinking of death. Bodies decay faster than you would ever think. Bugs come to melt them away.

I wondered what Robin saw when she looked down at millions of lives. Maybe she saw the beauty of the city; maybe she saw the bugs.

She smiled, her eyes sleepy, caught in a daze as she watched the crawling city below. I could finally see her clearly. We stood side by side until we became cold and the darkness swallowed up everything around us.

"That's it," Robin said, "time's up."

We climbed down the tower and with every step my feet became heavier.

Near the palace we found a tiny patisserie that smelled like blackberry crumble. "Foooooood," Robin said as she pushed open the door. The smell sent sugar sliding down my throat. It made me sick with excitement.

"*Bonjour,*" I said, "*je voudrais une—*"

"Yes, what would you like?" the baker interrupted.

"Oh," I said, "a *pain au chocolat.*" Robin tugged my elbow. "Two *pains au chocolat.*" I pushed my remaining euros towards him. I felt so faint I couldn't count them.

"*Non.*" The man smiled at the coins. "Sorry, it's not enough."

"Oh, sorry, *pardon*," I said, relieved he wouldn't serve me.

The man leaned into the kitchen and spoke in rapid, lyrical French. The second man, older, looked at me and patted his stomach.

"OK," the younger baker said, "you can have them."

"*Merci!*" I said.

"OK, bye," the baker said. He smiled and turned to the next customer.

The bag was greasy in my hand. If only kind Doctor Kahn could see me holding a greasy bag! Robin and I sat on the pavement outside and took a pastry each. I bit into it. It hit my mouth like a firework. I couldn't speak. "Man alive, I should stay here, eat this every day," I said, "stop looking like a prisoner of war."

"You could learn French," Robin said as she bit into her pastry, "get your strength up."

"God, this is good." I tried to slow down and savour every bite, but it was hard to not swallow it whole, like a pelican. I munched as quickly as I could to stave off the voices of the baby birds. "Almost as good as Greggs."

Robin laughed. She sucked flakes of pastry from her thumb. "Be fair, Greggs is wicked. Iced fingers."

"Yeah, yum-yums, epic."

"People keep giving us evils."

"Do they? We are pretty scraggly, to be fair," I said. "I can't remember the last time I washed my clothes. And I need to get my hair did."

Robin laughed. "Don't *ever* say that."

"What, get my hair did?"

"Stop it!"

"What's wrong with me getting my hair did?"

She hit my leg and laughed. "So, you think you'll still do your show? Your comedy thing?"

I shook my head. "Do you know which university most famous comedians go to? Where John Cleese and Sacha Baron Cohen and David Mitchell and Stephen Fry went?"

Robin curled her lip.

"Cambridge," I said, scratching the sweat off the back of my neck. "*Cambridge*. We were on track for Cambridge, you know. I was on track, and now I couldn't go to Cambridge on a bus."

"If Richard Pryor grew up in a brothel and Dave Chappelle never went to university, then you don't need to go to Cambridge," Robin said. "Anyway, you can go Cambridge if you want; it can't be that hard, it's all written down. I'd be more worried that you're about as funny as war."

I laughed. "I used to be funny."

"Yeah, well, I used to be prima ballerina. Shit happens."

"You could definitely do that if you wanted. You look like you can fly."

"I thought. . ." Robin said, looking at her arms, "I was going to be extraordinary."

"You are."

She laughed.

The last shred of pastry flaked from my mouth. I even

put my oily finger to the paper to pick up some last bits.

"Robin," I said gently, "why did you bring me here?"

"What do you mean?"

"I mean, why here? What are we doing here?"

"What do you mean?"

"I mean, you know, all the missions we've been on. This is another one of those, isn't it?"

Robin's face dropped. "What are you saying?"

"What? No. Nothing. I'm just saying that whatever this mission is, I'm cool with it. I mean, I'm fine with it."

"This was supposed to be an adventure."

"I don't mind, Robin. Whatever it is, I'll do it. I just need to know."

"What are you on about? Why can't I just be here to have fun? Don't trust me, is it? Think I'm up to something, is it? You daft racist."

"I'm not racist, I hate everyone equally."

"You," she said, slinging her bag over her shoulder, "can get back to London on your bloody own!"

She stomped off, and I headed back to the Gare du Nord alone. When I got to the train, it was so packed we had to sit where our tickets told us to. Robin kissed her teeth as I sat down next to her. She was back in her grey tracksuit and her braids were loose again.

"Time's up," she said with a yawn before she fell asleep.

I jolted in and out of sleep. I watched the tunnel rush past and tried to hold my breath. I imagined sleepwalking and trying to get out of the speeding train. I looked at

Robin's delicate hand spread out on the table. The tip of my little finger touched hers.

What I would ever enjoy if I couldn't enjoy a day in Paris with Robin Carter? I wondered why didn't I care if we got arrested at the border.

I couldn't bear to go back, not to London, nor to Paris, nor anywhere.

25

King's Cross was an agony of noise. The cars gunned for each other in trapped frustration. Pedestrians crowded the pavements. Every headlight hit a ghost bike surrounded by flowers.

"I hate it here," I declared, like a child. "I have to get out."

"You go Wimbledon on the Overground. I'll go Southfields on the District line," Robin said, heading into the Underground.

"No," I panicked, "let's go back together."

"Nah, that's bait."

She flew off. I had to run to catch up with her. "Robin, I'm sorry. What I said was stupid. I just wanted to help."

She flattened her hair and drew her hoodie so far over her head it covered her eyes. "God!" she said, walking with greater speed.

"Robin, please don't leave me."

"What did you just say?" She stopped and turned. "*Please don't leave me?*" She said it in agonizing slow motion. "What are you, in the Supremes or sammink? The world's shittest James Brown tribute act? *Please don't leave me*. What, are we married in the Forties or what? What is wrong with you?"

"It just came out wrong."

"*You* came out wrong," she yelled. "You don't even know me. You knew and you still did it."

"Still did what?"

She stopped and turned on her heel. "You went into the office of a boss and you planted a bug. What's wrong with you?"

I didn't know what to say.

"What were you going to do if you got caught?"

I couldn't lift my head.

"Why?" she said, furious now. "Why did you do it? Why did you go along with everything I said? You messed with very, very dangerous people, Jake. Why did you do it?" She sounded breathless. "And if you thought I was setting you up for something in Paris, why did you come?"

"Because you told me to," I said, my voice wavering. I didn't realize how pathetic it sounded until it came out of my mouth.

"You make me sick, you know that?"

"Don't say that."

"You do. Look at you. You'd rather throw your life away than be by yourself."

Under the lampposts the brown leaves looked like smouldering fire. She turned and disappeared into the darkness. I ran after her. "Take that back!"

"Where is everyone then?" She stopped and raised her hands. "Where are all your mates watching out for you? Look at you. You're just another lonely kid."

"Shut up, Robin."

"You should see yourself! Thin as death, muttering to yourself, hitting yourself in your sleep. See you when you're in your thirties? You'll be on the streets, fam."

"Shut *up*."

"They don't look after people like you, Jake. Not after you turn sixteen." She shoved me. "Stand up for yourself." She pushed me again. "Why won't you stand up for yourself? Jesus actually wept, the state of you."

Robin brandished her palms, shoved me to the ground, and walked away. From the ground I looked up at her and suddenly realized why she reminded me of the baby birds at the hospital.

"You're suicidal," I said.

She turned. Her eyes widened with fury. "I am *not* suicidal. I'm black. I'm a warrior. Black people do not kill themselves. Black people don't get depressed. You fucking lot get depressed."

"That's a myth," I said, "a really dangerous myth. You need to get some help, Robin."

"I don't need no one's help. This is armour," she said, slapping her arms. "And this city," she swung her palms towards the street, "is mine."

26

I rolled on to my side and put my knees to my chest. After some effort, I rolled to my knees and lifted myself up. I checked my jacket. Mud covered my back. This was just what I needed to add to the row I was about to get for being home so late.

On the Overground train I held my bag to my chest and watched the carriages like a tennis match, terrified of getting picked off by a roaming pack of hoodies. There's nothing worse than being cornered on a train. If you get kicked and you're down on the carriage floor, you can feel the tracks pummelling through your back. A very ancient part of your body thinks you're being dragged to death so you panic like a madman.

I pulled my collar and bolted like a greyhound as soon as I reached Wimbledon.

At the mouth of my long, dark road everything was quiet and empty. I put my head down and walked home as fast as I could. Once I spotted my house, I took my keys out of my rucksack and broke into a jog, the keys between my fingers like Wolverine. Outside the door I looked about before hurriedly putting the key in the lock and bracing myself for a wall of aggravation.

Inside the Death House the air was still. Nothing had moved. I looked upstairs and could see my parents' bedroom door was open. I went up. Empty. I checked the house phone. No calls.

I went to my room and looked out of the window at the Toad House. No one was there.

The pastry I had eaten rolled in my stomach, the oil coating my throat. I went to the bathroom and threw up into the toilet. I was sweating so much I took a shower. I was scared to be in the shower because the pipes made weird noises that sounded like someone breaking in. I washed my hair but the soap became rough. I worried that my body had grown that weird fur again, like that time I was in Meadow Gorge. I held up the soap and it was covered in hair. Not mine though. Gross, I thought. Dad never washed the soap.

I looked again. Blond hair.

I ran my fingers along my scalp. I pulled, looked at my fingers. Hair. It was coming out in clumps.

"No, no, please," I said. "No, no, no. Please."

I went to the mirror in growling panic. I squeezed my nose, certain I was dreaming. I didn't wake.

"No, no, *no*."

I washed the hair off my hands and ran downstairs to the kitchen. I rummaged through the cupboards and found a box of Frosties. I ripped open the lid. I took a handful and shoved them into my mouth. The sugar rushed to my head with such force that I buckled. I took a jar of chocolate spread, sank to the floor and ate it with my fingers. I pulled packets of meat and cheese from the fridge. I worked my way through the ham, even though the breath-smelling packets make me sick.

When the frenzy was over, I looked at the chocolate fingerprints all over the kitchen and the packets and boxes and empty pots of baby food. The cold of the tiles was creeping through my legs. My stomach raged war, and sent shooting pains to my heart and down my left arm. I took four of my diet pills and a handful of caffeine pills. They would keep me awake long enough to purge the crud from my system. My rabbit heart raced. As I made my way through a canister of black coffee and a bottle of mouthwash, I noticed Robin hadn't come back. I blinked and wondered why the night was so bright.

I couldn't believe it. Behind the mansions, the sun was rising.

27

On Saturday I slept in fits, barely able to get out of bed. I kept glancing at her window, her room unchanged.

Sunday: I paced the Death House, the sound of my footsteps hitting the walls. I hated that the house was so empty. A whole life chucked in a filthy skip. I returned to my window again and again like a trapped fly. Sometimes a small light pulsed beneath the mound of grey clothes. Her phone. She might as well have left behind a limb.

That's it.

Time's up.

I couldn't silence her words.

She'd been gone a full day. I went to the door of the Toad House. I looked up at the blinking red light and summoned all of my nerve to knock. It set off a cascade of screaming and barking. Screaming about who the hell it could be this time and who the hell was going to answer it and if it was the bloody police and rah rah if it was the bloody bailiffs rah rah rah . . . I scurried halfway down the path by the time Robin's mother threw open the door.

She had managed to get dressed today. She wore pink Aladdin trousers and a black sweater so large it grazed her knees. Her eyes were like washed-out ink, her skin flaky like pastry. The corners of her mouth hung down like kippers as if she didn't have the energy to lift them. "Who are you?" she said, baring massive white teeth.

"Uh . . . I'm . . . is . . . Robin in?"

"Robin's in when she wants to be. Who's askin'?"

"Oh . . . I'm . . . Jake. From next door?"

She threw a disgusted glance at my house. "That where all the bangin's coming from?"

"Um? Yeah, my mum's . . . difficult."

One of her kippers trembled as if trying to smile. "Yeah, well, no 'fence but she does look mad."

I did take offence.

"Robin!" she screamed. "James is 'ere!"

"It's, uh . . . Jake," I said.

"Ugh, *Jake* he's saying now." She tipped her head to the silence. Her pupils were the size of pinpricks. "She ain't 'ere."

"Do you know where she is?"

"No." She curled her lip.

"Do you know when she'll be back?"

"What? I ain't her blaaaaady secretary."

"When did you last see her?"

196

"What are you some sort of sort?"

"I don't know what that means." Cold wind rushed through my hair, stinging the patches of my scalp. I pulled at my shirt.

"You questioning me?"

"What?"

" . . . what?"

"You gan plaze?"

I didn't know whether she was saying plays, please, place, police.

"Well, you plaze?"

Rabbit heart.

"You better not gan plaze, you maga sort."

"What words are you saying?"

"You muggin' me off?"

"I'm just—"

"Just what? You know what 'appens to people rand 'ere who ask questions?"

"God," I muttered to myself.

"Oo? Go on, get off out of it!"

Slam.

I staggered backwards. "Charmed, I'm sure." I reached for my phone, thinking I could find Kane or Clarissa, but I had no phone, and even if I did, I wouldn't have their numbers. And even if I did, I didn't know them well enough to call them. And even if I did, they wouldn't come out to help me.

I went back to the Death House and phoned the hospitals. I called the police non-emergency line and asked if there had been any incidents at Wimbledon Park. There had not. I asked if anyone had been reported missing. They said no. They asked if I was all right and I said yes. They asked how old I was and I hung up.

I walked to Wimbledon Park. In the pale daylight the park was restful. I walked to the spot where that kid had been beaten up. Children were playing cricket with their father and laughed when he didn't catch the ball. They were too young to realize he missed on purpose. I looked all around. I didn't know what I could do so I went home and went to my room and sat by the window.

At sunset nothing in her room had moved.

28

On Monday morning I woke to harsh light streaming through my curtainless window. I licked my furry teeth. I checked Robin's landfill bedroom. Nothing had moved. I went to the bathroom and heaved.

I took a shower but only washed the lower part of my body. When I got dressed, my trousers wouldn't stay up so I tightened my belt into a tiny knot. I checked my parents' room: dead as a grave. I went downstairs and ate three red jelly squares. I went back upstairs and tried to see the back of my hair in the mirror. I prodded at the gaps. I went to look out of my window one last time then walked outside into the autumn light.

Leaves kicked about the road. I pulled my beanie cap over my head and coughed. The cough burned my chest. I put a fist to my chest and regurgitated the jelly squares.

It looked like I'd hacked up my liver. I looked at it for a while and then I went to school.

It was afternoon registration before I saw Kane. I didn't notice when he sat down next to me. He said my name like he'd been saying it for a while. "Jaaaaaake?"

I sat up with a start and met his brown eyes.

"Since when did you start wearing beanies?"

I scratched beneath the cap until a mumble came out. "Sorry?"

"Where were you all morning? Weren't you supposed to be in art? You were on the register."

I scratched my neck and tried to lean away from him. I was worried about him touching me, and about my breath. "Didn't feel like it."

"Where did you go?"

My cupboard.

For three hours.

That's why I smell like a tomb.

"Around," I said.

"Nutter. Art's all right," he said. "Miss Bailey's safe. It's quite relaxing."

"Was Ritchie Darscall there?"

"No, they don't let him do art because he kept ruining everyone's stuff."

"Charming."

Kane leaned closer. He smelled of trees, not just their woody scent but the coolness of the air around them. "You keep missing everything, your parents'll get a text message."

"Yeah, that text thing is a pain in the arse. I changed my mum's number on the thing."

"Did you?" Kane smiled. "You're suspect, Jake. You really are."

I was getting the shakes. They started in my chest and rumbled through my body. I jittered my leg to cover them up.

"What's wrong?"

"I'm not very good-looking and I have a terrible personality."

Kane laughed. "What's going on with the girl next door?"

"We spent the day together on Friday, and now she's gone. Like, gone gone. I went and spoke to her mum, but she just goes, 'I ain't seen her.' Like she really didn't care. But she went off to the park in the middle of the night, and now she hasn't come back."

"She probably round her mate's," Kane said.

"But why wouldn't her mum care?"

"Parents just give up, innit. When you're about eleven they think, Oh, sod this."

"Yeah." For the first time ever I thought about that look my mother gives me and felt calm. "Did yours?"

"No, to be fair, my mum and dad think I'm amazing."

I put my head on the desk.

A supply teacher bustled in and sifted through a stack of papers, breaking into a sweat under his thick hair.

"Supply!" the class screeched.

"You know any of her other mates?" Kane asked, concluding that we didn't need to listen to this particular teacher.

"No." I thought of her bare walls and abandoned phone. "I don't think she's got any."

"Everyone's got friends," Kane said. "You can't not have friends."

The world Kane lived in must be nice. I wished I could visit it. A land where making friends isn't a monumental effort, it's something that just happens. I bet he would go to Paris and have a grand old time. He wouldn't get to the top of the Eiffel Tower and see insects and suicide. He'd see world peace. To him the world was a lovely clear river and he was a fish. The world's most handsome and lovely bloody fish. "She didn't take her phone."

"How do you know?"

"I can see it ringing in her room."

"She's probably got more than one. Most girls do. Girls and drug dealers."

"Nothing in her room has moved. Kane," I said, looking around to make sure no one was listening, "what's 'jumped out'?"

Kane's eyes widened. "Christ," he said quietly, "why?"

"It's something she mentioned."

"Uh, Jake. . . " He started thumbing through his phone. "That's really bad."

Sean lolloped over like a horse and crashed into our chairs. "What are you gays up to?" He watched Kane tap out a text message.

"Shut up, Sean," Kane mumbled. "That girl Jake knows is going to get jumped out."

"Bait," Sean said.

"Will you please tell me what jumped out is?"

Kane and Sean exchanged infuriating glances as they decided whether I should be told this big huge secret. Finally Kane looked around and leaned close. His breath smelled of sugar. "'Jumped in' is joining a gang and 'jumped out' is leaving it. You literally get jumped out by the lot of them. Gang beating. To death a lot of the time. And if you're a girl? It's not good, Jake."

"Why would they want to jump her out?" I asked, rubbing my elbow that was on fire because I had leaned on it for all of two seconds.

Sean laughed. "Uh, she looked at someone funny, she wore the wrong snap-back on a Saturday, she farted in the wrong octave. . . Take your pick, innit."

"If they just abandon you," I said, "what's the point in ever joining?"

Kane said, "Most people do it by accident. You're getting bullied, or you're bored or skint, or whatever, and you blurt something stupid, then you're in."

"You get presents, protection," Sean said. "Someone to shave your tits on a Sunday, whatever."

Two serious examples and a joke. Sean knew how to time a laugh. Isaac and I were obsessed with working out the maths of comedy, the timing that was closer to music than it was to literature. Isaac said we had to learn how to play an instrument. Music, maths and comedy are all intertwined. I missed my brain being occupied with Mozart and Bill Hicks rather than violence and gang linguistics.

"Well, how can we get to them?" I asked. "How can

we talk to someone in her gang?"

"They ain't got a call centre, Jake," Kane said. "You can't go the comment section on their website."

"Yeah, you can't comment on their website," Sean said. "They ain't *got* a website."

Kane rolled his eyes. "Shut up, Sean, will you?"

"Maybe we could try and find someone who's been jumped out. We can ask them and. . ."

Kane became serious again. "It isn't survivable. They might not kill you but. . ." He shook his head. He had Dad's sentence disease, as if the words he needed didn't exist. "Jake, don't tell anyone I said this, but if you know she's been threatened, why don't you just go to the police?"

I shifted. "And say what? 'Oh, hi, this girl I barely know has gone missing. She may have done something massively illegal, but ignore that, can you help?'"

"What about Social Services?" Kane said.

"That bunch of meddling bastards?" I said. Bright flashes appeared when I blinked and remained when I opened my eyes. I shielded my face and shut my eyes until the flashing stopped.

"Are you having a breakdown, Britney?" Sean said.

"Girls' names aren't insulting," I said.

"What's going on?" Clarissa said as she joined us. The supply teacher was reading the newspaper while everyone went loudly about their business.

I buried my face in my hands and heard Kane say, "Jake knows this girl who's being jumped out."

There was a long pause. Clarissa didn't say anything

but I could feel her tense up.

"I'm not being funny," Sean said, "but I wouldn't get involved with this if my life depended on it."

The bell sounded. We collected our stuff, without a glance towards the teacher, and poured out into the hall. I tried to shift the weight of my bag off the bone of my shoulder. Kane took it from me and carried it.

"Make sure you don't do nothing with her," he said, "even if it seems innocent, like, you know, 'Oh, let's go down the shops, drop something off. Oh, let's just go drop off a bit of redirected mail.' Only thing getting redirected is your face . . . right up your arse."

"Yeah, be careful," Clarissa said, as we waited our turn to trudge down the stairs. "Don't get tricked into anything." We filed into the empty science room. "Definitely don't go anywhere with her," she said, throwing her bag in the corner and taking a seat at the back. Kane and Sean joined her, defiantly keeping their coats on. The seats in science are higher than anywhere else and it put so much pressure on the bones of my arse, I could barely sit down.

"Anywhere?" I said.

"Jake?" Kane said. "You haven't gone anywhere with her, have you?"

"I might have. . ."

"You might have what?" Kane said.

"You're getting done over, innit, Jake," Sean laughed. "Played like a banjo."

Bash joined us. "This is still a kid we're talking about," he said, "and torturing someone who's trying to get out of a gang is not uncommon."

"You think she's being . . . tortured?" I said.

"We need to get on the principal's email," Kane said, "use her ID to start asking round A&Es, police and Social."

"I can get myself sent to the principal," Sean shrugged. "It's a special skill."

"No," Kane said, "we're doing a lock-in tonight. Jake will bugger off like he always does and we'll all meet in the Conference Centre when the bell rings, and hide out there until everyone goes."

"Well," Bash said, "there go my election prospects."

His voice was so soft he made everyone giggle. He pocketed his notebook with a flourish and everyone giggled again.

"I'd vote for you, Bash," Clarissa said.

"Bash, you nanked your election prospects day you was born, son."

"That ain't true," he said, looking at our squawking classmates, who were threatening each other with rolled-up textbooks. "This place is exactly like Eton. We have boxing, fencing, debate club. . ."

"None of our parents work," Sean said.

"*Speakforyourself!*" we yelled at him.

"And we all live on estates," Clarissa said.

"Good one," I said, unable to think of a joke.

"Yeah," Bash laughed, "we all live on estates and none of us deserves to be here."

Kane threw his head back and laughed. It was as if the light came from him.

29

I spent the rest of the afternoon in my cupboard, editing the Apple Pie scene. Isaac's laugh played on a loop. I ate a cracker and three jelly squares. Jelly squares are quite grim but I didn't mind eating them even if they were warm from my pockets. Baby birds eat them because they're brightly coloured and they can use them as a marker for when they're throwing up different meals. Vomit geology. Vomology.

I stood up and wiggled around to get some blood to my toes. My trousers swam around the fall of my bum like a Southside rude-boy. I'd lost even more weight since the days Isaac's dad used to call us twins, or piglets, and later . . . twiglets.

Once, Ms Scabbard had called Isaac and me to the front of the class and made us stand face to face while she measured our combined waist size. She then measured the fattest kid in the class and announced that Isaac and I combined were thinner than Matt Manson. Matt's face fell and the righteous kids banded in support of him.

"Miss, it isn't his fault he's fat," Katie said.

"Miss, Matt's really upset," Amirah said.

"How would you like it if we calculated our combined ages?" I said. "And compared them to yours, miss."

"Right, that's enough—"

"Or our combined number of friends?" Isaac said.

"You be quiet, you—"

"Or our combined number of . . . uh . . . parents who are still alive," Shiloh said.

Uh, too far there, mate. Misjudged.

Ms Scabthroat inhaled the insult for a beat, her jaw hanging, then she lost it. And I mean *lost it*: yelling, sweating, spit spraying in all directions. She screamed so hard her ghost-white face bristled with purple veins. When she stopped screeching, she collapsed into a chair, glaring at us as if to decide whose head to rip off first. What followed was a silence so tense it could crack a mirror. She turned to the board and we all knew that whoever moved, squeaked, or sneezed next was finished.

"You know when we stood together. . ." I whispered to Isaac.

He scrunched his face and leaned away, knowing I would make him laugh, knowing that the next person to make a sound would split the atom and face the wrath of hell. But it was Isaac, and he couldn't resist. He took a nervous gulp of water. "What?" he whispered.

"Well," I leaned closer to his ear. "When we stood face to face? And she put that tape measure round us? My . . . uh . . . my winky moved."

Isaac sprayed his water over his desk, splashing Rosie in front, destroying his maths book, scrambling to catch the gobby fluid that came out of his nose. The sight made me grab my stomach in laughter.

Isaac howled and, scarlet and sweating, Ms Scabthroat screamed like a crazy pig: "Jones! Kaufman! Get OUT!"

I wiped my face and realized I was crying. A sharp, stabbing pain ripped through my hollow stomach. Isaac wouldn't believe I'd had so many fights. We'd never thrown or taken a punch between us.

A tiny twiglet. Less than half the size of poor Matt Manson.

I waited until the sounds of the school had faded away and then walked out into the dark corridor.

30

When Kane walked into the conference room, I was so relieved I couldn't speak.

Bash, Clarissa and Sean appeared behind him.

"Just so you know," Sean said, "I am already starving."

We waited in the conference room until the lights switched off around the school. There was a walk-in stock cupboard that we checked would fit us all in when the caretaker did his final sweep of the school.

Bootsteps approached and we tiptoed into the cupboard. It went dark and musty and Sean started to giggle. The door of the conference room was flung open. Sean clamped his mouth with two hands and we waited in silence as the footsteps entered the room. I could feel the others brace around me. The steps retreated.

Ahooo, said my stomach.

"Shut up, man," Sean hissed.

Ahoooooo?

"Shut up, Jake."

"Shut up. Stop sayin' shut up," Clarissa said.

The footsteps halted. Clarissa's heart beat against my arm. It pounded so hard it moved her tiny body. Her fingers found mine. Her touch sent a sensation like a burn across my palm. She probably thought my hand was Kane's.

"What now?" Kane whispered.

"Well, we can't stay here for ever," Bash said.

"My cousin hid in a service cupboard at the O2 for two days to see Beyoncé," Sean said, "but when he come out his eyes couldn't adjust to the lights and he slammed into this security guard stinking of piss, so he got chucked out before the support act come on, and he never saw nothing."

"Pikey bastard," Kane whispered.

"Oi, that's my cousin."

"Ain't he the one who got Community Service for eating a pigeon?" Bash whispered.

"No, that was his brother. And it ain't like he didn't cook the pigeon."

"Oh, well, if he cooked it then that's fine," Bash said.

The others giggled.

"We might need to go full cannibal locked in 'ere," Sean said.

"You'll be the first to go," Bash said. "I'm not even waiting till I'm hungry. Just peckish."

"Tell you who I would eat," Sean said. "Clarissa's dad."

The boys laughed. Clarissa told them to shut up. I tensed. I hated being outside of in-jokes more than anything in the world.

"Clarissa's dad is really fit," Kane said to me with a smile in his voice. "Drives her mad." I wondered whether I would have told them if it was my in-joke. People would beg me to explain. I never did.

"He's better looking than most women. It's a fact," Sean said.

"Yeah, yeah," Clarissa said in her soft voice. "I think that caretaker's gone, you know. I think we're all right."

"Tell you who is all right," Sean said, "your fit dad."

"Shut up, Sean," Clarissa said.

"Oi, Lissa, stop touching me up," he said.

"That ain't me," Clarissa said and the others giggled again.

"Stop touching me up. Ain't like you're Lissa's dad."

A noise.

We remained still and no one dared speak. As the silence became unbearable, a slow, rumbling fart clapped out of someone, like a car engine that wouldn't start. If injustice had a smell, this would be it. Kane slapped his hand to his face. Clarissa raised her chin to the ceiling and tossed her head as if drowning. Bash gripped his face as if he'd been burned. Sean threw open the door.

We gasped.

"My eyes!" Clarissa said.

"Someone farted out an actual dead person," Bash said. He mimed kicking Sean to the floor.

"Me?" Sean mouthed, his arms flying all over the place. "If it was me, I'd admit it. I'd take credit for that stealth bomber. It was like the fucking Blitz in there."

"Well, it wasn't me," Bash said, "because I know for a scientific fact that I don't eat actual gangrene."

"Whoever it was needs to say," Clarissa said, "because they need actual medical attention. I'm deadly serious. Am I going blind? Kane? Am I blind now?"

I moved to the window and looked down into the quad, flanked by estates and half obscured by trees. "Why have those bins moved?"

"So the runners can go out of view of the security cameras," Sean said, coming over. "That's were Darscall deals from."

"Say nuttin', Sean, innit," Kane said. "You wanna get us killed? *God!*"

"What? It's only him." Sean jabbed his thumb in my direction. "It's like telling a boil-in-the-bag cod."

"Darscall deals at the school?" I asked.

"Yeah, and his lot."

"Why the school?" I said.

"Prime real estate, innit," Sean said. "Free at night, no workin' CCTV and plenty of parking spaces. It's what they're fighting over."

"Let's get going," Kane said. "We're bait here. Old Wikileaks over there can tell you everything on the way."

In the corner, a tiny green light appeared. I recognized

213

it from the back of the camera we used to use to film our sketches. Someone was filming the quad.

I didn't say anything. I just wanted to find Robin.

Clarissa tiptoed to the door and nodded an all-clear. We glanced down the corridor. The change was dramatic. Shadows flitted at the windows and the corridors melted to darkness. I pulled up my collar. "It looks like an asylum."

"It used to be an asylum," Kane said, behind me. I looked at him in surprise. "They used to have all the crazies here," he said slowly, his hand trailing the wall as we walked the long corridor. "They had Big Nate Shrapnel, Eddie Breadknife, Mad Knock Hattie. The lot. Mad Knock Hattie had a mouth full of gold teeth. She would pounce on anyone who crossed her path and bite their cheek clean off the bone. The asylum workers had to carry cattle prods. The only warning you got was this knock. *Knock knock knock. . .*" Kane knocked the wall. "She had this nervous tic in her arm. It would jitter, so you could just hear this *knock, knock, knock . . . knock, knock, knock* as she walked along in the dark and—"

"RAH!" Clarissa jumped at me from behind.

"MUM!" I screamed and the others fell about laughing.

I slapped my hand to my chest and bent double. When I was sure my heart hadn't snuffed out, I laughed with them. I laughed and pushed Kane, who was so giddy he stumbled into the wall.

Clarissa edged down the corridor to the mouth of the stairs and looked down. She put her ear to the wall and waved for us to follow.

We giggled with nerves as we ran the corridor towards the principal's office. We checked the reception was clear and I opened the office door with a safety pin.

It worked. "Oooh!" they said.

We stopped giggling and went to work. Clarissa rifled through the files on the desk. Bash took the phone. Kane hacked into the computer. Sean just stood around and mouthed off.

I picked up a paperclip and used it to unlock the filing cabinets.

"That's what I'm sayin'!" Clarissa said as the lock popped.

I put my ear to the metal. I didn't need to, but I thought it would look quite cool.

"They should teach that in Life Skills," Sean said, "better than buttering eggs."

Bash motioned to us to be quiet. "Robin Carter," he said into the phone. He waited. "Castle Rise High School, yes. . . Our number identifier? Doesn't it come up on your phone? Yes . . . unidentified teenaged girls . . . or in the morgue . . . OK, thank you." He hung up. "Well, she ain't in the hospital . . . or the morgue. Not in Wandsworth, anyway. Shall I call King's?"

"Yeah," Kane said as the computer beeped to life. He opened the principal's email and found the address of Robin's social worker. He turned to Bash. "I'll be years trying to write this."

"Step aside," Bash said, taking the chair. "To whom it may concern," he said, with a broad smile. He pursed his lips while he typed and we all laughed. "To whom it may concern. We are anxious to know the whereabouts of Robin Carter, a minor under your charge. She has not been to school in a number of months and we have reason to fear for her safety. We therefore request a home visit, and copy of her files in order to coordinate our efforts to ensure this child is safe and has every opportunity to return to school. Yours most faithfully, Mrs Anderson, Principal, et cetera." Bash gave a decisive nod. "Then we block this email address from this account, we cc a ghost account, blind cc all of us, so when she hits Reply All, we get the response and it's deleted from this computer."

Silence.

"I don't get it," Sean said.

"Bash, you're a genius." Kane said.

"Yes, relatively," Bash said.

They laughed, but I was distracted by the files in a section labelled "At Risk". Sean was in there. Darscall had a huge file. So did Robin. So did I.

I lifted out a section marked MEADOW GORGE. I folded it and put it in my pocket. The sight of a section marked ACCIDENT & EMERGENCY INCIDENT made me feel sick. That's all it was, an "incident". I took that one out too. I left the expulsions there. A letter from my old school started, "Please be aware. . ." I screwed it up with quick fury. I threw it in the bin. Three points.

"I can't get this to work," Kane said, standing over the photocopier. "Four-number PIN. I've done all the obvious ones."

"Try 1988," Bash said. "It's the year half the teachers here were born."

Kane tried it and the machine beeped to life. "Bash for Prime Minister."

"Nah," Bash said, "that boy don't get paid enough."

"You know who don't get paid enough?" Kane said. "Clarissa's dad."

We all laughed.

Clarissa squealed, "Sean!"

Sean had his arse out, ready to press on to the principal's chair.

"Sean! Stop it!"

"Oh, go on, just gently."

"No!" Clarissa cried, before breaking into laughter.

"Just one cheek."

"No cheeks, Sean." Kane started to laugh. "Oh my days, he's doing it!"

Clarissa and Kane had their hands to each other's backs. I wasn't laughing. I wondered why I didn't find it funny.

"Let's go to the pool," Kane said.

"Yes!" said the others.

My stomach plunged. "No," I said, "we have to get out of here before they chain the doors."

"True say," Clarissa said.

Kane handed me Robin's photocopied file and we left the principal's office. I felt deflated. We hadn't achieved anything. I trailed behind the others, their faces lit by their phones. "Wait!" I said, my voice bouncing down the corridor. "Those texts!" They turned to look at me.

"Those texts the school sends when you're away. We can text everyone's parents."

Bash nodded, his eyes wide. "Brilliant."

"Come on." I ran back to the office. "We could start a revolution!"

I waited by the computer as they bundled back in the office. A strange warmth rushed over me. Their faces were bright and brimming with laughter. "Kane," I said, "get on to the messenger and see if we can send a mass text."

Kane sat down and jiggled the mouse. "What? 'Cos I'm Asian I should know how the computer works?"

They all smiled. Another in-joke.

"Asian?" Sean said.

"Are you Asian?" Bash said.

"Aren't you an Egyptian albino?" Clarissa said.

"Isn't he Puerto Rican?" Bash said. "Puerto Rican but with that Michael Jackson disease."

"I thought you was a robot designed to confuse racists," Sean said. "What are you, Kane?" he bellowed, and the others laughed.

"Oooh, look at this," Kane said, waving them off. "How do you work out how to. . ."

Bash went over to the screen to help him but Kane had worked it out before he got there.

"Right," Bash said, "we do this, then we run like hell."

"Safe," Kane said, rubbing his hands together.

"They should do this anyway," Clarissa said with a shrug. "Get her picture off SIMS and put that on there as well."

Bash scrolled through the database and shook his head. "It's got to be illegal to have all this information on us."

"Yeah, I've seen the Head of Year sitting with police going through everyone's pictures," Clarissa said.

Kane kissed his teeth. "They'll want our fingerprints next."

"We're getting that soon," Bash said. "They've already got it in schools round here. Electronic registration. They say it's to make registration easier, but how difficult is it?"

"Nah, nah way," Sean said. "They ain't getting my fingerprints on file."

"You could try not doing anything illegal," Clarissa said.

"Says you, trespassing," Kane said.

"True story," Clarissa said.

They smiled at each other.

Bastards.

Bash spoke aloud as he typed: "EMERGENCY. Missing child, fifteen, please call with any information. Answers to Robin—"

"Answers to?" Kane said. "She ain't a spaniel."

"Fair point." Bash turned to me. "What's your number?"

I swallowed. "I haven't got a phone."

"What?" they cried as if I told them I didn't have a soul.

"Are you five?" Clarissa said.

"Are you a ghost?" Sean said.

"Here, have one of mine." Kane handed me a smartphone.

I looked at the galactic handset. "Are you sure?"

"Yeah, yeah, have it."

Bash took the phone and typed in the number. He paused. "Are we really doing this?"

"Do it," Kane said.

Bash looked at me. "If we do this, we're exposing her. Everyone will know who she is. She can't hide any more. She might be in danger, and if so, this could save her. But she might be hiding. She might be underground. She might be on a job. If she is doing any of those things, this will ruin her."

I looked at Bash, then Kane, then Clarissa. Their faces told me that this was my decision. I needed something, something away from this madness to reassure myself that I wasn't overreacting.

"And you'd be involved, Jake," Kane said. "You have to be careful."

I thought of her pushing me to the pavement outside King's Cross. It was her version of Mad Knock Hattie. She was just trying to scare me.

"She really is in trouble," I said. "Besides, what choice do we have? And everybody should be . . . involved. Everybody. I'm not going to be like those people on the bus who just sit there while you're getting . . . whatever."

They nodded. I hated that they understood all that.

"Four thousand three hundred picture texts," Bash said. "Hope they ain't on Pay As You Go. Soon as we send this, the teachers will know what we've done."

"Right, ready?" Bash clicked the mouse. His finger

hovered over the Enter key.

"Get ready to run like riots," Sean said.

"Shut up, Sean."

"Shut up, Sean."

"Shut up, Sean. You never rioted. You went down Wimbledon and bought those hi-tops. Shut up."

"I never!" Sean said.

"Sean! Your mum was with you! You bought them in TK Maxx, you massive tart."

They all piled in and Sean relented.

"Ready?" Bash said.

"I'm gunna do a stress poo," Sean said.

"Ready?"

"Yes! *God!*"

Oh, my rabbit heart.

Bash pulled on his sleeve, wiped his prints from the mouse, stood, checked we were all ready, clicked enter with his knuckle, and yelled, "Run!"

31

We bolted out of the office, along the corridor and down the stairs to the double doors. Kane got there first and threw himself on to the bars to open them. The doors opened a sliver, then hit something hard. Kane grabbed his shoulder and seethed in pain. "Shit!"

On the ground was the shadow of thick chains binding the doors from the outside.

"We're trapped rats!" Bash said.

We ran to the other door, slammed against it, and hit chains.

"Help!" Sean cried.

"Shut up, Sean!" Kane yelled.

They growled, hit at the walls, grabbed at their hair and swore, pacing the short walk between the corridor walls. I looked at the lock. I was embarrassed that I still carried Kane's permanent marker with me. I took it out of my pocket and bit out the ink pad. I eased the casing through the gap in the door.

"I can't believe you can get your arms through that gap, fam," Clarissa said.

Kane was smiling up one side of his mouth.

"Thin as wages," I said, using Robin's joke.

The face of the lock was too far away and my thin hands dropped the pen. I cursed. I lay on the cold floor and tried to reach it. But it was useless. From the floor I could see the padlock. Louisiana Yale. The kind they use in prisons.

"Can't," I said, "even if I could get an angle on it, I'd need my tools."

"Tools?"

"Yeah." I shrugged. "Rake keys, calipers, all that stuff."

"Where did you learn how to pick locks?" Kane said. He sounded concerned, which was strange, because people almost always sounded impressed when they asked that. The only other person who had been concerned was kind Doctor Kahn, but she was concerned about everything.

"Vauxhall," I said. No one laughed. "Uh, my mum had me learn because she's a property developer. It's a legitimate skill. People make a living out of it."

"Yeah," Kane said softly behind my back and I could tell he'd just exchanged a glance with Clarissa.

"We need bolt-cutters," Sean said.

"Bolt-cutters?" I said. "That's a round section, boron-iron chain."

223

"A round what what?" Sean said.

"A . . . it . . . it just means it's impossible to cut. No one could cut it. Even if we had bolt-cutters, which we don't, you couldn't get purchase on it, because it's round, and even if you could get purchase, you couldn't cut through the iron. They can't be frozen and smashed either. Impossible."

"How do you know all this shit?" Kane started, but he was drowned out by their panic.

"Oh, God." Clarissa held up her phone. "We've just announced to everyone that we've broken in here."

"OK, everyone, think," Kane said, and we all paused.

"We're gunna die," Clarissa said.

"All right, everyone calm down," Kane said.

I wondered about suggesting that we hide out in the stock cupboard until morning, but my mouth wouldn't move.

"We could batter the door off its hinges," Sean said.

"With what?" Bash said. "Someone will know we've been here. And we'll break our shoulders . . . and arms . . . and spines."

"Could we cut it somehow?" Kane said.

"It's iron," I said again.

"No, the door, I mean."

"It's a fire door. Insulated," I said. "They must've fitted it after—"

"Listen to this door-shagger," Sean said angrily. "Why do you know so much about doors? Are you married to one?" He paused. "We could burn it down."

"Yeah," Clarissa said, folding her arms, "that's exactly what we need to do when we're *locked* in a building, Sean. Set fire to it!" She shook her head. "How are you still alive? How do you cross the street? You mug!"

"All right, I was only saying. Keep your wig on."

"Wig?" Clarissa smacked Sean's head and he ducked.

Kane started kicking the door with impressive might but it was no contest with the lock.

"God Almighty, it's like the Avengers if the Avengers were shit," Kane said, kicking the door. "Two minutes and we've turned on each other."

We laughed and calmed.

Sean scratched his bottom lip in thought.

"While Einstein over there has a think," Bash said, "we need to talk about smashing a window and getting out of here."

"The windows are reinforced plastic," I said.

"SHUT UP, JAKE!" Sean screamed.

"He's only sayin'," Clarissa said. "Ain't his fault."

"It's all his fault!" Sean cried. "He's moist, fam. He'd get us killed given half the chance. He's like the Grim Reaper. Look at him!"

"Calm down, will you," Kane said, holding Sean back as he gunned for me.

"We could call the caretaker," Sean said. "We don't all have to get in trouble. I'll say it was me. I slept here once. I'm on CPR."

My mind reeled. What was CPR? That thing you do when someone has a heart attack?

"We're not letting you do that, Sean," Kane said.

"*Speakforyourself*," Clarissa said. "Knock yourself out, Sean."

"No," I said, "if anyone has to take the blame for this, I will."

"No, you won't," Kane said.

Sean slapped his hands together. "I'll go chemistry, get some acid and we'll burn through the lock."

"God, Sean," Clarissa snapped, "it's like you're five."

"I've seen acid dissolve a whole car, haven't I?" Sean yelled.

"Yeah, good idea, Sean," Bash said. "And while you're up there, go and see if they've got any uranium next to the goggles and the Bunsen burners."

Sean headed off resolutely.

"No, that was a . . ." Bash shook his head ". . . joke."

"We're doomed!" Clarissa said.

"Wait, what if we don't leave?" Kane said.

"Stay here all night?" Bash said.

"Fine by me." I shrugged.

"We'll be freezing and, knowing us, we'll all starve to death or get attacked by bears. And what do we do in the morning? You know, some teachers get here at seven?"

"Seven?" Kane said. "What are they even doing?"

Sean reappeared, his skinny arms loaded with bottles. "Here!" he said.

"Oh, that's just brilliant," Bash said. "Liquid ammonia. Watch as this slightly stronger version of piss burns through iron." He pulled the cork out and chucked the liquid through the gap in the door. Nothing happened but I still took a step back. "Oh, look! Look at the fire door melting away like the Wicked Witch of the West. Cover your eyes, everyone! Careful it doesn't melt your face off."

"Yeah, yeah, all right." Sean curled his lip.

Bash took another bottle. "What noxious acid is this? Dio . . . chloro . . . ethane. Ethane your arse, Sean." He unscrewed the cap. "Let's look at it burn through cast iron. Ooooh, everyone. . ." He threw the liquid. "Run for cover, Mother—"

BANG!

The air exploded. Clarissa screamed as we were thrown to the floor. We scrambled up and bolted down the long corridor, finally diving into an empty classroom.

"Oh, God! Oh, God!" Clarissa yelled. "They'll think we're terrorists!"

"I am not dying in this budget school!" Kane shouted.

"We're gonna get deported!" Bash cried. "I can't go to India, there's too many people! I'll never get into university!"

"Uni?" Kane said. "You're worried about *uni*? What about me in Nigeria? I'd be sold for scrap."

"You'd be dead, Kane, be fair. You wouldn't last five minutes," Sean said.

"Swear down," Kane said.

"Swear down," Bash said, and they launched themselves at the window. It held. "You'd be executed twice. Once for being British, the next for being African."

"And again," Sean said, "for being gay."

Clarissa grabbed a chair and smashed it into the window. The chair shattered but the window remained unscathed. The impact sent her tiny body flying to the floor. Kane laughed maniacally as he helped her up. "Is . . . this . . . life?"

"These windows won't smash!" Sean screeched.

"I'm not gonna die here with you muppets, no way!" screamed Clarissa.

"Mother!" Sean cried. "Mother Mary!"

Kane grabbed a fire extinguisher and launched it at the pane. It bounced back and sent him sprawling across the room.

I walked out of the room and put my hand to the floor. It was freezing cold. The fire alarms were still silent.

I returned to the chaos.

"Look at what you're using!" Bash cried as Kane picked up the fire extinguisher ready to hurl it again.

"Fumes! It's the fumes that kill! *Fuuuuuumes!*" Sean said, coughing. "It's happening! I'm dying! Tell my mother I love her." He slumped to the floor, taking a dying breath.

"What are you doing?!" Bash shouted at Clarissa.

"I'm saving the books!"

"Never mind the books!"

Clarissa dropped the pile she was carrying. "OH, GOD! I never got a tattoo with Keisha and them!"

"I never kissed a girl!" Bash cried.

"Kiss Kane!" Sean shouted from the floor. "You pair of benders!"

Kane looked at me and his face immediately calmed. We watched our dishevelled, panicking compatriots, streaking across the room, hurling themselves and anything they could find at the window. The room was destroyed. Books strewn. Chairs broken. Desks tipped over.

Kane fell to his knees with laughter. "Sean, there's no fire."

"You saw it, you bell-end!" Sean's strained neck looked like rope, popping with veins and bone. "Bash's gan Guantanamo. You're gan Africa to get executed. Jake's gan back to whatever asylum he escaped out of. We're doomed. . . And I can't go prison. I'll get buggered."

"No one's buggering anyone," Kane said, laughing.

Sean stopped. Bash stopped.

A temporary calm.

"Aaaaaaa!" Clarissa yelled as she ran once again at the window with a chair. The window fought her off easily.

Kane put his hands to his knees and laughed. I joined him. Bash started chuckling.

"No fire," I said.

"But it exploded," Sean said.

"Everything's fireproof," I said. Thank you, Robin.

"This is bait, man," Sean said. "I saw my life flashing."

"You saw your dad flashing," Bash said.

"I can't breathe," Sean said, his hand flat over his chest.

Kane shushed him. Footsteps.

We looked at each other in horror. Our eyes flitted across the destroyed room. The footsteps were coming from the end of the long corridor but they were getting louder and louder. *Knock, knock, knock.*

"Can't stay here," whispered Bash. "We'll have to make a run for it."

We went out into the dark corridor.

"Oi!" came a belting yell.

"Oh, God!" Kane said.

"Oi! You kids. I know who you are!" the voice boomed down the corridor.

"Ohh," Sean said, grabbing at his bony arse. "Stress poo. Oh, God, I'm going to stress poo. I ain't even lyin'."

"Make it go back in," Clarissa said, her teeth gritted.

"How!" Sean wheezed. "How does that work?"

"Shut up, will you," said Kane.

"I'm gan prison. They've got my number. Oh, bait, man. Oh, please, God, save me from this stress poo. Oh, my dignity."

"He's turned around," I whispered. "But he must have opened the main door to get in here."

"True," Kane said. "Everyone, hoods up and run. Ready?"

They pulled up their hoods; I pulled up my collar and cursed myself.

"Oh, I can't run. I swear I'm going to shit myself," Sean said.

"Fuck you, Sean," Clarissa said so calmly the rest of us smothered our laughter.

"OK," Kane whispered, "on three. One . . . two . . ."

"Oh, my dignity," Sean said.

" . . . three."

We ran for our lives, back down the corridor, blasting through the door and out into the school yard.

"Oi!"

As we ran for the fence that surrounded the school, I slowed in horror. It was taller than anyone's reach and had no bars or locks to use as footholds. If I jumped I could maybe catch the bar that ran across the top of the fence, but even if I could do that, it would be useless, as my Kit-Kat arms couldn't lift my own weight.

Clarissa reached the fence first and, without breaking her stride, pressed her foot to the railing and jumped to catch the top bar. She looped over the top and landed on the other side. "Jesus," I said, my lungs weak. Kane and Sean were helping Bash pull himself over the fence.

"Oi!" the yell came across the yard. "I know who you are!"

"Come on, Pie and Bash. God," Sean said, straining under Bash's weight, "pissing me kidneys here." Finally Bash grabbed the top bar and launched himself over, landing painfully on the other side.

Kane held his hands out for me to step up. I couldn't even move. "Leave me here," I said, my head swimming.

"Come on," Kane laughed.

"Come on, you skinny tart!" Sean cried. "I just gave birth."

"Oi!" The yell was closer.

I put my hand on Kane's shoulder and my foot in his cupped hands. When he had lifted me to the top of the fence, he put his hand to the back of my shin to ease me over the top. I thought of when Isaac got stuck on top of that fence, and I had laughed so hard I had to lie on the ground like a starfish.

Kane boosted Sean, then slung himself over the top and caught me as I came down on the other side. Sean jumped to the grass and we ran just as the caretaker breathlessly reached the fence.

When we reached the end of the road, out of sight of the school, we stopped and stood in a circle with our hands to our knees, our chests heaving.

"Anyone got pants?" Sean said.

"Pants?" Kane said. "As in out of breath?"

"No, pants as in *pants*," Sean said, "because I've shit myself."

We laughed.

I took the phone out of my back pocket and looked at the blank screen in disbelief.

"Has anyone replied?" Bash said quietly.

"I got the text," Clarissa said, checking her phone.

"Yeah," Sean said, "but we're closer to the computer."

The three of them fought to slap Sean's head. As the circle broke up, I turned to Kane. "Thanks for that," I said. "For that . . . for. . ."

"It's all right. You weigh nothing," Kane said. "You all right walking home?"

"No. Yeah," I said.

"Where do you live?"

"Rancome Road," I said.

"Ransom Road? That's rough, man. You sure? I don't

mind walking that way. It cuts through my estate. And I am the right colour." He pointed his two thumbs at himself. He must have meant the Brackley Estate. I didn't realize he lived there. It was so strange for a boy to be offering to walk me home.

"Kane?"

"Yeah?"

"What's CPR?"

"Oh." He kissed his teeth. "Child Protection Register."

"Oh." I tried to stitch together everything Sean had said over the last few days. "Oh. Is Sean's dad . . . weird?"

"No, his mum's just a bit out of it. Forgets who he is and shit like that."

"God."

"Innit, though."

I kicked a tiny stone ahead of us. Kane caught it with the side of his foot and kicked it ahead of me. "Did we do the right thing?"

"We did something," Kane said.

Even after we said goodbye and I walked off, I felt like he was watching me.

When I got home I called out to my parents, but there was no answer. I went to my window. Robin's things were in the same place. Kane's phone rang and rang, but I let it go to voicemail. All night I read the incoming texts and listened to voice messages, writing them all down. I went downstairs and fetched some of Mother's blueprint paper, drew a giant grid and began cross-referencing the calls and texts. Most were infuriating texts of support that offered no information. I switched on Mother's police scanner. After a while, I went back downstairs and used the house phone to check the hospitals again. Perhaps she had run away to safety. Perhaps she was already dead. Perhaps she was being tortured. No one recognized her even though she went to Cattle Rise for two years and ran in the track team and won gold at Crystal Palace.

How could someone just disappear?

I found the scrap of cardboard where her number with its funny sevens was written and used Kane's phone to call her. Each time the small light came on in her room. I thought maybe her parents would hear it and realize she was missing. I scrolled down the call list, alarmed at the number of times I had called her.

ROBIN

ROBIN

ROBIN

Wait.

A nervous prickle of energy brushed against me, like the tail of a cat. I stood up.

Why the hell was her name in Kane's phone?

32

I went to my dad's cupboard and dragged out his cardboard boxes. I ripped the tape from them with my keys. The boxes were crammed with old, battered clothes, unread books and discarded astronomy tools. I started pulling out the clothes. They smelt of lemon and vinegar.

I had always got annoyed when Mother called Dad the Portuguese Widow, but she did have a point. He always wore black. In the sixth box there were flashes of colour: orange, white, some grey. The clothes were dusty and damp to the touch, but they didn't smell. I rifled through, throwing clothes over the floor until I found it: Dad's old snap-back. The Boston Red Sox, the logo had faded, but it was better tended than the other clothes, the peak still curved after two decades. I fixed it over my eyes, threw on a hoodie, and ran out of the house.

Rancome Road fed through three estates. The last, the Brackley Estate, was the only one hidden from view of the main road. It sat at the apex of Ransom Road and Cattle Rise Road, like a nut waiting to be cracked. The neat brick wall running along the side of the road deceptively swept you into the gaping shark's mouth of the estate.

I didn't allow myself any time to think as I pushed open the heavy door into the first block. The window of a ground floor flat was plastered with pictures of Mickey and Minnie Mouse. Faded stencils were on the door, stuck inside the windows and on a greying towel which hung below the window box outside.

We were always told that you never, ever go near flats that have cartoon characters plastered over them.

Come in, come in, little children. . .

I grimaced and forged on, ignoring the hastily repaired iron doors and the smell of piss. In the stairwell there were buzzers for more than one hundred different flats. All the name boxes next to the buzzers were empty. I checked it was safe to bring out Kane's smartphone and scrolled through his Doomsday Book of contacts. I wondered who I could call. Bash might not know. Sean would ask too many questions. That only left Clarissa. I looked at the green phone icon beside her name and hesitated before I pressed it. It would be the first time I had ever called a girl. I looked around again, checking no one was watching me. I thought of Robin, and pressed call.

"Shaka Kane!" Clarissa said before I could interrupt her. "Sugar Kane! Kane Austen. Oh my days, what did we do? That was gas! I've been beakin' ever since, I'm so—"

"Clar—"

"Who's this? Oh, Jake. Jake, Jake, Jake. Oh, shame." She laughed. "Did anyone call? Has anyone seen her?"

"No, Clarissa, listen. I need to give Kane his phone back."

"What's the matter with you?" she said.

How I hated that people always asked me that. They'd look at my dumb face and think something was wrong. It was as if my misery was so epic, it had seeped into my face and was sitting there like water in a potato, immovable even at times when I felt sane. I didn't know my voice had the same problem.

I pressed my hands to my eyes. "Nothing," I said irritably. "I just need to know Kane's door number."

"He lives in Brack, you can't go there. Just wait until tomorrow. He won't mind."

"No, I need to see him now. I'm already here."

"Jake, you've got to be careful." Her voice was measured.

"Clarissa, will you just tell me, please? And I mean, *please*?"

"No, I'll call him and he'll call you if he wants to see you." She paused. "You're standing in the middle of Brack with a phone out? In the dark? Are you dumb?" She spoke the questions backwards, the inflection at the beginning, indicating they were not just rhetorical, but a certainty.

"There's no one out."

"*Eastenders* is on," Clarissa said. I could hear tapping.

237

"Are you calling him?"

"Yeah? Are you mad? That place is bait."

"God, the paranoia. So stupid." I looked at the phone in my hand, my long thumb over the screen as it went to black. There I was in a stairwell, talking on a phone to a girl. Like a proper person. "Tell him I'll walk around this whole place looking for him if you won't tell me."

"What's wrong with you? What's happened?"

"I'll yell out his name if I have to."

"Jake, what's happened?"

"*Clarissa!*"

"Three five seven. *Is this life?*"

I hung up.

When I reached the flat, the front door was open an inch, and Kane's darkened face was pressed through the gap. "Are you mad?" he said quietly. "Are you *mad*?"

I thought of the sweat stains on my grandfather's net curtains and wondered what it must be like to have your door in view of hundreds of beady eyes. I looked back around the estate. Iron security grills that covered every front door. In the courtyard, a motionless car had its headlights shining.

I lit up the phone and waved it in front of his face. "Let me in or I'll make a scene."

"Are you mad?"

"Yes," I said. "I have a certificate."

He unhooked the chain and shouldered me into the flat.

"You're a rack of bones, man. What are you *doing* here?"

His room was barely bigger than the bunk bed within it, which was strewn with clothes and school books. I could stand in the gap between the bed and the wall, but Kane had to twist his body and lean on the top bunk. "Do you think this is a game? You're a tourist, fam."

A small version of Kane wandered into the room wired into his PSP.

"GET OUT!" Kane yelled and the little one jumped at the sudden rush into reality. He gave me a filthy look, checked Kane, then ran out and slammed the door.

Kane squinted at my cap. "Red . . . *sex*?"

"Red Sox. Boston."

Kane kissed his teeth and checked the window. "You're bait, man."

I shoved him against the wall. He pushed me away easily. "What the hell?"

He turned and I flew at him. I went for his face with the flat of my hand. He didn't move. His expression didn't alter. "Are you serious?" he said as he held my wrist.

"Why is Robin's number in your phone, Kane?"

Kane rolled his shoulders. He looked warily round the room. "You don't know how much you don't know."

"Where is she? I swear I'll kill you."

Kane laughed. "Have you ever had a death threat?"

"Of course I have."

"I mean . . . a real one?"

"Yes."

"One you actually believed?"

"Yes."

"So do you think I believe you?"

I relented. He pushed me backwards. His hand slipped under the zip of my hoodie and pressed on my shirt.

"Don't touch me."

He recoiled. "Are you all right? You're so thin."

"Why don't you mind your fucking business," I said, straightening my shirt.

"Kwame?" A slim, elegant lady in a grey niqab rushed in and said something in soothing Arabic. Her hands were worn and strong, wrung together as if praying. Kane spoke softly and guided her away without touching her, his face comfortably close to hers, their eyes locked. She gave me a wide-eyed look, the desperation framed by her grey head scarf. When she had left the room, I took my hood down and drew the collar up to my chin.

"Jake, listen to me, you cannot get involved in any of this."

"Give me names," I said. "Give me names and addresses."

Kane laughed with exasperation.

"Give me the names of everyone in that stupid gang. Give me the name of someone who's been jumped out."

"Jesus." Kane spoke in a hiss. "I joined when I was ten. Ten. You know why? Because Tox gave me a pair of trainers. And that's it." He levelled his eyes with mine. "No one has seen her. They're looking for her, but no one has seen her, all right? Because of the text they're afraid to be seen with her; they think the police are watching for her too. And you did that. So that's good.

Because you should hear the way they talk about her. You should see it. . ."

He scrolled through his text messages

Snake. . .

Skank. . .

Nanks. . .

Shanks. . .

Clapped . . . clapped . . . clapped . . . clap her.

I put my hands to my knees. A slow, rolling pain came from the depths of my stomach.

"Jake," Kane said, "stop cryin'."

I wasn't crying. The pain was like waves breaking. I shuddered and stood up. "Where is she?"

"I don't know, mate, I swear to you. God, will you stop it, Jake. You've gone ghost-white."

"Where is she?"

"I don't know."

He put his hands to my shoulders and it burned right to the bone. I shrugged him off.

"You have to let this go. She's gone and she doesn't want to be found, you get me? If you find her, they could find her. You have to let this go."

A pain sharked through my stomach, sending me to my knees. This kind of pain is from the liver. The bailiff of hunger pains. The liver, and its tree of nerve endings, sends a blast of pain that can knock you out.

I saw black, bent double and howled.

"Oh, my life," Kane said.

"I will scream," I said. "I'll scream this entire place

down if you don't tell me where she is."

"Jesus, you've got to go hospital, fam, you look like you're about to pass out."

I went to the window and tried to open it. I hit the lock with the side of my hand and it opened. Kane finally panicked.

"Jake, don't!" He easily prised my hand away from the window and closed it. "There' a big deal going down. Every member of the CRK is gunna be there. That's where she'll be."

"Where is this happening?"

"Where do you think?"

"At school?"

"At school."

The bailiff shuffled testily around the pulp of my stomach, giving me a few minutes' reprieve. I scrambled up like the evolution of man, and headed for the door.

Kane blocked me. "You can't just walk out of here," he said.

I surged forward and made it out of his claustrophobic bedroom. I didn't care about Kane or the estate outside. Nothing in the world was happening except this brutal pain in my liver.

Kane blocked me at the front door and looked out across the estate. He narrowed his eyes and followed any movement within the dark mouth.

"Jake, it's dark and it's . . . you can stay here if you want."

I shook my head.

"At least take this." He looked through coats on the

rack and fished out a grey hoodie. I looked at it sleepily before taking it from his hand. I said nothing as I walked out of the flat.

By the time I reached the stairs, I had to sit and press my stomach, to stem the agony. The last time I had been bent double like this Robin had run to get me an inhaler. The thought made me miss her even more.

I dragged myself up. Movement helped the pain and shrunk my mind to a pinpoint, one step in front of the next. I blocked out the wide spaces in which children were playing in the dark. They spotted me and sped over, circling me on their scooters. I pulled up my hood and they drifted off. It was like having a superpower. It made me feel so good I was able to keep walking.

I left the estate unscathed and walked up and down the roads that fringed the park. I checked out the leads people had texted: a sighting at a corner shop near Wimbledon Park Station, another at the corner of South Park, heading towards the bustle of Haydon's Road. I walked until a fiery pain ignited in my ankles.

I thought of the time when Isaac's parents had bought us scooters and I had played on mine until I felt faint. Isaac's mum said it was all right to play all day but I had to stop to eat and drink. She told me once you're thirsty it's too late, and she gave me purple squash to drink through a swirly straw. I really liked that straw.

I got Robin's picture up on my phone and, as I walked towards Collier's Wood, I asked everyone I passed if they had seen her. No one had. After a while I asked every other person, then soon I didn't ask anyone. I walked to Tooting and went into St George's Hospital to see if she was there. A nurse told me, no, there were no unidentified youngsters. She smiled and I lingered at the desk. She asked me what happened to my arm; she asked me when was the last time I ate something, and I left.

I walked towards Alexandra on the road that cuts through the graveyard. I reached the police station. I told the large policeman behind the desk that I had a friend who was missing and what should I do. He said *friend* as if it was some big question. "Are you missing?" he asked me. He said it very carefully. I looked at him with my arms raised and my palms turned to the ceiling. "I'm not missing," I go. "I'm standing right here." The policeman goes, "Yes." He said he couldn't search a house without a warrant or the owners' permission, and I told him good luck getting that, and he goes, "Tell you what, I'll go round and have a word if you like," and I said, "Thanks but no thanks," and I walked off. He asked if there was something I wanted to tell him and I said, "No." "You want a lift anywhere?" I said, "No" but he was still behind me and he said, "People have to want help," and I said, "All right," and kept walking.

When I reached the Death House, the clouds filtered sunlight into grey and rotten apples had fallen to the wintry mud. I felt I was watching myself in a film, standing in the cold, unable to open the door. I thought about how miserable I looked, and then I wasn't really sure why I was doing it, so I went inside.

Sickness bloomed in my stomach. My liver must be fat with toxins. Liver bailiff is a hell of a stage to get to. I went straight to the fridge, empty except for corned beef, which I taunted my stomach with before I rained my fists down on the countertop.

The big time marker for a missing child is four hours.

After four hours, the chances of finding a missing child roughly halve.

The chance of finding a missing child decreases at a steady pace as each hour passes.

The chances of finding a missing child after 72 hours are minimal.

Robin had been gone for four days.

33

The next morning it took me for ever to find the front door key. I was trapped in the stupid house and steaming by the time I found it, wedged behind a stack of old newspapers. I looked around for signs of Mother. Some cereal had gone, so she must have been back at some point. I hesitated by the door, and left.

I reached Cattle Rise with highway blindness. I couldn't remember walking there. There was a hollow, nervous feeling in my chest. I came out of registration with my head down and waited for the crush in the corridors to die down before going to look for Kane.

"Gay," someone said as they passed me.

"Not an insult," I said.

Darscall thundered towards me and grabbed me by my collar. "Holding price, just gone up," he grunted and shoved me against the wall before stomping off. "Thanks a lot," I said.

The loudspeaker announced an emergency assembly. I imagined we were going to get the Riot Act read to us because of last night but as we shuffled to assembly the air became alive with talk of a shooting.

A teenager had been shot dead three streets from the school. Kids relayed the story over and over, with warring theories and competitive knowledge about gangs, drugs, weapons and teenage suspects.

"It was a girl," someone said.

"A girl."

"A girl."

I scratched at my neck to get a grip of my collar, but realized the top button of my shirt was already undone. Once, Mother had been away on a build and I had eaten nothing but jelly squares for three days. I was in the bath and I had left the hot tap on. I liked how the water made red sleeves on my arms. When I got out of the bath, all the water in my body made a wave from my feet to my head, and fell like a rollercoaster. I fainted and crashed back into the bath. When I woke up, I was underwater. I panicked and took in a lungful of boiling water. I kicked and plunged my head deeper into the bath until a great surge bolted up my spine and sprung me upright. And that was how I felt in that moment, like waking up underwater.

My ears popped. "Who was she?"

"We don't know."

"Black? White?"

"Black," Clarissa said, shaking her head.

"What's her name, do we know?"

People turned to tell me to shut up, but when they saw my face they went back to their phones and to see if any of the papers had named her. They searched, texted, refreshed web pages until her name was released: Epiphanie Emery.

It was a morbid relief. A crash of emotion is not good when you haven't eaten. Your signals go haywire.

Clarissa checked around her and used her thumb to wipe a tear from the sallow dip of my cheek. Quickly, surreptitiously, she ran her fingers down the side of my face. I opened my mouth to speak but she hurried off.

"Epiphanie," Sean said, "I found her Facebook page."

I held my breath before I looked at it. It was another pretty girl with a face full of lipgloss giving attitude to her webcam.

"How they spelling 'Epiphanie'?" Bash asked, his arms firmly crossed.

"With an 'h'," Sean said.

"She won't make the news then," Bash said.

Sean looked sadly at his phone. "Weird to think yesterday she updated her status, and now she's dead."

"What was it?" I asked.

"*Nandos is siiiick*," Sean said. "Got seventy-four likes. Seventy-four! I haven't *met* seventy-four people. Not much of a what-you-call-it. . ."

"Epitaph," I said.

"Epitap. God keep her." He shook his head. "Her whole life is on here, there's four thousand pictures. Isn't it so weird? I'm looking at her Facebook page, and she's dead."

"There are twenty million dead people on Facebook," I said.

"How do you know that?" Sean stopped. "*Why* do you know that?"

I shrugged.

The meaty corridor felt even smaller. All us dirty-haired kids had things to do, places to be, people to talk to. I needed to get the hell out of there and find Robin. We needed reassurance, we needed to see our friends, we needed to know the story of this girl's death and what it meant.

I broke from the crowd and went into the toilets. My phone was filled with hundreds of texts that read, "Hope you find her", "God bless", "Will keep a lookout, hope she is OK", but nothing about where she was. A wave of texts said they hoped she wasn't the girl on the news.

I emerged from the toilet and was swept back into the crowd. "Hall," barked a teacher.

"We're going to get our arses handed to us," Kane said, appearing at my side.

I ignored him.

"I'm not friends with Robin or anything," Kane said. "I don't know her."

I turned away.

A police officer approached us and looked so severe

that we shuffled out of his way.

Kane looked around, his flawless face agitated for the first time since I had met him. "This is about that girl. They're looking for something."

I wanted to ask him what he was thinking, but I didn't trust my voice.

As we were herded into the hall, Kane's hard body pressed against mine. In the scrum I no choice but to sit next to him. "Sniffer dogs. They're keeping us all in here so they can search our lockers."

I turned in horror. I'd forgotten the package Darscall had made me keep in my locker. "They can't do that!"

"Yes they can."

"They can't! There's . . . pro . . . pre. . ." I couldn't think of the word. "Rules."

"No, there ain't." Kane fussed with his rucksack. "This is for you," he said, pressing something into my hand. "Put it in your bag, quick."

I braced. This was all I needed. Another banger making me hold something for them, so I'm the one getting felt up at the Detention Centre. I looked down at a plastic box he had handed me. It was filled with crispy brown chicken and golden sauce.

"What's this?"

"Jerk chicken," Kane said, "my dad makes it. It's the best thing in life."

I looked at it in horror.

"Put it in your bag," Kane said, checking around him.

"Has it got drugs in it?"

Kane turned slowly, his face long with shock, his voice low. "That . . . is . . . some . . . *old*-school racist shit right there. I thought you just looked hungry, that's all."

"I am *not* racist." I shoved the box of food across his legs and back into his bag. "And I am not a charity case."

"Who said you were?" Kane blocked my hand. "Just so you're not eating Twizzlers or whatever you people eat." He put the food in my bag.

"You people?" I muttered, remembering Isaac's joke. "*I'm not white*," he would wail, and everyone would laugh.

Out in the corridor I could see two police officers making their way down the row of lockers. Mine was located at the very end of the row. "We have rights, don't we?" I hissed. "What's the . . . how does it go? My something something's locked, so's the boot in the back, and I know my rights so you'll need a lawyer for that—"

"Please, stop." Kane put his hands to his face.

"*Aren't you a shark and attack I know*—"

"If you keep rapping, I'll kill myself."

"So you'll need a warrant for that." I clicked my fingers, which hurt quite a lot. "They'll need a warrant."

"Yes. That's exactly what Jay Z said: 'One knows one's rights so I'm afraid you'll need a warrant for that, old chap'." Kane coughed back a laugh.

The officers and their sniffer dogs made their way down the row of lockers, opening and slamming them, one by one, edging ever closer to mine. "Hep, hop, ho," the tall officer said to his Alsatian. The dog looked

251

like an absolute bastard. Its tongue hung from its gaping mouth and was the size of a basketball shoe. It confidently dispatched of each locker and the officers moved on to the next, and the next. If you think sniffer dogs can't find pills, you're mad. Sniffer dogs can find pill residue on clothing that has been *washed*. My stomach became water. A heat spread from my chest down my Kit-Kat arms. I rubbed my scars.

"But they need a reason? A warrant?" I said desperately.

"That's in America," Kane said as he followed the progress of the officers. "This is here. You don't think they can search your locker and throw you in jail? You can go to jail for writing something on Twitter." He turned to me and his face dropped. "Why are you so worried anyway? What have you . . . no. No. Don't tell me. I don't want to know."

I looked at him sideways.

"I hope you like carrots, fam, 'cos that's all they've got down the Detention Centre."

"Don't joke." My head swum.

"You all right?" Kane said. "You've gone ghost."

I felt faint as the officer and his beast of an Alsatian opened the locker next to mine. I prayed for a miracle. Perhaps they would find what they were looking for in the pink gym bag the Alsatian was getting his snout around.

The gym bag was replaced and the locker was closed. Mine was next.

I held my breath as the key went into the lock. The

policeman pulled out my rucksack, looked inside, replaced it, and shut the locker without a second's thought. He moved on to the next row.

"You coming to English?" Kane said.

I could feel my heart beating in my ears.

"You coming to English? Jake?"

I blinked, looked into his brown eyes. "What happened?"

"When?" Kane said.

Everything was wavy. Maybe Darscall knew we were getting searched today. But why would he bother saving me? Maybe he didn't want his drugs taken as evidence and destroyed. Maybe it was Robin who had taken the package. Maybe it was in there but wasn't what the police were looking for. I needed to check.

The lockers were cordoned off. I scanned the crowd penned into the assembly hall. The same people who usually got indignant about being told to put their leftovers in the bin were not objecting to this search.

"What's happening again?" Kane said.

"What?" I woke up to myself.

"You was just muttering to yourself, *It's happening again*."

"Was I?"

"You're like my granddad after he swallowed them worming tablets and gave the dog his Alzheimer's pills. Come on, old bean –" he put his arm around me "— let's go to English before you start clucking like a chicken."

34

In English, Miss Price gave in to the chatter and let us talk about Epiphanie. My head was screaming. It wasn't just any headache, it was an M&S headache, where your head feels like it's been split like a coconut and you're amazed that your brain can hurt this much and you can still be alive. My stomach forwent the traditional rumbling, and was bullying my liver into sending shooting pains through my nervous system. I wished I didn't know stomachs have neurons in them and can pick up signals, send signals, have feelings. "Butterflies" in the stomach isn't your brain telling your stomach to react, it's your stomach reacting by itself. The kneading tremors you get when you're scared, or have just realized you've done something terrible, are the neurons in your stomach reacting. The stomach brain. The fingernails. I dug my fingers into my gut to confuse it.

Ahoo.

Ahoooo!

Miss Price asked us all to write about a kid our age being shot in the street less than a mile away. She asked questions. Where was the girl from? When Raizer told her how Epiphanie had got shot for being in the wrong "territory", she asked, "You're talking about boroughs?"

"Nah," Raizer said, "I'm talking about ends."

"Ends?"

"Yeah, that's why Epiphanie was killed," Raizer said. "She crossed a boundary. She shouldn't have been there."

"At least you know her name," Nickola said.

Kane piped up. "Yeah, some fucking – sorry, miss – white kid – sorry, Jake – gets killed and it's all headlines like 'So-and-so Smith is slain'; a black or Asian kid gets stabbed and it's like 'Number 23 killed'. We're like meat off a Chinese menu."

"None of us lot dead would make the news," Bash said.

"Oooooooooooooooh!"

"Allow it!"

"*Evening Standard*, maybe? Three hours over the lunch time," Miss Price said with a grin.

"Jake would," someone said.

"Nah!" someone said. "He's been expelled. He's too rough for people to care about."

Rough?

"And he's a boy," someone said in agreement.

I didn't know which I'd prefer, to be on the Chinese menu or to make the news.

"Yeah, but he is white."

"He is white. True."

"*I ain't white!*" Isaac would wail as if he had never noticed. It would send everyone into fits of laughter. "*Read the melanin, my friends,*" he would say, before eventually looking shocked by his own arms. Finally, he would crane his neck, put his face to the ceiling and cry "*Nooooooo!*" and you had never heard such laughter.

"This is all because the CRK elders and youngs are getting together on Friday to end their beef," Raizer said.

"This Friday?" Miss Price said. "Where?"

Raizer shook his head, screaming with laughter. "You wouldn't believe what goes on, miss!"

"Say nuttin', innit, Raizer. You *snake,*" the class said in chorus.

"Has anyone threatened you?" Miss Price asked.

"Not me, miss. It's the wannabes you wanna worry about."

Miss Price shook her head. "You all deserve so much better than this."

There was a silence then the bell rang. Miss Price clapped her hands together. "Remember, at the end of term it's. . ." She paused and raised her hands with excitement. "Pip-Pop Day!"

The class groaned.

"Come on, it's everyone's chance to express themselves. Remember there's a top prize for the best poem or rap."

I felt dizzy as I stood up.

At that moment, Ritchie Darscall darkened the door, and grinned.

Darscall and his minions followed me down the heaving corridor. I took the twenty pounds I had leftover from Paris to pay him for my phone. I didn't look him in the eye as I held out the money.

"That was a one-time offer," he said, snatching the note. "Holding price."

He lumbered closer. I put my hand to my head. My gluey hair was wet with sweat. Robin was right. You can't pay the ransom and you can't run away. "You'd better still have my gear," he said.

We reached my locker. I had no idea if the package was in there or not. I didn't know how it could be. I nodded, giving myself a few safe seconds. Darscall and his minions twitched with anticipation.

"Give it here then. Bait round here."

"Aren't you worried they'll check the lockers again?"

"Are you talking?"

My hands shook as I opened my locker and retrieved my rucksack. I unzipped it slowly and held my breath as I reached down and — I couldn't believe it — the package was still there.

He snatched it from me and weighed it in his hand.

"Rich—" The word spilled out of my stupid mouth.

"*What* did you say?" Darscall's massive head did a sweep of the corridor. He needed attention.

I swallowed. "Do you know anyone who's being jumped out?"

"What did you just say?" he laughed.

"It's just that . . . you'd have the most . . . street knowledge."

"Go on." He swooped breath-close to my face. "Keep talking."

"Do you . . ." I sighed. The words wouldn't form themselves. " . . . jumped . . . out?"

"What do you know about being jumped out, flower?" His finger prodded my forehead. "Something you're not telling me?"

"Ritchie, if someone is getting jumped out around here, where does it happen?"

"Are you dumb?" Darscall said. His minions giggled.

"None of you can *laugh* properly," I could see flashing lights and I bent to slow the pain in my liver. "What God-awful lives do you have not be able to laugh properly?"

Darscall stared at me open-mouthed.

"Where does it happen?" I persisted. "Is it always in Wimbledon Park?"

He turned to his minions. "Is he still talking?"

Lights are the last warning. You've ignored your stomach, your liver, and here comes the brain with the eviction notice. I tasted metal. I saw my second birth. Fading brake lights. Blood with pieces in it. "Rich," I said again, "if anything happens to her, you'll have to deal with me."

Darscall's eyed widened. He smiled maniacally. "I'll let you have that one, treacle, because you look like you're being swapped about, and I feel sorry for you boys, I really do."

"I mean it, Ritchie."

"Who's asking?"

I rolled my eyes. "I'm asking," I said.

He took a full lunge towards me and grabbed my collar. I couldn't breathe. My shirt was bunched in his paw, forcing my arms out at right angles like a scarecrow.

"Tourist," Darscall said. "Village piece of shit."

He dragged me along the corridor and into the toilets, his minions scuttling excitedly behind us. He grabbed the back of my thin hair and shoved my face down into the rancid bowl, pulling and pulling the chain. The minions laughed. I panicked, retching and unable to breathe. I could feel Darscall ripping at my clothes and yanking my belt. My belt, so tight with its extra knot, tugged against my stomach and withstood his attempts to get my trousers down. I remained dead still, struggling to breathe.

"The Beast," I said.

It stopped.

"What did you say?"

"The Beast," I coughed. "The Beast is asking." I blinked within a sudden release. "If he ever finds out about this, you're dead."

Darscall drew back. Reassessed me. "Who are you?"

I felt a tingling sensation, like wings spreading across my back. "Yeah," I said as I got to my feet, "you just made a big mistake. Fatal."

Darscall grunted to his minions and they all left. "You tell him that that skank will be all right as long as she shows up on Friday."

"I'm not passing on any messages for you."

He took the smallest step back. "Whatever," he said in

a smaller voice.

"And I want my phone back."

He looked at me. "Fine," he said. He slapped the phone into my hand.

"And I'm not from some village," I said as I straightened my shirt. "I'm from Brixton, so fuck off."

He scuttled off. I steadied myself, putting a hand to the wet wall. I felt sick and so lightheaded it took me right back to the top of the Eiffel Tower, looking down at all those bugs and that murderous taper, with a girl who barely left her own street.

"Time's up," Robin had said.

I inhaled.

I knew where she was.

35

Exhilaration lifted the burning weight from my matchstick legs. Rain pasted my clothes to my skin, but I didn't care. I ran in through the door of the Death House, ignoring the gutted living room, the dust on the kitchen counter, the empty fridge. No one had been home. I raced upstairs. The chair was still under the hatch in my room. I climbed up and put my moon head through the ceiling, but I couldn't lift myself any further. With the last of my strength, I took Kane's phone out of my pocket and shone it into the attic.

"Hello?" I said. "I'm alone."

I hung there like a budgerigar. "Hello?" I said.

A pulse beat beneath the base of my skull. My joints protested and threatened to drop me.

Silence.

I felt like screaming. I was certain I'd solved the mystery. I tried to lift my pitiful weight into the attic. I tried again. My Kit-Kat arms burned and lost their grip, and I grimaced as the chair teetered beneath my feet. I dropped the phone and as I tried to catch it, the chair fell. My fingers shredded on the ancient floorboards as I scrabbled for a grip. I slipped and landed on my back in the middle of the room. The impact arrested my lungs and filled my eyes with dust.

I didn't dare move. I didn't know where my phone had fallen. If I tried to move and found that I couldn't, and if my phone was out of reach, I would surely rot here.

A head appeared above me. "Jake?"

"Jesus!" I yelled, and made her jump. She came into the light, her head bobbing down from the hatch. I was faint with relief. "Robin," I said.

"Oh, my life, Jake, what happened?"

"I went for a walk."

"Where? A swamp?"

"I think I've broken . . . all of my bones."

"You're bleeding."

"Robin, it—"

"Jesus, your skin is like. . ."

"Robin."

"I got scared, didn't I," she said. "I had to hide out. Sorry I couldn't tell you. If you got involved it would be so bad for you."

My heart broke for her, but I couldn't feel it. The pain in my joints burned to the shin. I had so many things to say to her, but it all came out as, "*Aaaaaaaaaaaa.*"

"Jake," she said as she peered down through the hatch, her head hovering above mine, "are you dying?"

"I don't think so." I scratched my scrawny neck and this hurt my neck and my fingers and my wrist and my elbow and my shoulder. "I'm just really unattractive."

Robin giggled nervously. "Where are your parents? You need to go St George's, you know. I ain't even lying."

I groaned.

She couldn't come down because there were no curtains, and I couldn't raise myself up on my poor bones. So there we lay for quite a while, her face above mine, words exploding into black space.

"Seriously, you need to phone your mum. You don't look right."

"I don't know where they are."

"How can you not know where they are?" Robin said.

I squirmed on the floor. I didn't know how she could possibly care. "They're probably at my nan's. She likes to see the baby."

"What baby?"

"My baby sister."

"You've got a baby sister?"

I nodded.

Robin flicked away some braids. They fell in front of her face again and she flicked them away more forcefully so they flew around her neck and hit her face from the other side. I realized it was Robin who had been eating the crackers and cereal, which meant that Mum hadn't been back at all.

Robin looked at me. "I ain't never heard no crying."

"What crying?"

"The baby. I ain't ever heard no crying."

"No," I said, "she's a good baby. Reboot."

"What?"

"They reboot. . . They rebooted me."

Robin shook her head. "You look like the last chicken in Lidl."

I laughed as much as my chest would allow.

"You're going to have to find something to cover that window," Robin said.

I nodded.

"Get some food while you're at it, I'm 'ank."

I took my time peeling myself off the carpet. Down in the kitchen, I searched slowly, then frantically, for food. In the fridge everything except the jam was irretrievably out of date. The skyline of condiments and pickles was useless. The yoghurt had gone to water and the chicken was reanimated with mould. Maybe I could search my parents' room for some loose change to buy food from the corner shop, but I remembered immediately what I had said to Darscall. It was too dangerous to go outside. I felt a rush of anger: this is what house arrest feels like.

I picked up a nail gun that was lying on the newly exposed floorboards and struggled back upstairs. I fetched a sheet from Mother's cupboard, went back to my bedroom and tried to position it over the huge window.

"Careful," Robin said from the hatch.

"It's only a nail gun," I said.

I held the sheet in place and pressed the nail gun against the wall. I counted to three and fired. The force of the nail shooting out the gun rocketed up my arm and knocked me backwards.

"Jesus!" Robin yelled.

I hit the floor and the gun fired a nail straight through the window. In my panic, I fired the gun again. The nail hit the wall at an angle and shot back at me, missing my face by a breath. "Aaaa!" I cried as the sheet fell, bringing a gob of wall down with it.

"Watch your head," Robin cried. "Watch your stupid massive head!"

I looked at the small hole in the window. I tested the glass. It felt like the strange wobble when you get out of the bath. "Another job well done."

Robin laughed. "Try hanging the sheet from the jagged bits. And where's the food?"

"There is no food," I said quietly.

Robin jumped from the hatch without breaking her legs. "Man, am I hungry. Have you really got no food? Like, none at all? I'm Starvin' Marvin."

I shook my head, mortified.

"I just have to lay low for a few days, until all this blows over, and then I'll be all right. My people will take care of me. The school sent this text looking for me so they're all off my back. Everyone is too scared to be seen with me. I know my mum wouldn't have sorted that.

One of my bredrin would have seen me right. Now it's just the Beast I have to worry about. I know you think they're a bunch of criminals but—"

"I sent that text," I said.

"What?"

"Me and a few others broke into the school and called the police, and the A&Es, and Social Services, then we used their system to text every parent and child in the borough, and I read every single text that came back and fielded every phone call. I walked all over Wimbledon, Tooting, Earlsfield . . . I went to St George's twice. I went to the Brackley Estate, checked all your contacts, tried everything I could think of . . . which is not much." I yawned. "But I tried."

Robin sank to the floor. "Why?"

"I was worried about you."

"*Why?*"

"Because."

"But I was so horrible to you."

"You had your reasons."

"But why would you put yourself in that situation? For *me?*"

"Because . . . chicken!" I said triumphantly. I dug around in my bag and held up Kane's plastic box like that monkey holding up Simba. The light shone through the dark golden sauce. "Circle of life!" I sang.

"Is that what I think it is?" Robin sat up like a meerkat.

"Jerk chicken."

"*Jeeeeeeeeeezan!*" Robin said. She stuck her fingers

into the box and her words became slow and heavy with pleasure.

"Does 'Jeezan' mean chicken?"

"Nah, it means, like . . . 'look'."

"Oh. What's chicken?"

"Chicken." She laughed, struggling to keep the food in her mouth. "Gimme the hot sauce. You can't handle the sauce!"

"Oop, racist," I said, gladly handing it over. Even pepper gives me palpitations.

When something pressed against my teeth, I realized I had put the edge of my thumb to my mouth to catch the paste. The paste was on my thumb and had oil that could easily have been put onto a napkin. I thought quite highly of myself for doing this and licked my thumb again.

Cold meat and rice would usually shudder down my throat like sick in reverse, but this felt like comfort, and I ate slowly, savouring the dancing flavours.

"Where's your mum anyway?" Robin said.

"Who knows." I pushed the box over to her. "Everyone's buying in Norbury, and she's waiting on a cancer patient."

"Charming," Robin said. "Oh, my *actual* days, who gave you this? It ain't paste."

"This . . . this girl at school. It was her birthday."

"You couldn't lie down."

I smiled. She was too excited to interrogate me. It was tempting to tell her to just stop being so silly and force her to go outside. It was difficult to not think of gangs as something that only existed if you allowed them to exist, and that if Robin walked out of here, nothing would really happen to her. Gangs were like fairies, or voodoo: if you just stopped believing in them, they would go away.

"Yeah, but Tinker Bell don't usually come back and slash your face, you get me?"

"Did I say that out loud?"

"God, you're weird." Robin shook her head. "But I haven't spoken to anyone in days so I'll take what I can get, innit."

I looked up into the hatch and remembered Isaac's camera. "Did the camera work?"

Robin shook her head. "Nothing. Not a damn thing. He keeps everything out of view of the window." She put her head in her hands. "There's nothing from the pizza place either. I'll never get anything against him."

"You've got the guys on camera dealing drugs," I said.

"There's no use curing ninety-nine per cent of the plague when you only need one rat to infect everyone. But I'll get him," she added, looking up. "Even if I die trying."

By nightfall it was clear my parents weren't coming back and Robin slept in their bed, until she changed her mind and climbed in with me. Man, she really did reek. My hair was shedding all over the place.

"We're like a pair of badgers," she said.

"Royalty," I said and she laughed. "Robin, what's

going to happen to us?"

"We have to keep everything normal. We have to lay low. You have to go school. We can't risk Social coming round."

"Bloody social workers," I said.

"Social workers are amazing," Robin said, and I immediately felt guilty and childish. "I can't go to school, it's Pip-Pop Day. I haven't written anything for it."

"Pip-Pop? What the hell is that?"

"Hip-hop but with poetry."

"Take one of them poems from your grey book, they're well good."

"Stop looking through my stuff!"

"I like your stuff," Robin said.

I struggled out of bed. The moon was a glow through the bedsheet curtain. I went through mine and Isaac's stuff and found our projector. I hooked it up to my computer and aimed it at the sheet.

"What are you doing?"

I didn't answer. I let the waltz play as the pale dancers dissolved on to the sheet. "The Royal Ballet," I said. "It's not live, but it's good enough."

Robin reached for my hand and I sat beside her in bed. She touched the soft skin of my wrist, tracing the cuts on my arm until she reached the nine lines I'd scored into my shoulder. "I'm glad you're still here."

As Robin fell asleep on my shoulder, I couldn't sleep thinking about what would happen to her.

In the dead of night, I thought I heard a noise.

My bedroom door opened and closed itself. I turned and heard the unmistakeable sound of a rake key.

36

I pressed my hand over Robin's mouth. The house creaked as heavy footsteps treaded the floorboards downstairs.

"Someone's here," I whispered.

I took my hand from her mouth and she rolled out of bed.

A noise came from the stairs. Robin stood on the chair and pointed desperately at the window. I refused to go. As the footsteps came nearer, she relented and hauled me into the attic. She closed the hatch without a sound. As my eyes adjusted to the darkness, the window let in enough moonlight to see her face. Her eyes were wide; her fist was pressed to her teeth.

My rabbit heart beat into the floorboards. At my feet were smashed bricks, the chest, and the discarded pickaxe.

We heard doors being opened, one by one, then

footsteps entered my bedroom.

Robin looked at me and drew wild circles around her face to say: Do not let him see you.

I felt him stop and look around. A knock came on the hatch, once, twice. Another knock. I heard him drag something across the floor. Another knock: small, as if made with a knuckle. He threw open the hatch. Robin scrambled away. I grabbed the pickaxe and swung at him with a great yowl. I missed and planted the axe in the floorboard, barely missing my own stupid foot.

"Who the hell are you!" he yelled as I toppled backwards. "Get down here!" He balanced on the chair but couldn't lift his weight into the hatch. He swatted at us like a caged bear. "That dizzy bitch is up there, ain't she?" He took another swipe.

"Leave us alone, Marcus," Robin said.

"You better show yourself at the meeting, Robin."

"They'll kill me, Marcus."

"I'll drag you there myself. I'm not taking a hit for you."

He climbed down from the chair and out of sight. I heard a small whirr, like the winding of a clock. He appeared beneath the hatch once again, playing with a lighter.

"I will smoke you out, Robin." He flicked the lighter. "One . . . two. . ."

Robin prised the pickaxe from the floorboard and aimed it at his head. "Put that down."

"Don't, Robin," I said.

He grinned up at me. "You're going to let her do the dirty work, are you? Just like your granddad," he said, "soft as shit. He used to do everything I told him to as well." Robin shot me a glance.

"Shut up," I said. My voice was squeaky.

The Beast roared with laughter. "Who's this queer, Robin? Scraping the bottom of the barrel. Christ."

"Don't talk to him like that," Robin said, adjusting her aim. "I got you right between the eyes."

"You en't got the balls for it." With a great yell, he heaved himself up and grabbed her ankle.

She fell to her knees, raised the pickaxe, swung, and plunged it into his shoulder. He yowled and stumbled from the chair. He pulled the axe from his shoulder with a piercing cry. The axe left a deep, bloody crevice. He staggered across the room, disorientated by pain and rage, and hit the window. He rolled in agony against the windowpane. I looked at his huge shoulders, his barrel stomach, and his handprints, bleeding across the sheet. The glass wouldn't hold his weight. I let out a cry but it was too late. The glass shattered and fell from the wall. The Beast stumbled, seethed, and fell to the garage roof with a smash.

We climbed down from the attic and edged to the window. The Beast was howling and squirming on the roof. Robin grabbed my arm and mouthed, "Run."

37

We ran from the house and down the long road. Robin turned down a narrow side street and I followed. She stopped suddenly and leaned against a car. The door opened. She looked wildly around to see if anyone was watching us.

"What are you doing?"

She slid into the car.

"You know how to steal a car?" I said as she flung the passenger door open.

"Oop," she said, reaching under the seat for the keys, "racist."

The engine revved. I panicked. "Do you know how to –" we screeched off and sped down the road, "– drive?"

There was no response.

I strapped myself in. "Slow down, we'll get stopped."

"Slow down and we'll get caught. What were you thinking!" she screamed. "I have a plan, Jake."

My knees locked together. "I'm going to have a heart attack."

"Well, that's one way out."

"Robin. We have to call the police now."

"We can't."

"Why not?"

"Because I've done terrible things. I'm guilty. I'm an accessory. Every night, I've gone out running, running until I want to die, cutting my feet, throwing up. I throw up in my dreams. It's like I'm throwing up concrete. It's killing me. Being pure evil. It slayed me. It's like it's killing me."

I nodded and wanted to tell her that I understood but I couldn't find the words.

The engine screeched like a wounded animal. We sped past the park, the boarded-up shops, the underpasses. At the lights, Robin braked so hard we lifted out of our seats.

"He knows who you are?"

"I . . . think he must do."

She slammed her hands on the wheel. "—you stupid cracker!"

"I wasn't thinking." I wrapped my arms around myself. "Don't . . . just don't panic," I said a little louder. "Don't panic. We'll get nowhere by panicking!"

"Hush up, will you? You're like a horse."

"Horse?"

"Horses are scared of everything."

"I'm scared of horses."

Robin rolled her eyes. "Jesus."

"We could tell the police now."

"That's our house, Jake. My mum lives there. I'm not telling the police nothing until I catch him out on a deal with his stupid, stupid gang."

"Robin, slow down. You're going to hurt someone."

"I know exactly where we're going," she said, her fingernails white on the steering wheel.

We drove down a long road that had been carved through a housing estate. The roads became wider, the shops smaller, the traffic heavier. The old buildings were beautiful and the new ones ugly. The streets were alight and alive.

Brixton.

"Robin, you are sick. You're a sick, sick person. Don't you dare stop here."

"What happened here?" She took the left turn so sharply I had to grab the dash. "What happened?" She screeched left again. "You're a zombie, you know that? I see you. I see you in your sleep. Crying, kicking and screaming. You've got the devil about you. You're dead inside."

I turned to throw up, but my body was too weak to do it.

"What happened here?"

The knives came out, screaming down my face. I fought them before I realized they were my own godforsaken hands. My hands. They'll be the death of me.

They belong to someone else.

When I woke up to myself my face was burning and Robin had stopped the car. Her lips hung as she breathed through her nose, her neck expanded, her shoulders braced. I got out and slammed the door. This was worse, because I was alone and in the middle of Brixton. I put my hand on the street sign and threw up over the scrap of grass. My sick was acid, and throwing up felt like setting myself on fire. I let out a guttural wail that brought Robin rushing out of the car.

"Oh my God, Jake, what happened?" Her face was ashen. "What happened?"

She crouched beside me and held my shoulders, shaking them with her strong hands to make me look at her. When I finally looked into her eyes, she was crying. "Jake, tell me what happened here."

"Are you crying?"

"Jake, what's wrong with you? What happened to you?"

"Nothing happened to me."

"Jake."

"This is none of your business, Robin."

"But why are you so miserable all the time?"

"I'm not," I said.

"Why are you so ill?"

"I'm not," I said.

"Why don't you eat?"

"Because," I said, trying to get away.

"Because, why?" she pleaded. "You can write your sketches and your jokes. You can make a name for yourselves, you and Isaac. Go to Edinburgh one day."

I shook my head. "We can't."

"Why not?"

I shook my head.

"Jake, you can't give up on yourself. You can work this out. You can do anything you want."

"I can't."

"Why?"

"Because he's dead."

"Who's dead?"

"Isaac," I said. "Isaac is dead."

Robin pressed her hands to her mouth. "How?"

"A car hit us," I said. "He died and I survived."

"Jake," she said softly, "is that where you got that scar?"

"If it wasn't for the paramedic —" I shook my head "— I would have died too. I was screaming, 'Help him, help *him*.' Isaac was in the middle of the road. He was twisted up and the paramedic was, like. . ." I couldn't finish the sentence. All I said was the truth. "I hate that I survived."

"Well," Robin said calmly, "you didn't, did you?"

"Don't talk to me." I went to the car. "What do you know about anything?"

Robin followed me. "Do you think it was your fault?"

"I know it."

"Jake, he was old enough to look after himself."

I shook my head and got in the car. "He was only eleven."

"Eleven?" Robin said as she got in the driver's seat. "But I thought you were in school together?"

"We were. We were inseparable."

"So he was younger than you?"

"No," I said.

Robin was quiet. She seemed to be watching the lights of the cars, her eyes flitting back and forth. "This happened four years ago?"

"Four. Almost five," I said.

"You've been like this for five years?"

I didn't answer.

"Where did it happen?"

I shook my head.

"You should go there."

"Not in this lifetime."

"In counselling they take you to the place where it happened, so you can see what actually happened, not what you think happened."

"I know what I think. I'm sick of people telling me what I think or what I'm supposed to think."

Robin started the car. She tapped something into her phone.

We turned into a small dark street lined with brownstone cottages. The car stopped and I pressed back into my seat in horror, speechless and unable to fight for myself.

"You . . . had *better* turn this car around."

"It wasn't your fault, Jake."

"You had better turn this car around, I swear to God."

"It wasn't your fault he died, Jake." Robin got out.

She went around the car and opened my door. "You didn't push him."

"What are you talking about?" I pulled at the lock on the door.

"You didn't push him," Robin said. "I need you to say it."

"You knew all that already? You read my stuff."

"I just wanted to read your poems and then I found everything else."

I didn't know why she was so upset. All I knew is that I had scarcely been so angry.

"Please come and see the road."

I clamped my eyes shut and thought of all the things she must have read. All my poems, all my prayers, my suicide notes. I couldn't fight her as she dragged me out of the car. "Jake," she said calmly, "you asked me to do this. You asked me to not let you end up like your granddad. All alone. Just an empty shell of a man. You looked me in the eye and you said, 'Don't let me end up like this.'"

"God, I didn't think you'd take it seriously," I mumbled.

"You talk about Isaac like he's still alive. Like he's just angry with you or something. You keep calling him."

"I do not."

"You talk to him. I've heard you."

"I do not."

"You do, Jake." Her voice quavered and I couldn't stand that she might cry again. "Why do you think he's going to answer you?"

"I don't. I'm not insane. I was there. I saw him die."

"But why do you call him? Why do you think he's going to answer?"

I took a breath. "Because it can't have happened." I scratched my patchy head. "I know it happened. I'm not mad. It's just illogical. Why would he have died? We had things to do. He was the nicest person on Earth. And I'm not saying you can't die if you're nice but I'm just saying it doesn't happen, that's all." I stopped and tasted the cold air. I had never heard that thought out loud.

I looked out at the road. It was the strangest feeling, like shrinking. The road boiled to a sudden stop. I traced the tarmac until I was sure I was looking at the spot where he fell. I held out my hand. People walked down it every day and had no clue that the ground had opened up here and killed the one person who made the world bearable.

And she was right: the road was much smaller than I remembered.

The air was ice. My ribs and throat ached. My palms, rough, scraped at my cheeks.

In drama club, a boy called Jesse, a beautiful kid by anyone's standards, was wearing his hair down when he usually had it up in a girly ponytail. I'd often looked at him and wondered what it would be like to stroll around looking like a perfume ad. You wouldn't want for anything your whole life. Girls would ask *you* out. Imagine.

In a daze and without any thought I said to Isaac, "I

prefer him with his hair down." Talking to Isaac was like talking to myself. It was so natural I did it without thinking.

Isaac turned, slow, beaming. Delighted. "Ooooh," he lisped in an effeminate voice, "you like 'im wiv 'is 'air down, is it?"

The teacher gave us a glare. "Shuddup," I said.

But it continued all lesson.

We were in pairs, improvising a set where someone accuses someone else of stealing their shoes and wearing them.

"Uh, those are my shoes," Isaac said.

"No." I looked at my trainers. "They're mine. That's why I have them on."

"Oh. Sorry." We both laughed. "Tell you what else I like," Isaac said, "that Jesse with is 'air down."

I laughed each time he said it but was surprised to find that it bothered me.

That evening I convinced Isaac to come and see a film and afterwards we went back to my house, even though my parents were away. We came back in the dark and I became worried about gangsters hiding behind cars or lurking in gateways, so I walked down the middle of the road. Isaac joined me. I told him I'd liked the film and Isaac said he liked that Jesse with 'is 'air down. I told him shut up. I nudged him, and that was it.

The car hit us. Two tonnes of metal versus two kids half the size of poor Matt Manson.

I felt the cold ground and tasted blood. I watched the eyes of swerving taillights. I saw Isaac twisted in the road. I saw his eyes close. I saw the ambulance. I saw the paramedic hover over me, his eyes wide, saying, "Jesus."

I saw his parents, their mouths drawn in horror. They would never speak to me again.

I really wished the doctors hadn't told me he'd broken his neck. He was dead, but he was also broken, paralysed.

I missed Shiva because I was in intensive care, and I didn't get to say goodbye.

The wind was wet. I stepped into the road. In my mind I had pushed him into the path of a car, but on this narrow road, any car would have hit both of us. Headlights grew behind us, the driver beeped and Robin stormed at him, "Back up. Back up! We're busy!"

"You back up!"

"I'll back UP YA LIFE!" Robin yelled. The driver backed down the road. I couldn't help laughing at how quickly she calmed down.

Kind Doctor Kahn once told me that the only other animals that commit suicide are dogs. She had seen it with her own eyes. She had asked me if I knew dogs were bilingual, and I said, yes, I knew that. Wild dogs don't make that weeping sound when they cry; domestic dogs have learned to do it to communicate with humans. She said I was very clever for knowing such a thing. I said everyone knows that. She said very few people know that. She said that dogs find a way to express grief, but crying isn't grief. They're bilingual, did I understand? Yes, I said, dogs are highly evolved parasites, but she said that wasn't the point she was trying to make, and I said talking about dogs killing themselves is a messed up thing to tell a depressive, because it's probably the most depressing thing in the world and of all time.

Dogs don't really kill themselves. They waste away. I don't believe everything people tell me.

"I don't think you believe everything people tell you," Robin said.

I flinched. "What was I saying?"

"You speak to yourself all the time," she said.

I stretched out my legs and my knees clicked. I liked the sound.

There was a sudden breeze. The rain stopped. I slowly walked back to the car and sat in the passenger seat.

"Hard, innit," she said.

I nodded. "I lost everything."

"I know."

"Social Services got at me. My mum's never forgiven me. They took me away from my family."

Robin climbed into the car. "Social Services don't investigate kids, Jake. They were investigating your parents."

I looked at her.

"They were trying to help you. You almost died because your mum and dad weren't looking after you."

"Don't say that."

"Why not? Why should you take all the blame? They didn't look after you. And they still don't."

"Shut up."

"I swear I've never let anyone tell me to shut up as

much as you have without punching them right in the face. But I'm telling you, Jake, your parents neglect you. And they might be ill or stressed or whatever, but they still have to look after you."

"You've only known me for a week. You don't know anything about me and you don't know anything about my parents."

"I knew in five minutes. Page one of the bad parent handbook: teaching a child criminal activity."

"Stop it."

"Obvious, innit." She spread her hands out like a magician's. "It's why I can drive."

"Stop talking."

Robin started the car. "Leaving you to look after a baby, not providing enough food or a safe space, and being so neglectful they don't even notice their child is . . . dying."

"Who's dying?" I picked at the knees of my pyjamas.

Robin reversed out of the road so as not to drive over the spot where Isaac was killed. I tried to contain my thoughts. It took so much concentration I couldn't even blink.

Robin smiled. "We could go Scotland if you want."

"We could go *to* Scotland," I snapped. "*To* Scotland. You go *to* places."

"All right, we could go . . . *to* Scotland."

"Right, I'm going to drive to Scotland with someone who thinks Edinburgh is somewhere near Kent." I shook my head. I could barely look at her.

We turned out of Coldharbour Lane. Brixton was

mine again, a living space, and I was grateful for that feeling. I began to feel sleepy, the lights in the car went off and Robin pulled over and looked anxiously in the mirror. "Shit, man, we gotta bounce."

"Why?"

"I did nick this car."

"God, Robin! I'm not running through Brixton in my pyjamas."

"We won't be the first," she said, "and we won't be the last."

"We can't walk home," I said. I thought about what I had said to Darscall, and I saw the fury in the Beast's eyes as he looked down at me. "We can't go home."

"What choice have we got?" Robin said.

I stood cold in thought. There must be somewhere we could go but the world had become so small. She was right, we had no choice. We had to go back. "Jesus, Robin, we can't go back there. It's too dangerous."

"You got any friends, have you? Lovers? A secret set of parents squirrelled away somewhere? Who'll sew your fucking socks and make porridge and listen to all your stupid problems or something? No, you don't. No one does. This is how it is, Jake. You get the shit kicked out of you in a house you have to go back to. Welcome to the world."

"There . . . we could . . . we could try . . ."

"Did Jake break? Did I break him? Yes, he's broken."

"Will you stop your incessant jabbering for one second?" I pressed my hands to my mouth. The solution was unthinkable but we had no other choice.

38

We walked to Isaac's house. I hadn't seen his family since the accident. I didn't know if they still lived there. I didn't know if they would retch upon seeing me, fly into anger, call the police, break down in sobs, or perhaps welcome me with open arms. I didn't know.

The house was nestled in a beautiful row of Edwardian houses on Shakespeare Road. The front door was a calm teal colour with a black knocker and I remembered how much I used to like this door. I put my hand to the knocker and froze. I couldn't wake a peaceful house, return as a reminder of the horror they had endured.

I looked at Robin, freezing and tired, took a deep breath and knocked. The lights came on and the door was opened by Rabbi Kaufman. He was just as I remembered him, large and bearded, with big arms and a broad smile, despite being woken in the dead of night.

"We got lost," I said.

"Jake!" He drew me into a hug. "And who is this?"

"Robin," Robin mumbled.

"Robin, how pretty," the rabbi said as he ushered us in. "The bird of Thor! A majestic and fearless bird. How I love robins!"

Robin smiled.

"Jake!" Mrs Kaufman said from the top of the stairs. "Oh, is that you?" She was slight and graceful still, with an incongruously loud voice. She didn't look any older, but there was a darkness somewhere behind her eyes, a sadness, as if a light had been turned out. "Jake, you're so thin. Joshua, look how thin he is. Well, I'll get you something to eat right away. Look how thin you are."

"She thinks you're thin," the rabbi said. I smiled.

"It's not healthy," she said. "It's not good for a man."

"Leave the boy," the rabbi laughed. "Do your mothers know where you are?"

"Yes," we said.

We sat down at the kitchen table. Mrs Kaufman was already cooking. She handed us a cup of tea and a ham omelette each.

"Thank you," Robin said.

"We don't want to be any trouble," I added.

"What a pretty broach," Mrs Kaufman said, looking at Robin's spider broach.

"Jake gave it to me," Robin said. "It's my favourite thing."

They cooed admiringly and drew lines between us

with their eyes. "Are you . . . ?"

"No, no," I said.

"No, no." Robin's eyes widened. "God, no," she said, long after the point had been made. "No, no, no. God. Imagine. *God*, no."

Shoshana, Isaac's sister, shuffled down the stairs, sleep slowing her movements. The last time I saw her she was an awkward, skinny kid with braces. Now she was long-limbed and curvy, with big curly hair and a glowing, beautiful face. "Sosh," I said.

"Jake," she said, "what's happenin'. You look terrible."

"Cheers," I said. "You look nice."

"Yep, puberty has been quite a success. Nothing too drastic." She clicked her teeth and pointed to her chest. "All present and correct."

Her parents laughed guiltily and looked away.

"Well, congratulations," I said.

"Cheers," she said. "Right, I'm going back to bed. I thought this was going to be one of your desperate converts with their mad eyes and dying ovaries."

"Sorry to disappoint," the rabbi chuckled.

"Night-o."

"Was that Isaac's sister?" Robin said. "She's funny." She read the sudden silence. "Sorry, should I not have said his name?"

"No, no," Mrs Kaufman said with a smile. "We say his name all the time. *Isaac would have liked this. Isaac would have found that funny. Isaac would have. . .*" She smiled but couldn't keep talking.

My hand wrapped over my mouth and I started to cry. It didn't come with panic. I didn't hallucinate or feel faint. Instead I felt the warmth of Mrs Kaufman's hand rubbing my back. "We have certainly missed you, Jake."

"Don't tell him he's thin," the rabbi said.

"I wasn't going to say that," Mrs Kaufman said, "but look how thin he is! He needs looking after."

"Don't start that again, mother dearest," Rabbi Kaufman said with the gentlest of laughs. "He's a fine young man."

We were ushered upstairs and Robin was shown into the spare room. Rabbi Kaufman asked gently if I would like to sleep in Isaac's room. "We kept it the same," he said, "but not in a creepy way."

He opened the door. All of Isaac's things had gone but the brown furniture and the blue wallpaper and the mounted toy aeroplane I was always so jealous of were still there.

As I climbed into his bed I sobbed a great deal, but I managed to keep quiet so I didn't disturb anyone.

It didn't take long for Robin to scurry into the room and climb into bed with me. I wiped my eyes. "What do you think he meant when he was, like, *don't start that again*?" I whispered. "She was, like, *we need to look after him* and he was, like, *don't start that again*. Did you hear it?"

Robin shrugged with one shoulder. "They tried to get custody of you."

I sat upright. "*What?*"

"It's in your mum's stuff."

"Jesus, Robin, you're like the world's weirdest cat

burglar. You're like a gateway Jeremy Kyle."

"It doesn't matter," Robin said. "We're the same person." She smiled and this immediately stopped any anger I felt.

I ran my hand down the wallpaper with its tiny pictures of rodeo cowboys. "It is weird, isn't it. He seems so young now."

"Nothing weird. It's a tragedy. All you need to do is remember him in, like, a better way."

"I've been trying to." I turned to her. "Since I got out of hospital I've been editing our stuff so it's perfect. I've just got this one scene I can't get right. I can't edit this corpsing out. Look at it."

Robin watched the twenty-second clip. She laughed as Isaac so carefully approached the apple pie and again as my laughter cut across the soundtrack.

"You should keep it in," Robin said, "it's funny."

"No, it ruins it."

"It doesn't ruin it. I love it."

"Really?"

"Really. Now, we need to get some sleep. I imagine I'm going to have to pretend to go to school tomorrow or else they'll call Social Services. They seem like proper parents and all."

"They are. And they have normal conversations with their kids."

"I know!" Robin turned to me again. "Did you see that girl, just cracking jokes in front of her mum and dad like that? And she was fit. And she had nice skin."

"I know, and did you see how the kitchen was full of food and pots and pans and shit like that."

"I know, and did you see how there wasn't no condensation on the windows or bits of food and shit all over the floor."

"I know, and guess what they do in the evenings?"

"What?"

"They all sit around and have a meal together. Every day."

"Every day?"

"Every day. We should cut our losses and stay here."

"You should stay here. I bet they'd let you, and you don't owe anything to some gang and you certainly don't have to go to some sort of trial tomorrow and try and prove your own innocence."

Robin turned over. She was like one of those fairy-tale mirrors, you could only say so much before the face faded.

"Don't go to that meeting. If you got jumped I'd be really . . . I'd be really devastated."

"If I don't go, I'll lose face."

"But that's better than losing your actual face, Robin."

She looked around the room and her breathing slowed. She turned and put her arm around me. It made me squirm but I let her. "You're right," she said quietly, "I won't go."

"Good," I said.

The rain came down in sheets and I liked the way it sounded on the window. "Goodnight, Ise," I said, and I was so thankful to not be trudging through the bowels of Brixton that I feel into a deep, peaceful sleep, and I didn't wake until morning.

39

The Kaufmans cobbled together uniforms for us from Isaac's sister and brother, and from Isaac's old shirts, which I still fitted into. I saw the rabbi glance at Mrs Kaufman to remind her to keep a lid on the things she desperately wanted to say.

They drove us to school and Robin giggled as she walked towards the gate. "Check me out, going to *school*."

"What are you going to do?"

"I'm getting my arse out of here before anyone sees me, then I'm going back to yours."

"It's dangerous there."

"I'll stay out of sight."

"CRK-K-K-K," someone said excitedly as they pushed by. Robin dipped her head but then she looked up, slowly and suspiciously, in a way that made my stomach heavy.

"Jesus." Her eyes widened. "He wasn't talking to me. He was talking to you."

"Robin, I can explain."

Sweat shone on her neck. I had never seen anyone become so angry, so quickly. "Talk fast before I slap that dumb look off your dumber face."

"Darscall was attacking me. It just came out. I just said that I knew the Beast and he left me alone. I didn't know what else to do."

"Oh, you didn't know *what else to do*? After everything we've been through, you thought you'd dabble in affiliating yourself? You've seen me being maimed by the crocodiles so you thought you'd dip a toe? Well, I'm going to have to go to that meeting now, aren't I, because they'll come after you like dogs on heat."

"No! God, no, you don't have to do that."

"You stupid, ignorant cracker, you pasty t—"

"Don't call me a tourist."

"You—"

"Don't call me a tourist."

"*Tourist*," she said.

"I am not a tourist. I've been arrested. I've been in hospital. I am a danger."

"To yourself," Robin wheezed. "You got arrested to save you from your*self*. You know what happens to tourists? Here? Do you know?" She leaned in and spoke slowly. "They get cut open, hosted and sold for scrap, Jake. That's what happens." Her voice was low and slow, and so threatening I retreated a few steps. "I found the barbiturates you hide under your floorboard. I don't even know how you got hold of them, but they're gone, so now if you want to kill yourself you'll have to do it with sleeping pills like everyone else, with a ninety per cent fail rate and in screaming fucking agony."

It left me so cold I couldn't speak until she started walking away. "Robin, I'm sorry."

"Stop saying my name, you dick."

"You can't go to that meeting, you don't know who the snake is."

"No," she held out one hand, "but I know what the youngs are up to in that pizza place." She held out her other hand. "And I know what the Beast is up to –" she put her hands together "– and as soon as one finds out about the other. . ."

I didn't dare speak.

"Pwcch!" she said. Her hands blew apart.

"Robin, you can't be serious. If you plan goes wrong and they catch you, they'll eat you alive."

"What choice do I have?" She pulled her braids further over her face.

I reached out for her. "What does that mean?" But she ran and I knew I wouldn't be able to catch her. I would never, ever be able to catch her.

40

I went to registration and all four morning classes. In biology we had a supply teacher but I stayed put and asked the stick thin white girl next to me if I could borrow her book to catch up. In one school year she had written:

Wednesday 3rd September
Pla
BRING dem SOMALI BOYZ
BAG O MAN

4October

Gluse is the
%

SKANK!
SKANXXX! Xxxxo
lol.

At lunchtime Kane took me to the canteen and shared a box of jerk chicken with me, and I told him about Isaac.

"I didn't know he died," Kane said. "What a tragedy. That's rough, mate."

"Who died?" Bash said as he sat down next to us.

"Jake's best friend from primary school. He was well funny. I didn't know."

"When?" Bash said.

"Four years ago?"

"You look like you're grieving, to be fair," Bash said.

"Weight of the world, innit," Kane said. "When my cousin's friend died, my cousin went mad."

"It was her fault though," Bash said.

Kane paused. "It weren't her fault though."

"It was her fault though," Bash said.

"It weren't her fault though," Kane said.

"It was her fault though."

"It weren't her fault though."

"A bit."

"Yeah, a bit." Kane relaxed. "I mean . . . she was driving, yeah . . . but . . . but it was that Nicky – Nicky died – who got them tanked in the first place. So. . ."

"That's awful," I said.

"Yeah, well, she can't walk or wipe her arse no

more, and she talks like she's pissed, so that's punishment enough."

"Jesus," I said.

"You were there?" Kane asked me. "When. . ."

I nodded.

"That's rough," Kane said. "That's rough. Seeing stuff. My cousin Taze saw his mate OD, swear down. He's mash up because of it."

"Is he the one that beat up that kid in Burger King?" Bash said.

"Yeah. This kid called him a Paki so my cousin smashed his face into a table. Broke his nose and teeth."

"Double Whopper," I said.

They laughed.

"You feel a bit better then?"

"Yeah, I'm sorry about . . ."

"'Allow it," Kane said with a dismissive wave of his hand as he cleared his mess away and headed out. "Looks like it's all done with now anyway."

I followed him out of the canteen, desperate to ask what he meant and if he knew what was going to happen tonight. But I remembered my promise to Robin, and kept my mouth shut as we climbed the stairs to English.

A huge banner had been placed over the wall I had destroyed:

Do not go gentle into that good night.
Rage, rage against the dying of the light.

"Welcome to Pip-Pop Day, everyone!" Miss Price said.

"How are you doing?" she asked me.

"Yes, fine," I said.

"What happened to the girl next door?"

"She's fine. She's in my house now," I said, suddenly desperate to talk to someone about it, but the rabble piled in and Miss Price had to deal with them.

"OK!" Miss Price enthused. "Everyone ready for Pip-Pop Day?"

There was a murmur.

"I *said*, is everyone ready for Pip-Pop Day?"

Everyone cheered.

"Boo," Bash said in a little voice, and everyone laughed. I laughed with them.

Miss Price had us do a breathing exercise where we took long breaths in and out until we felt relaxed. She explained that what was said in this room would stay in the room. She asked us who would like to read a poem and no one volunteered.

"Bash? Would you like to read your poem?"

Bash shifted in his seat. "None of you lot laugh," he warned. "It's not clever or funny or anything."

There was an "*Ooooooh*" from the room.

"I should have written a funny one," he said, opening his little black notebook.

"READ!" we all said.

"It's not. . ." He fussed with his tie.

"Get on with it!" Sam yelled.

"Are You a Supply Teacher, Sir?
by Mohammed Bashir

'Are you a supply teacher, sir?'
'Yes,' he smiled, dead to me.
'Welcome to biology.
Your teacher is off.
She tried her best but the stress
Of you lot got to her.'

This room could be filled
With doctors and nurses,
Radiographers and researchers,
And Nobel Prize winners,
With saviours of blood,
And experts on brains.
She can imagine
the cure for famine.
She could make the icecaps freeze.
He could sign decrees to save the trees.
She could ask the world: if the drought's in Africa
Why're the pumps we make over here not made over
there?
This vanishes in this pit
Of mess and poverty and sloth.
'Are you a supply teacher?' we sneer.
'Yes,' he says. 'Our supply is cut off.'"

"Innit, though," Mo said, and everyone agreed. "That

was wicked, man."

"That was excellent, Bash," Miss Price said.

"Bloody supply teachers, man," Raizer said.

"That weren't the point of the poem," Clarissa said.
Her turn. "This is about my . . . dad," she said with a
cheeky twist to her mouth.

"Oooooh!"

"Fit!"

"Peng!"

"Chung!"

"Buff, man. Big man ting."

"Biiiig maaaan tiiiing!"

"Shut up, man," Clarissa said.

"Boo!" Bash said.

"Get on with it," Raizer said. The laughter was
enough to lift the mood and Clarissa was off:

"Queen
by Clarissa Simone Neale

When I say Jamaican, you say queen.
Jamaican
'Queen!'
Jamaican
Queen!'
I don't care me dad's from Cyprus Park,
'Cos he's got more soul than Clark's
And more wrap than Smith's
And more fizz and energy

Than a truckload of Pepsi.

He richer than the Ivy.

He's bright white he right love me.

It don't matter to me

that me mummy crossed a sea

from Jamaican sands,

I'm both at the same time. I ain't no 50 Cent. I'm two hundred per cent.

I'm black and white like old movies about Egyptian queens.

And I have dreams.

Black and white drama

Like Barack Obam-AHHHHHHHHHHHHH!"

There was belting applause. Clarissa put her head in her hands. She had a big smile on her face.

No one wanted to follow that. Kane grudgingly accepted but stayed seated as the class cheered him on. He looked suddenly upset. Quickly and in a whispery voice he read:

"Puppet
by Kane Rajmansingh

Every day I wake up,

And get this puppet out its box.

I dress it in my uniform,

And send it out the door.

I send it round the school and make it talk.

It laughs at the right time, snarls at the right time.

It's rude and offensive and teases too much.
The puppet comes home in one piece.
I sigh with relief.
But I'm lonely and wishing I was free."

There was silence.

"Bait, man," Sean said and everyone laughed.

I forced my eyes away from Kane. I wasn't happy, but at least I didn't have to do that. It felt strange. I felt sick, but good sick. He stopped and smiled at me. I held up my phone. He posed. I took a picture of him.

Miss Price's big, expectant eyes turned to me. I opened my grey notebook. I stood up and the class was silent.

"This is called 'Once' and it's about . . . well . . . it. . ." My voice felt distant. I stopped and glanced at Bash's generous face, his eager eyes.

"Boo," Bash said softly and everyone laughed, so I read.

"Once

Once it seemed that in this world
I needed no one else.
You were once my better half,
My sun, my second self.

Once the wake of Sunday rain
Wouldn't change my mood,
In the peace of knowing I had
that day, each day, with you.

But no season seems like summer now.
No sun could light the day.
Because at once my life was lost,
When yours was stole away."

I looked up, terrified they would laugh because tears had filled my eyes. They weren't laughing: they looked sad, compassionate. I looked into Kane's forgiving eyes and at Clarissa twisting her mouth in an effort not to cry. I glanced at the blank page.

"Now it seems broken trees
Still reach for the sky
In their dreams, of blooming leaves
They have to say goodbye."

No one spoke. Miss Price gave a dainty clap and everyone joined in.

"It was like . . ." Nickola said, clicking her fingers, "oh, it was like that poem we done it at my last school. What's it called. . ."

"'Perhaps'," I said, "by, um. . . Miss, who wrote the poem 'Perhaps'? It was in the war poetry anthology?" I couldn't believe my brain wouldn't allow me to see her name. I had read that poem hundreds of times.

"Ooh, I'm not quite sure," Miss Price said. "We can look it up." She tapped on her computer. "Vera . . ." she peered closer, "Brittain."

"That's it," I said.

"Who wrote that?" Nickola pointed at the Pip–Pop banner.

"Does anyone know?" Miss Price said.

I put my hand up.

"Jake?"

"Yeats," I said.

"Lovely, well done."

"No," I corrected myself, distracted. "I mean, Dylan Thomas, sorry. Yeats is the other one."

"What other one?" Miss Price said.

"Miss, who wrote that?" interrupted Clarissa, pointing at the wall.

"Have you only just noticed that?" Miss Price laughed. "Does anyone know?"

I said nothing.

Miss Price looked desperately at me. "No one? I think it's Oscar Wilde."

Wrong.

"It's his most famous quote."

Wrong again.

The noise fell away until I heard only my own heart. I looked up, my eyes wide.

Miss Price beneath her careful calligraphy:

There is another world, but it is in this one.

I looked again at her muscled shoulders, her calm demeanour, her constant questions about local gang culture, her requests for letters on thoughts and feelings. I thought of her restraining Darscall, of how quickly the paramedics came when I fainted, of her comforting me as if unburdened by oaths and puritanical guidelines. Of – my eyes widened – of her turning up at my house after I'd changed my address on the school system. Of her teaching stuff that wasn't in the exam. Of a teacher who didn't know how to calibrate a white board. Of her saying she had actually bothered to read my transcript. Of the drugs mysteriously disappearing from my locker as the police searched for them. Of people being arrested. Of Cattle Rise having an informant. I looked at this room – so carefully decorated, so different to the other rooms – and back to Miss Price. Something had always bothered me about the way she stood, leaning forward, with her hands behind her back. Police. "Oh. My. God," I said.

"Sorry, Jake?"

"N . . . nothing," I said as I fumbled for my phone.

"I really did love your poem," she said.

"Thanks," I managed as my red fingers texted Robin. The police must be waiting for the CRK tonight. Why else would they be here?

POLICE. DON'T GO. THEY KNOW.

Out in the corridor I searched on my phone for Bettina's pizza place. Suddenly I stopped dead, staring at the tiny screen, the kids flooding past me like a river around a stone, because the picture on the news feed was that of a burned–out shell and of police appealing for witnesses.

Robin, I thought with horror, what have you done?

41

"The number you have called has not been recognized."

I pocketed my phone and broke into a jog. I thought of running with the baby birds for all those miles, one hundred calories per mile, or eighty-six at my weight. I thought of walking with Isaac, the endless treasure hunt. I remembered moving to Acton and walking the streets by myself, as I had never done before. I thought of walking the boulevards of Paris with Robin.

I dialled again and got a new message: "The telephone number you are dialling has been switched off. Goodbye."

Once I'd passed the park, I started running. I liked the way my heels felt as they hit the pavement, and the way that light thud loosened my shoulder blades and popped my spine. I hit the ground harder, testing my pelvis, my left femur, quietly impressed by its stamina.

I took my key out of my bag before reaching Rancome Road and kept it balled in my fist. On the doorstep I checked for movement in the Toad House, terrified the Beast would recognize me. I opened the door and ran inside.

A smash came from the kitchen, then another, and I panicked before I recognized the yell that came with each throw.

"Mum?" I said as I went to the kitchen.

She spun around. Her face was red and harried. A madness had come about her. Her hair, usually perfect, had wormed up into a wiry mess. She grabbed my shoulders and it bloody hurt because my shoulder bones are like those things they use to squeeze the juice out of lemons; if you touch them, they liquefy my flesh. I yelled in pain and twisted out of her grip.

"What the hell happened to the window upstairs?"

"I'm fine, thanks."

"Jake, listen to me, this is very, very important. Have you touched anything in this house?"

"No."

"And you haven't brought anything in? You haven't made any mess? I'm not cleaning up new mess!"

"No. Stop yelling. Your fillers will slip."

"Christ, Jake, will you listen to me and do what I ask for once in your life."

"Listen to what?"

"Your grandfather – he left us money, Jake. A lot of money. And not exactly money that you can . . . *declare,*

OK? And we have to find it. Mummy has to find it."

The word made my stomach churn. "There's no money here, Mum. Look at it. He ate corned beef every day. He had no help."

"He had thousands, Jake, hundreds of thousands." She worked the panels of the kitchen cabinet loose with her bare hands. "And we have to find it. We need that money."

"Well, it's either gone or it's been stolen, Mum. You could break into this house faster than it would take most people to find a key."

"I know it's here!" she screamed.

"Maybe you should have visited him once in a while," I said. "Maybe he would have told you."

She chucked a cabinet door like a discus and, fair play, it flew through the open door into the centre of the skip.

"Three points," I said quietly.

"Three points," Mother said, her mouth growing fat with misery. "When I was your age, all the girls wanted to be Darcey Bussell or Madonna. I wanted to be Michael Jordan."

"How did that go?"

"Can't tell us apart, can you?"

I stifled a laugh and climbed the stairs.

Mother followed me, her heels clacking off every surface, holding a small package wrapped in blue paper. She handed it to me on the stairs. "Take it," she said.

"Mum, I haven't got time."

Her forehead creased down the middle and this seemed

to make her eyes even larger. I took the package and opened it, my cold fingers faltering on the tape. Inside was a flat white box. I opened it and pulled out a silver photo frame, wrapped in tissue paper. My breathing quickened. I knew from the smallest corner of colour what was on the photograph.

He's smiling, I'm laughing.

"It's a new frame," Mum said. "Look, there's the box."

"I like it," I said. My voice was small. I ran my thumb down the frame.

"I miss him," she said, "and I miss you with him. I should have been there."

"There's nothing you could have done," I said. "There's nothing anyone could have done."

"But you blame me. It's like you hate me."

"I don't blame you. No one is to blame. Even that idiot driving. It was no one's fault. It was just a terrible thing."

Mother looked at me and ran her crucifix along its chain.

"What?" I asked.

"That's the most I've heard you say. In years."

"Well," I shrugged, "I find it hard, speaking."

She nodded. "I haven't been patient with that."

"You should have helped him," I said, looking at the blank walls around us. "He was your dad." I climbed up the stairs. "It wasn't his fault he was ill."

"He was ill, and it is a real disease, I know that now."

"You won't even say it."

"Depression. I know it's real. Chronic depression. Atypical depression. . ." She shifted. "I bought a book."

"It's like being underwater," I said, "trying to talk, trying to live, underwater."

"I know that now. I should have helped you. Both of you." She nodded. "I cleared everything out of the loft," she said to my back as I turned away from me, "so careful of the dust."

My stomach contracted. That meant Robin had gone and there was a lifetime of photographs in the skip. I looked at my phone and knew it was useless to try to get hold of her. I would have to go to the only place where I could be sure I would find her. I would have to go back to school.

I took a shower and did a good job of scrubbing myself and washing my hair. Not much hair came out in my hands. I took a second to look at my scars in the mirror. They were no longer a rainbow of colours. They were all the same pink colour and I felt quite proud that I hadn't added to them since I came out of hospital.

As I got dressed I told myself what I would do: go to the school after dark, sticking to the main roads, scale the fence and wait in the bushes until I saw Robin. I needed just thirty seconds to talk to her. Tell her everything, get out, and it would be done with. I would take my mother's police scanner in case she didn't believe me.

I put on clean socks and underwear, my black school trousers, my plain white trainers, a white T-shirt and the grey hoodie Kane had given me. As I pulled it over my head I got the sudden scent of trees. I bunched the material to my nose but the smell had vanished. I put on my dad's baseball cap.

I took the scanner, my wallet, my phone and shoved them in my rucksack. I dug through Mother's tools and took her small magnets and electrical charger. I called to her that I was going out to see a friend and left before she could reply.

When I reached the ugly towers of Cattle Rise, the grounds seemed empty. There were just five cars on the lot and I couldn't see anyone milling about. I waited.

In the distance a man came out of the third tower and climbed into a large red car, one of the two left on the lot.

The red car approached the gates and I pressed myself flat against the fence. The driver leaned out, keyed in the code and waited for the gate to open. He drove out slowly and turned right. I froze as the light licked across my face. The gates hesitated and left gate began to swing back. I dashed through them as they closed, the left gate nicking my ankle. On the other side, I waited in the shadows for the car to come back or for an alarm to sound, but it didn't.

I was in.

The darkness was shocking. London is never truly dark and never before had I not been able to see my own feet as I walked. I hadn't brought a torch or any gloves. A master criminal.

The locks on the school windows were so old they

could be opened with a magnet. I crouched by the window of the history room and fixed the small magnets to the battery. I had one chance on this battery charge so I took care fixing the wires. I charged the magnets and put one over the barrel of the lock, and the other at the other end of the handle. I waited for the charge to build and held my nerves as I moved the magnet upwards. At first nothing happened, and I cursed quietly at myself, but then the handle jumped a little, and as I eased the magnet slowly upwards it began to lift. I pushed the window and it opened. I took a quick look around to check I was alone and climbed inside.

In the dark hallway, I remembered Kane's tale of the asylum and jumped at every sound.

I made it to the stairs and felt a cold wind brush my back. I braced. Nothing. I heard someone padding behind me. I turned but there was only darkness. I lightened my tread and kept walking. Another sound. I stopped in the silence until my breath slowed enough to stop the beating in my ears. I took another step forward and was spun and slammed against a soft body with a hand fastened over my mouth. I struggled but kicking my legs only served to help my attacker bundle me into a classroom. I was thrown from the hold and stumbled backwards before falling hopelessly to the floor. I looked at the figure in the darkness.

Robin. She was so angry she could barely speak. "What the *hell* are you doing here?"

"Robin, wait—"

"Nah, nah, nah, you don't speak." She looked around and spoke in a hiss. "You promised."

"No, but Robin—"

She grabbed my wrist and pulled me out of the classroom.

"Robin, wait!" I dug my heels into the floor but it was no use. She dragged me like a child would a doll. "Robin, the police are all over this." I put my hand over hers to try to prise her grip from my wrists, but it was as if I wasn't there. She didn't loosen her grip or slow her pace. "There isn't a snake. There's a teacher at school, undercover. That's how they know everything that's going on, and they'll be here any second, so don't do anything stupid."

"And where did you hear this?"

I saw a darkness about her eye. "What happened?"

"Nothing," she said. "Where did you hear this?"

"What have they done to you? What have you been doing?"

"Negotiating," she said. "Now where did you hear about this undercover teacher? In one of your night terrors? In an elastic band? In a smoke signal?"

"Nowhere, I worked it out."

"Well, it must be true." Robin sped up and I was swept along with her, her grip burning my wrist.

"I'm telling you the truth. It's my English teacher. She didn't know where 'Do Not Go Gentle' came from."

"Someone don't know who? Dylan Thomas?"

I nodded.

"And that makes them a copper?"

"No, wait, Robin, I can prove it." I pulled my scanner out of the bag. Then I realized I'd have to get a plug and fuss with it to find a frequency.

"We're bait here," Robin said.

"No, wait. I'll find a plug."

She finally let me go and I crawled around looking for a socket. "James Bond over there. 'Ah, Dr No, prepare to die . . . as soon as I find a Wi-Fi signal."

I scrabbled hopelessly with the wires, trying to fix them into their little sockets. "Just let me *find* it," I said. I could feel Robin's anger. "I have to *tune* it."

"We haven't got time for this, Jake. You're going to get me killed!"

"Give me one second to find the setting."

"I should have let you die on my doorstep."

I caught a frequency and missed it. My massive hands were shaking. "Just let me find it."

Robin paced the corridor and kicked the wall.

"Come on." I tried to placate her. "When have I ever been wrong before?" I heard her laugh but only with exasperation.

The scanned crackled.

. . . *10-4 receiving.*

"Oh, well done, Jake, you found a cat up a tree, you stupid cracker."

Brigley approaching now, over. Vasso with him, looks like.

. . . *Marcus "the Beast" Brigley . . .*

Robin stopped.

. . . *The Beast on the approach. Have him in my sight, over.*

"Who's—"

"They're here," she whispered, her eyes wide.

10-4 we have the Big Fish walking in now. All units stand by.

"*Shit*," Robin hissed. "Come." She ran down the corridor and I grabbed the scanner and ran after her.

We reached the main door and heard grunting voices. A group of older men was walking towards the yard. We turned on our heels and ran. At the other door we saw torchlight. We turned and ran again.

Trapped.

We ran up the stairs. I concentrated on keeping up with Robin. I noticed she wasn't carrying anything. "What are you planning on doing, Robin?"

"Burn Baby Burn."

"Robin, you're insane."

She pushed me backwards. She moved so quickly I only saw the lights change. I was in complete darkness when I heard the locks switch. The cleaning cupboard. It stank of bleach and toilet water. I wrestled with the door. It was locked. "You can't get involved, Jake," she called from behind the door.

I coughed and panicked. "Robin!" I called. "Robin you're a prick, you know!" Then it hit me: the strange chemical smell in the attic. "Robin, if you burn this place down with me in it, I will haunt you for ever." I took my phone out of my pocket and used the light to look around. Rancid buckets and mops and bottles of bleach. On the shelves there were jars. I put the phone in my mouth and began to open them, finding screws and hinges and old locks. I opened a jar of washers and found a length of chicken wire. I bent it into a tiny "S" shape with my weak teeth. I slid it into the casing of my marker pen and fed it into the lock. I found the bite easily, turned it and the door opened to darkness. I grabbed a bottle of bleach from the shelf and stepped out into the corridor, sweating like an idiot.

The empty school was horrifying. I took off my shoes and ran silently up to the top floor. I lay flat on the tiles of the corridor and listened for footsteps. I couldn't hear anything.

I went to the Conference Centre where Sean had pointed out of the window to the quad where Darscall dealt from. I couldn't see anything until a small shape shifted in the blackness of the bushes. I prayed that Robin was safe. I saw Darscall, with his unmistakable lumbering walk, shuffle back into the courtyard, flanked by seven question-mark kids, all hunched over cigarettes.

A shadow fell across the window. I closed my eyes and flexed my grip on my bleach bottle. I turned.

"Robin," I said.

"Why . . . won't . . . you . . . flush!" she said, throwing her arms above her head. She could hardly speak. "How the . . . how did you get out?"

I mimed using a key.

"Really?"

"If you knew how useless locks are, you'd never sleep."

Concern travelled across her face and she pressed her

back against the wall. I took the scanner out of my bag. "You could call to them now," I said. "Warn them. Robin? You could all them right now."

Robin looked out of the window and spoke after some time. "No. They'll think it was me anyway." I saw she had liberated a camcorder from Media Studies. "Good lock, bad hinges," she said. She nodded at my bottle. "Going to wash them, is it?"

"Bleach."

"Put it down before you burn your hand off with it."

I did as I was told.

The quad was busy now. We watched boys, semi-hidden by the bushes, dealing to kids who slouched across the school grounds from the estates nearby or pulled up in their parents' battered cars.

A black van pulled up outside the quad. Robin switched on the camcorder. Men with hunched shoulders and crooked spines poured from the van. Even from high up I could tell it was the Beast who led them across the quad to where Darscall was standing.

"If they don't have enough and he gets away," Robin said, aiming the camcorder, "I am dead. Swear down."

The gathering in the quad became heated. Robin turned and looked at me but she didn't say anything. More cars pulled up.

"Two cars," Robin said, "and six men in there. They're not taking it seriously." We watched in silence. "I was trying to help you," she said. "Darscall's found out you were lying about being with us and your name's being passed around like chicken wings. If the Beast finds out he'll pull the switch. They'll snack you. You can't be here."

My stomach went to water. I couldn't believe she could care about me at a time like this.

On my command said the scanner.

"God help us," said Robin.

A truck quietly pulled up and police spilled out of the hatch, armoured with shields and batons. The officer raised his arm, then after a beat flung it down, and they burst into the quad.

A series of piercing cracks whipped the air, the unmistakable sound of guns firing. Pockets of light blinked on as the estates opposite awoke. A gravelling holler of discontent erupted.

Robin covered her mouth.

We've got the Big Fish, 10-4. Immediate back-up required. All units.

Firearms. Firearms, be advised.

Two hulking men were thrown to the ground. Three, four, five . . . all with beer bellies and tattoos.

The police were dragging a couple of black-suited men from their BMW. A third emerged, his head held high, his grin so wide we could see it from our high window.

Not a hoodie in sight.

"Look!" Robin cried suddenly. "He's getting away!"

She pointed the camera. A man was making his escape over the fence just as a second riot van screamed into the street. He was stumbling and holding his shoulder.

"No!" she cried. "He can't!"

"Who is it?"

"The Beast! He's getting away!"

I watched in horror. I couldn't believe the swarming police hadn't seen him and headed him off. Everything would be ruined. I grabbed the scanner, fixed the wires and did something very, very illegal:

"All advised, the Beast headed over fence east, east, suspect on foot Cattle Rise Road."

"CASTLE!" Robin screamed.

"Shit, Castle Rise Road."

10-4, who is this? Over.

Robin shook my shoulder. "Say it again."

"We can't."

"Do it!"

"Give them time." I bit my thumbnail.

"Say it again. He's getting *away*."

I grabbed the scanner. "10-4 he's a big fat bastard and he's running down the bloody road, get after him!"

The scanned crackled. *State name, over.*

"Get after him, for fuck's sake!"

The beast hobbled surely on, looking into the window of every car. "Bloody coppers," Robin said, kissing her teeth, "state of them they can't run after him!" I panicked before I spotted a spritely figure hop over the fence, one leg looping over the other, and landing with such deftness he was able to launch straight into a full-bodied run. He was joined by another, a straight-backed man who ran with his fingers straight, an aerodynamic run; his fingers were so straight you could see the cut of his uniform: police. "Go on, lads," I said to the policemen as the honed in on the Beast. "Go on, lads."

The hobbling Beast mounted a motorcycle. The police gained on him. As the motorcycle revved, the officer grabbed the Beast's shoulder, yelled, and threw him to the ground as the motorcycle screamed off on its own and crashed into a parked car.

"Yes!" we cheered as the scanner buzzed with excitement.

10-4 be alert. Top floor. Open projectile. Two suspects. Code Purple.

It took Robin seconds to blink. "Jake." Her voice was tiny.

"Yeah?"

"What's Code Purple?"

"Gang activity," I said. "If we get caught up here we're—"

She snatched the camera from my grip, whipped out the chip and threw the casing through the open window. She tipped the scanner over the ledge and we watched it sail to the ground and smash into pieces.

She shot out of the room and started down the five flights of stairs. I felt dizzy as I matched her, leap for leap. She reached the fire doors and I chased after her. The fire escape dropped us to ground level and we ran. I felt weak at the thought of the fence. Robin cleared it as if it was a child's safety gate then put her hands through the railings and boosted me up and over the top. We ran down the dimly lit road. "The park," I yelled, "run for the park!"

"How the hell did they see us?" Robin screamed.

Only then did we hear the whump of a helicopter circling overhead. "It must have been the scanner."

The helicopter dipped and its underside blinked red, as if a missile was attached. "No," I said. "Body heat."

We hit the park, scaled the gate and pitched into endless tunnel of darkness. "The lake," I yelled, sensing Robin behind me. "Quickly!" The helicopter edged closer. "Get your clothes off!"

"Why?" she yelled.

"Get 'em off!"

"It'll be freezing! You've lost your tiny mind!"

"It's body heat!" I tore at her grey hoodie. "That's how they can see us. They've got thermal scanners. Quickly!"

"I can't see! I can't see!" Robin cried.

I fumbled in the dark, grabbed her arm and hurled her into the lake. We both swore as the ice hit our nerves. Robin squealed as something brushed past us.

"Get under the dock," I gargled.

"What duck?"

"The *dock*! Get under the *dock*!"

"Gross," Robin spluttered.

"We have to time it right." I heaved us beneath the dock. "We've only got seconds before we heat up again. One . . . two . . . breathe. . ." We gulped the pungent air and put our heads under, sinking into black ice, our eyes closed. The cold stilled my limbs. I could feel she was there, and I felt the sudden calm of another world. I told my rabbit heart that if it would just survive this, I'd treat it properly. I stopped struggling against the icy water.

Lightly, Robin's lips touched mine. She breathed air into my body for seconds until we crashed to the surface.

The helicopter was gone.

"It's heading back to Southfields," Robin said.

"We'll have to go up the hill."

Robin picked up her clothes and held them in front of her shivering body. "You pulled yourself out of the lake."

"Ha!" I said, then shook my head. "Probably just adrenaline."

"Yeah, adrenaline," she said. She looked at the ground and smiled, biting the corner of her mouth to hide it.

The Cyclops glare of the helicopter circled on the lower road. We heard the roar of police cars in the distance. We scaled the fence and ran down the long street. I didn't feel anything but hunger. I wasn't worried about the darkness. I smiled for the briefest second before I saw Robin's face thinning with horror. The Toad House bubbled with fire.

42

The police were waiting at the Toad House. Gloved forensic officers carried out boxes and firefighters surveyed the wreckage.

A police officer wandered over. "Do you live here?" she asked, pointing at the blackened Toad House.

Robin shook her head.

"Are they all right?" I said. "I live next door."

"No one was hurt." The officer gave us a quick up-and-down. "You kids all right?"

"Yeah," Robin said. "Dandy."

"You bin for a swim?"

"Water fight," I said. "It got pretty Eighties."

She laughed because people born in the Eighties like it when you talk about the Eighties.

She was joined by a male colleague. "You live next

door?" he said, gesturing to my house.

I nodded and kept my hand on Robin's shoulder.

Robin and I went upstairs and took turns in the shower. I made Robin go first because I didn't want her to find any clumps of hair.

When I came out of the shower, she was wearing one of my school shirts. "Better not get hit by a bus wearing this hot mess," she said. She pulled up the shirt to reveal my purple boxers.

She picked up a pair of scissors from my desk and began to cut her braids out of her hair. The fluffy hair underneath sprang up with relief. She scratched her head, her shoulders raised to her ears with the pleasure of it.

"What are you thinking?" I asked.

"They won't be able to hold him. They won't have enough evidence."

"What are we going to do?"

Robin turned to me. "There is one last bit of evidence," she said.

"What's that?" I said. "Anything, anything."

She turned to me and lightly tapped the side of her head.

I blinked at her while my flaccid brain computed what she was saying. "You can't give evidence. You'd have to incriminate yourself."

"It's the only way," she said. "They'll need a witness and I've seen everything."

The light behind her picked up the fine hairs on the back of her neck. She looked like she was glowing. I wanted to beg her to not go through with it, but she looked calm, and determined, like the statues in the Louvre.

She took a red rubber band from her wrist and fixed it on to mine. "So you can find me," she said.

I smiled.

"Also, I'll text you," she said and I laughed.

She looked at my desk and noticed the picture Mum had given me. She picked up the nail gun and fired a nail into the wall next to the window. The reverberation didn't send her sprawling backwards on to the floor.

She hung the picture. "It looks good there," she said. I nodded. She reached for my phone and took a picture of herself, then tapped in a number.

Then she put an arm around me and took a picture of both of us.

"You're the bravest person I know," I said.

"I'm the only person you know." She put her arms around me and I put my arms around her.

"Gross," I said, and we laughed and broke away.

43

I sat on the stairs while Robin talked to the police officer in the kitchen.

I took out my phone and looked at Robin's picture. I liked her with her hair short. I saved the picture as my screensaver. I flicked to the picture I had taken of Kane and saved it under his number. I scrolled through my new contacts: Robin, Kane, Clarissa, Bash, Sean.

I scrolled back to Isaac's number.

I pressed the menu button.

And then I pressed delete.

I exhaled. I hadn't realized I had been holding my breath. "Goodbye, Isaac," I said. "I miss you."

I looked in amazement at the screen. Kind Dr Kahn's number appeared where Isaac's had been. His final gift. Nothing could have been clearer. I had to text her:

*Dogs express grief with starvation. I was grieving. I was
trying to tell them but they wouldn't listen. I understand what
you were saying now. Please help me. I want to live.*

She texted back immediately:

You are wise. Come back.

I walked outside to get some air. Robin came out and
sat beside me on the scrappy patch of grass. "They said I
got five minutes."

We looked back at the officers milling about the house.
I looked at the ground.

"Robin," I said, my eyes wide. "Robin, what did you
do? To Bettina's?"

Robin shrugged with one shoulder.

"Transmitters?" I said. "Firecrackers on steroids, more
like."

The police officer came outside and handed me a cup
of black tea. "I couldn't find much in the way of food
there," she said. She turned to Robin. "Are you ready?"
Robin nodded.

We were surrounded by detectives and sergeants in
their black suits. "Keep that safe," Robin said, handing
me the spider broach.

"No, you can have it."

"But he left it for you."

I took the dumb-looking spider and smiled. I liked

that it now reminded me of Robin and of my being capable of loving someone unconditionally. As Robin was handcuffed I pinned it to her collar. "It's for you."

"You won't be able to take that," the detective said. "You should leave anything that expensive safely at home, unless you want it processed."

"Expensive?" I said.

"Expensive?" Robin said. "It's a stone and a few crystals and bits of plastic."

"That's plastic and those are crystals but that isn't a stone." The detective took a closer look and almost cracked a smile. "That's a raw diamond."

Robin and I looked at each other. She beamed. "You gave it to me, remember!"

She laughed as she climbed into the back seat of the police car. "I'm coming to live up the road with you in Edinburgh."

The spider weighed on my hand. I looked up just in time to watch the car disappear down the long road. Autumn leaves danced at its wheels. I looked at the spider's legs painstakingly glued to its little body. The next time I wanted to die I would remember being underwater, and I would remember that I had fought and fought to survive, and that's when I called Doctor Kahn, and told her I was on my way.

ACKNOWLEDGEMENTS

To Genevieve Carden, my brilliant agent and personal Springsteen: a grand total of seventeen lines made it, intact, from first to final draft so I should thank you, and Scholastic, for your patience and expertise. Thanks especially to Genevieve Herr and Alice Swan for believing in me and getting me out of the habit of using ellipses and saying everything twice . . . twice, I tell you!

To my mum, Lesley, and my sister, Danielle, for not saying things like "get a proper job" and instead saying things like "why don't you just eat the whole packet?"

To Laura Gilmore, for general Julia Robertsness, and for saving me from living in that garage with all the lovely slugs.

To the Longhorns: Sarah Solidum, Kawika Solidum, Annie Chan, and Robb MacDonald. To Sarah Wilshaw, Eoin "what do you know about any of this?" Meade, Michael Graham, Felicity Jones, and the wonderful Mark Strathdene. And finally to the humans born in the time it has taken me to write this: Anna, Sidney, Lennie, and Noa. May you live long, prosper, and one day do battle for my estate.